PRAISE FOR
SHE DIDN'T STAND A CHANCE

"The brutal desert heat meets a cold-blooded killer in this taut mystery from Stacie Grey. A Palm Springs setting, rich people behaving badly, and the laugh-out-loud family dysfunction made this a winner for me. I couldn't put this book down."

—Joshua Moehling, *USA Today* bestselling author of *And There He Kept Her* and *Where the Dead Sleep*

"For *She Didn't Stand a Chance*'s engaging outsider Gertie, the inhospitable and deadly desert is nothing compared to the suspects trapped with her at her dead father's estate. Clever, atmospheric, and sizzling with suspense, this book is an addictive binge."

—Heather Chavez, author of *Before She Finds Me* and *What We'll Burn Last*

SHE LEFT

"Deliciously twisty—Agatha Christie would be spellbound."

—M. M. Chouinard, *USA Today* bestselling author of *The Dancing Girls*

"In this engrossing mystery, a vividly drawn cast of characters, claustrophobic setting, and propulsive pacing will keep you flipping the pages until the final twist that will leave you reeling. Grey skillfully and lovingly plays within the rules of the genre while also bringing a fresh voice and perspective to the *And Then There Were None* premise that will delight not just Agatha Christie fans but fans of tense, clever, and goose bump–inducing stories as well. Clear your calendar for the day, because this is a one-sitting read!"

—Brianna Labuskes, bestselling author of *A Familiar Sight*

"*Knives Out* meets Lucy Foley's *The Hunting Party* in this tense locked-room mystery. Be wary of invitations where everyone could be a suspect."

—Georgina Cross, author of *One Night, Nanny Needed* and *The Stepdaughter*

"Readers who were raised on a steady diet of Agatha Christie will find much to love in *She Left*—the intriguing cast of suspects, the red herrings scattered through the story, and the sleuth who has to put it all together to get herself to safety. Grey's story is a satisfying riff on the classic mystery story structure that will keep readers guessing until the end."

—Eva Jurczyk, author of *The Department of Rare Books and Special Collections*

"In *She Left,* Stacie Grey combines a clever setup with all the excitement of a classic whodunit, complete with a compelling cast of characters (and suspects). The tension grabbed me from the first page and ratcheted up relentlessly with each scene."

—Elle Grawl, author of *One of Those Faces* and *What Still Burns*

"*She Left* by Stacie Grey, with its sharp writing, a cunning locked-room setting, and eerie atmosphere, reads like a modern-day Agatha Christie and has all the hallmarks of a can't-put-it-down thriller."

—Ashley Tate, author of *Twenty-Seven Minutes*

"Immersive and hypnotizing, *She Left* is the effortless summer read that will enthrall you from the first chapter. Suspense and mystery lovers will find each character to be convincingly suspicious and the decades-past crime to be full of compelling unanswered questions. Start this in the morning because Grey's taut writing will drive you to finish this book in one sitting."

—Elle Marr, Amazon Charts bestselling author of *The Alone Time* and *The Family Bones*

SHE DIDN'T STAND A CHANCE

SHE DIDN'T STAND A CHANCE

A NOVEL

STACIE GREY

Poisoned Pen PRESS

Copyright © 2025 by Stacie Grey
Cover and internal design © 2025 by Sourcebooks
Cover design © Lisa Amoroso
Cover images © Andrew Holt/Getty Images, ArisSu/iStock.com, Wildroze/iStock.com

Sourcebooks, Poisoned Pen Press, and the colophon
are registered trademarks of Sourcebooks.

All rights reserved. No part of this book may be reproduced in any form or by any electronic or mechanical means including information storage and retrieval systems—except in the case of brief quotations embodied in critical articles or reviews—without permission in writing from its publisher, Sourcebooks.

No part of this book may be used or reproduced in any manner for the purpose of training artificial intelligence technologies or systems.

The characters and events portrayed in this book are fictitious or are used fictitiously. Any similarity to real persons, living or dead, is purely coincidental and not intended by the author.

Published by Poisoned Pen Press, an imprint of Sourcebooks
P.O. Box 4410, Naperville, Illinois 60567-4410
(630) 961-3900
sourcebooks.com

Cataloging-in-Publication Data is on file with the Library of Congress.

Printed and bound in the United States of America.
PAH 10 9 8 7 6 5 4 3 2 1

For Rumpole.
May your pillow always be in the sunbeam.

Fire and Ice

Some say the world will end in fire,
Some say in ice.
From what I've tasted of desire
I hold with those who favor fire.
But if it had to perish twice,
I think I know enough of hate
To say that for destruction ice
Is also great
And would suffice.

—ROBERT FROST

LETTERS FROM GERTRUDE GLASS (AGE TWELVE) TO ARNOLD GLASS

Dear Mr. Glass,

I need to ask you a favor. Carla says I'm not supposed to contact you, but I don't know who else I can ask. Andy Burnett is my stepfather, and he is a photographer for the newspapers. He was working in Peru, and he got arrested for taking pictures of a protest. The man who called said they were doing everything they could to get him home, but I don't think they're trying very hard. I have tried to contact people in the government, but they don't listen to me. But I know you know a lot of people, and they might listen to you. Can you ask someone in the government to do more to find him?

Andy is a good person, and we need him back.

Sincerely,
Gertie Glass

Dear Mr. Glass,

I am writing to thank you for helping us. I know I did not get a response from you, but when Andy got out of jail, the people said he must have very powerful friends, and I think that must have been you. I know you don't want to hear from me, and I won't bother you anymore. I don't have any way to pay you back now, so I am including an IOU you can use in the future.

Sincerely,
Your daughter,
Gertie

EXCERPT FROM ARTICLE "TOP 75 MODERNIST HOUSES IN AND AROUND PALM SPRINGS," *DESERT STYLE MAGAZINE*, SUMMER 2018

#68 THE GLASS HOUSE

Perched on the edge of the Valley, between the Palm Springs city limits and Vista Seco State Park, there's a window-filled house that stands on its own. Literally—the land it was built on wasn't intended for development, and it remains unclear how it was permitted. Built by its current owner, the appropriately named retail property developer Arnold Glass, the main part of the building is enclosed on two sides by full story-height windows and is known as the Glass House, for obvious reasons. Evoking, depending on who you ask, either van der Rohe's Barcelona Pavilion or the shopping malls that made Mr. Glass's fortune, there's no arguing it's not a striking design.

The Glass House was built in 1976, a late addition to the modernist oeuvre, and the pictures of the original styling from that era show it in every detail. Later renovations replaced the parquet floors with white marble and the shag-carpeted walls(!) with simpler plaster effects, but the central conversation pit and the "floating" plexiglass stairs leading to the central tower remain. In one concession to current trends, the five acres of grounds have recently been converted to a low-water planting scheme.

Situated behind security gates and only rarely opened by the very private Mr. Glass for press photographs (and never to the unwashed masses!), we turn to public records for the gritty details. According to the Riverside County tax assessor's office, there are seven bedrooms and four bathrooms in the main house, plus one outbuilding with another bed and bath. No major renovation work has been done since 1992, when the shape of the pool was changed and the kitchen brought up to modern code.

The architect, Richard Gunther, was more known for his work on shopping mall design; the Glass House was his only residential project. A historic building dating to 1906 also sits on the property.

1

They saw her coming.

On either side of the front door were walls of windows, double height and interrupted only by supporting pillars. The reflected light of the morning sun made the figures inside little more than shadows to her, but Gertie would be clear to them. She knew what they would see—a slim figure with short hair, dressed in black jeans and a gray cotton blouse and carrying an oversize tote bag as a purse. What she didn't know was what they would be thinking when they saw her. Gertie composed her face into the impenetrable expression she had been practicing since she was eight and pressed the doorbell.

The door was answered by a woman in her early sixties with bobbed hair, which had been expertly dyed blond, and a linen jumpsuit in bottle green. Maryann, Gertie thought, lining her face up with the pictures she had found online.

"Gertrude," the woman said, with a smile that was only a little forced. "We're so glad you could make it. Please come in."

"Thank you. And please call me Gertie."

Coming inside from the heat of the desert was like dipping into a pool. No small feat of air-conditioning, Gertie thought, given the walls of windows and the size of the place. The room she entered was enormous, more car showroom than living space.

It was a place Gertie had been before, but not since she was three years old, and if she had been hoping for a flash of familiarity, she would have been disappointed.

But she wasn't here to see the house. It was the people Gertie was interested in, and she didn't recognize them either.

Aside from Maryann, there were three other people present, two men and a woman, all sitting in a conversation pit that was sunk into the middle of the room like a dry lake bed with throw rugs. They stared at her openly, sharing glances as if daring each other to speak first. Gertie decided it would have to be her, but for once in her life, she was at a loss for words.

What do you say to four siblings you don't know?

"Sorry I'm late. Traffic was worse than I expected."

"That's all right," said Maryann. "We aren't starting until eleven. Jules wanted to make sure you had time to get settled first."

Jules was their father's lawyer, the only person Gertie had been in contact with since Arnold died. Or while he'd been alive, for that matter.

"You drove? But why? There's a perfectly nice airport, and we could have sent a car." That was Jennifer, the other woman present. She was ten years younger than Maryann and doing her best to make the most of it. Her pants were probably designer—Gertie couldn't imagine wearing anything so ugly if they weren't—and unlike the others, she was barefoot, her chipped toenail polish looking out of place against the sleek marble floor.

"Thanks for the offer," Gertie said, though the idea of taking a plane to travel slightly over a hundred miles was as absurd to her as if Jennifer had suggested she bunny hop the whole way. "But it's not a long drive, and I like to have my own car. Considering the circumstances of this visit, it seems prudent."

One of the men burst into laughter.

"Looks and talks like him! Remind me why we spent all that money on DNA tests? My God, she's more his child than any of us."

"Neil, honestly," Maryann admonished, and Gertie was finally able to sort the two men into their names. The speaker was the younger brother, so the other one would be Brian, currently leaning back on the white leather sofa with a glass of brown liquor resting on his belly.

"Oh, come on, you're all thinking it," said Neil. He was the most relaxed of the four, lounging in an amoeba-shaped plastic chair as though it were comfortable and cracking and eating pistachios from a glass bowl on a side table. He dropped a shell on the floor and turned back to Gertie. "You have to understand, the last time we saw you, you were toddling around, and now here you are, all grown-up and looking so much like the old man, I'm inclined to wonder who we're burying."

Brian snorted, but as he shifted forward to rest his elbows on his knees, he studied Gertie's face. "You'll have to excuse my brother," he said. "Nobody ever told him he wasn't funny."

"I'm her brother too," Neil retorted. "And I've been thinking it's time for an upgrade on siblings."

"Boys! Enough," Maryann said. "There'll be plenty of time for you both to demonstrate your personal failings later. Let's give Gertie a minute to get her bearings."

She picked an invisible bit of lint off the bodice of her jumpsuit and glanced up at the giant clock hands on the wall above the stairs. (They might have been pointing to five minutes to ten; it was hard to tell without any numbers.)

"Have you had breakfast?" she asked Gertie. "I'm afraid we've already eaten, but I'm sure Eddie could put something together for you."

"Thanks, I had something on the way." A double-double with grilled onions, fries well done, and a strawberry shake, eaten at the In-N-Out drive-through as soon as she was out of range of her mother's endless calorie talk. Gertie had been blessed with a vigorous metabolism and a love of long runs, but a lifetime of fad diets had left her mother, Carla, with the ability to smell french fries on her breath, and no meal was worth another lecture on the evils of the carbohydrate.

Gertie hadn't been exactly looking forward to this visit, but there were some upsides.

"So, what do you think of coming home?" Brian gestured at the room. "Is it just like you remember it?"

Gertie studied Brian's face and decided he wasn't joking.

"I'm afraid I don't remember it at all. As you say, I was only three when we left." Gertie had more to say about that, but the nervous tension in the room made her cut her answers short. Gertie did have what could be called memories, but she couldn't be sure which of them were real and which had been built up by years of her mother telling her the same stories and showing her the pictures of the house every time it showed up in a magazine. So the room they were in looked familiar to her, but not in a tactile way. The only image that stood out in her mind without the glossy-paper reflection was of a chair with spindly legs against the background of a patterned carpet. In friendlier circumstances she might have mentioned it.

Instead, Gertie looked around with calm interest at the marble floor, handrail-free stairs, and open drop into the conversation pit and said, "Is this what it looked like then? It seems like it would be hard to childproof."

From the way the four siblings looked at the room and each other, it was clear this hadn't occurred to any of them.

"Well, you had a nanny, and Mrs. Phan, to look after you. I'm sure they took care of that sort of thing," Neil said uncomfortably. "I know my kids haven't had any trouble."

"Didn't Lief fall into the pool when he was two?" Jennifer asked. "It was lucky there was that guy on the staff who'd been a lifeguard."

Neil bristled. "Dad never should have let that nanny bring them in. Anyway, he was fine. Nestor had them both signed up for baby swim classes when they were eighteen months."

Gertie recognized the name—that would be Neil's husband, Nestor Zanes, who had recently been elected to the state senate.

"You said you didn't drive far—are you living in the area now?" Maryann was back in hostess mode, which made sense, but Gertie found it disconcerting. She had thought a lot over the years about what it would be like to meet her father's other children, but she hadn't anticipated it being so similar to the small talk at the beginning of a job interview.

She decided to test how far that went.

"Just over in Laguna Beach. I was in Boston for law school, but since I graduated, I've been staying with Carla while I study for the bar. She has an apartment a few blocks from the ocean."

Gertie didn't expect that innocuous statement to get an equally bland response, and she was right. No one said anything, but the reactions varied between the siblings, ranging from Maryann's pressed lips and Neil's flaring of nostrils, to Jennifer snorting and crossing her arms and Brian draining his glass before looking deliberately out the windows. Clearly, her mother's name still had an effect here, even after twenty-five years.

It was Jennifer who recovered first.

"Well, I suppose everyone has to live somewhere, don't they? Did you have any luggage?" she said in a voice that was only slightly strained.

"Yes, someone met me when I arrived. He said he was taking it to the pool house?" It had been an absurd scene, the sharply dressed young man standing by with a cart to receive Gertie's lone piece of luggage, an old duffel bag that had belonged to her stepfather.

"Yes, that's where you'll be, since you're staying for the

memorial service," Maryann said. "I think you'll find the accommodations adequate for that much time."

"I'm sure I will." Gertie noticed something—amusement, maybe?—in Maryann's tone, but she was relieved that she wasn't going to have to be staying in the same building as these people. Before she had arrived, she had toyed with the idea that coming here might mean she would get some of her questions answered. Like why Arnold had summoned her after not seeing her for twenty-five years, or if in all that time he had ever spoken about Gertie or known anything about her life.

But the reception she had gotten so far had put that hope out of her mind. The bitterness that had characterized her parents' divorce clearly lived on in Gertie's half siblings, and she was no more welcome in her father's home after his death than she had been in his lifetime.

As though he could hear her thoughts, Neil dropped another pistachio shell back into the bowl and smiled up at Gertie from his seat in the conversation pit. "Don't take it personally," he said. "We've never been big on guests around here."

"I understand," Gertie said absently. She was gazing at the set of floating glass stairs in the middle of the room, and the strange grouping of plants at its base.

Because there was at least one more question she didn't know how to ask. All Gertie knew about her father's death was that he had fallen in his home, and the police were declining to call it an accident.

2

Gertie thought she would be able to find her way to the pool house on her own, considering the pool was visible through the patio doors, but Jennifer offered to show her.

Stepping out the sliding doors was like walking into a wall of heat. That wasn't a surprise, but the noise was. The hot, dry air was filled with buzzing, like the world largest faulty fuse box. She had heard it when she arrived as well, and she couldn't figure out what it was or if she should be worried.

Jennifer must have heard it too, but her expression as she led Gertie across the courtyard was vacant and unconcerned. She had passed through the outdoor dining area and was halfway down the length of the pool, pointing out features like she was leading a guided tour.

"The pool was originally kidney shaped, but that was changed in the nineties. We usually have Christmas out here, with a tree from a farm near Mammoth, and they decorate all the palms with lights. It looks really nice, actually."

Gertie imagined it did. The courtyard was enclosed on two sides by the house and surrounded the rest of the way by a wall rendered in pale stucco, high enough so there was no view of the desert beyond. The whole thing was about the size of a basketball court, though between the swimming pool and the succulent-heavy landscaping, it would be hard to get a game going. There was even a patch of lawn, incongruous among the more naturalistic planting.

As out of place as that looked, it had nothing on the building that was their destination. At the far end of the courtyard, a small brown-tiled-roof building squatted like a toad in a bathtub. Gertie had seen a few pool houses in her life, but none of them had so thoroughly rejected the concept of pools.

Jennifer saw where she was looking and nodded.

"Funny place, right? It was here when Dad bought the property, and part of the deal for building the house was it couldn't be torn down. It's like, historical or something. Anyway, it worked out, because my grandma had to move in with us, and she hated the main house. So she could live there, and it worked okay because there aren't any stairs." Jennifer gave her a sideways look. "She was the original Gertrude, you know. Dad wanted to name one of us after her, but Mama wouldn't let him. He had to wait for someone who really suited it, I guess."

"Seems that way," Gertie said neutrally. She was aware Jennifer was being snarky, but it was going to take more than that to get a reaction out of her. When the plain daughter of a gorgeous woman has a name like Gertrude, she learns how to stare down a lot.

Gertie said, "She must have died before I was born. I don't think Carla ever mentioned her."

Again, the mention of her former stepmother's name caused Jennifer to draw in her breath sharply. "Did she tell you a lot about us—I mean, about living here?" she asked, trying to sound casual and failing.

"Oh, you know, some. It was an important part of her life." Carla Di Luca had married Arnold Glass when she was twenty-four and he was sixty, and their only daughter had been born two years later. Three years after that, they were bitterly divorced. But the time Carla had spent in the house outside of Palm Springs had been her one experience with the life she believed she was supposed to live, and she had spent the two and a half decades that followed talking about it.

Gertie wondered if there was something in one of those stories that was making Jennifer look so nervous.

They reached the pool house, and Jennifer waved at the door, suddenly in a hurry to get rid of her.

"Anyway, here you are. I assume Juan or whoever put your stuff inside. Sorry there isn't any air-conditioning, but it usually cools down at night."

Gertie thanked her and put her hand on the doorknob before the absurdity of the situation overwhelmed her. It wasn't the sort of thing you just brought up—ten minutes earlier she hadn't thought she would be able to ask about it at all. But she couldn't leave the question hanging in the air, not when she had so much riding on the answer.

Since there was no delicate way to approach it, she went with the direct method.

"He was killed, right?"

"What?" Jennifer's shock was genuine and faded quickly into anger. "What the hell are you talking about?"

Having gotten started, Gertie found it easier to go on. "Arnold's death. There wasn't much in the papers, but everything I've seen says the police are still investigating. They don't spend that much time investigating natural deaths, do they?"

"*My father* died after falling down the stairs from his office. The police don't know what they're doing. They'll say anything if it gets them publicity." Jennifer spat out the words, her voice shaking with fury.

They stood staring at each other until Gertie looked away and shrugged.

"If you say so," she said and started to go inside, but Jennifer stopped her.

"Why did you come here?" she blurted.

Gertie looked back at her steadily. "I was invited."

3

Once she was alone, Gertie took stock of her temporary accommodations. She understood now what Maryann meant when she said the pool house was good enough for a short stay. It wasn't as hot as outside, but still more than hot enough. As the sweat started to run down Gertie's back, she made her way around the building, opening every window that wasn't stuck and hoping for the best.

In a way, she almost had to respect Jennifer and the others for putting her here. Gertie might have been invited to stay, but her half siblings were leaving no question of where they thought she belonged.

Even the building itself looked like it was from a different world than they lived in—it would have been hard to imagine something more different than the modernist minimalism of the main house. The windows were small and set deep in the thick walls, which were painted dusky pink, and the mismatched furniture was all heavily polished dark wood and thick upholstery.

The pool house was divided into three rooms, with a bedroom

with an incongruously grand four-poster bed, a small but functional bathroom, and a main living space. The kitchen was at the far end of the room, with well-worn butcher-block counters and a window that looked out onto the landscaped grounds. Beyond the cacti, another wall ringed the property, one that looked less decorative than functional, and for a moment, Gertie imagined herself being in a very high-end prison complex.

Shaking off the feeling, she went back to examining the space. A small table separated the kitchen from the living area, which was furnished with a love seat facing an old CRT TV, a coffee table, and what could be described only as "stuff." Books, magazines, dolls, and candlesticks—all the clutter that had been banished from the main house must have found a home here. Even some office supplies had made the trip, with a metal filing cabinet in the corner that held some old marketing materials and a stack of laptops that had probably been manufactured before Gertie was born.

There was even a framed photograph left facedown under a pile of paperback books. Gertie picked it up and looked at it.

It was a family grouping of Arnold, his first wife, Doreen, and their four children. Based on the background, they were at a resort somewhere, around Christmastime. And based on the hairstyles, it was the eighties, with Maryann and Jennifer wearing crushed-velvet dresses with puffed sleeves as big as their permed hair. The boys were looking equally of the moment: Brian in a pink suit with the sleeves rolled to his elbows and Neil in head-to-toe stonewashed denim.

Doreen's dress was dark blue with a flower print, a

lace-trimmed collar, and shoulder pads. Looking at her and her children, Gertie could understand why everyone had been talking about family resemblances. The five of them all had the same square faces and wide mouths—even their round blue eyes all matched, in contrast to their father's, and Gertie's own, narrow gray ones. That wasn't the only way Arnold stood out, and Gertie spent some time studying the man who had cursed her with her face and name, who hadn't seen or spoken to her since she was three years old.

He must have been fifty in the photo, noticeably younger than in his wedding pictures with Carla. By then he had been almost entirely bald and his face more deeply lined—here she could see traces of her own fine light-brown hair, and the sharp angles and long nose that defined her face were hard to miss. And, of course, her forehead (so tall that a college classmate with aspirations to comedy had dubbed it a "fivehead") was very much present and accounted for.

All told, she didn't blame Neil for making the connection. She wouldn't have thought she was anyone else's daughter either.

She knew Arnold's first wife had passed away during the time her parents were married—from the way Carla talked about it, it was like she thought Doreen had died intentionally to spite her. In the picture she looked healthy enough, a round middle-aged woman with a hairstyle she had probably had for decades. Gertie thought about the pictures of her own mother from around the time she'd met Arnold, ten years later than this. Young, slim, tanned, and bottle blond, Carla had been working as a swimsuit model and spending her weekends at the sort of parties where rich men and young women mingled. Poor Doreen had been doomed from the start.

And now here was Gertie, with Doreen's children resenting her for existing. She put the photo back where she'd found it, pausing only to look again at the books that had been stacked on it and wonder who in the house was a fan of paperback horror novels.

Her bag was in the bedroom, sitting on the end of the bed. Both the closet and the dresser were already full of old clothes, so Gertie cleared out a drawer and a few hangers, then unpacked. Her hosts might want to make sure she knew she was unwelcome here, but Gertie had known that all along, and she had her standards.

There was still nearly an hour until she was needed for the reading of the will, and though she knew she would be expected to return to the main house before that, Gertie wasn't ready to go back yet. So, despite the heat, she took a little more time to explore her surroundings.

A closer look confirmed Jennifer hadn't been exaggerating when she said the building was old. The walls were adobe, at least a foot thick, with a rough whitewashed surface, and dark beams crossed the ceilings.

The walls of the pool house might have been designed to keep some of the heat out, but what got in, they held. An electric fan sat by the bedroom window, but after examining the state of its power cord and plug, Gertie decided she would rather feel like she was just figuratively burning, rather than make it literal.

That reminded her of something, and Gertie went back to

where she had left her bag on the table. She didn't actually think fire was much of a danger, but there was no lock on the pool house door, and that made her uncomfortable. Ignoring her wallet, her phone, and her laptop, she reached into an interior pocket of the bag and took out a slim folder.

Inside, there were two sheets of paper and an envelope. Gertie looked at them individually as she took them out of the folder and tucked them between old advertising flyers in the filing cabinet.

The first was an obituary, printed off a newspaper website:

> Arnold Glass, shopping mall magnate and patron of the arts, died after a fall in his home. He is survived by his four children—Maryann Glass-Coleman, Brian Glass, Neil Glass-Zanes, and Jennifer Glass—and six grandchildren. He was preceded in death by his parents, Arnold and Gertrude Glass, his brother, Edward Glass, and by Doreen Glass, the mother of his children. In lieu of flowers, donations can be made to the Coachella Valley Sculpture Garden.

Then, a letter from her father's lawyer that had arrived two weeks after the death, requesting her presence at the home in Palm Springs on the following dates. Gertie had nearly thrown it away, but something stopped her—curiosity, or maybe just concern for what would happen if Carla found it on one of her regular hunts through the trash. Then, the next day, there had been another envelope, with only one thing in it and no accompanying explanation. Gertie took it out of her folder and looked at it again, for what was now the third time since she had last seen it, sixteen years before.

It was a sheet of lined paper, torn out of a spiral-bound notebook, with the fringed edge carefully trimmed off. The writing on it had originally been done in pencil, then gone over in pen, with a signature that dated from before Gertie had mastered the cursive capital "G."

And above her name, printed clearly, were three letters: *IOU.*

TEXT MESSAGES BETWEEN GERTIE AND CARLA GLASS

how much do you get? Is it a trust with rules or just cash?

The meeting with the lawyer is in an hour. I don't know if I'm getting anything. The drive was fine by the way. And I'm staying with a bunch of siblings I haven't seen since I was three.

you had better be getting something. If you don't we'll sue. My new lawyer thinks it should be good for at least ten million.

What new lawyer? Is this the guy you met in Riverside?

Don't sign anything

relax, Kyle isn't like that. Shaman Lindsey said he had very pure vibes

...
...
...
Just don't sign anything, okay?

4

"What the hell do you people think you're doing?"

The interruption wasn't exactly courteous, but it couldn't have come at a better time. Having run out of ways to avoid returning to the main house, and concerned that she was going to sweat though all her clothes, Gertie had come back inside to find the size of the party had been reduced by half. Neil had gone to make some phone calls, and Jennifer was resting in her room.

That left Gertie to spend some quality time with her two oldest half siblings, and it wasn't going well. Maryann wandered around the room, checking every decorative item for dust, while Brian focused on his fresh glass of liquor and his phone. Every attempt Gertie had made at conversation had died on the vine, and she'd been about to have another try at asking about their father's death when a new arrival delayed that conversation.

The voice that interrupted them was shrill and at the same time pouty, and before she even turned to look, Gertie had a pretty good idea of what she was going to see.

The speaker—shouter, really—was a young woman with bright blond hair, wearing a mismatched selection of designer clothes and a look of serious displeasure. She was coming down the stairs from the second floor, brandishing a cell phone.

"Who the hell turned off my credit cards? I want them back on right now!"

Maryann was unmoved by her hysterics. "I don't know who could have canceled your credit cards. No one here has that ability. We did put a hold on all of Dad's cards, of course, since he's no longer with us."

"How dare you!"

It wasn't kind of her, and Gertie knew better, but the first word that came to mind while looking at the woman was "buoyancy." Puffy lips and overstuffed cheekbones drew whatever attention was left away from the two giant globes that floated under the woman's thin cotton crop top. Even her shoes looked inflated—giant marshmallowy wedge sandals that made wheezing noises every time she took a step.

"It's my card! Arnold wanted me to have it." She gave Maryann a calculated sneer. "He said I earned it."

Maryann was unmoved by the insinuations.

"Did he put it in your name, Haylee?" she asked, and when the other woman didn't respond, Maryann replied with a smile of her own. "I didn't think so. The household accounts can cover your day-to-day costs for the time being. But I think you might want to look into making alternate arrangements for the future."

"Oh, you think so, do you?" Gertie had to hand it to the

woman—she was a fighter. She gave her mane of yellow hair a vigorous toss, nearly tipping herself off her shoes, and went on. "Maybe you're the ones who'll be having to make some changes. My Arnie said he was going to take care of me, and I think you're all going to find out he did."

She ran her hand over her flat stomach with a slyly triumphant look that faded into confusion as Maryann and Brian laughed.

"Sorry, hon, but Dad went in for the snip twenty years ago," Brian said. "He got caught that way once already. And one thing you can say about Dad, he learned from his mistakes."

Neither he nor Maryann looked at Gertie as he said it, but she knew a challenge when she heard one. She set down her tote next to an end table and approached the new arrival.

"Gertie Glass," she said, maintaining steady eye contact as she held out her hand. "I don't believe we've met."

The woman stared at her face, and then her extended hand with an expression of incredulity. "Are you fucking kidding me!" she said, then turned around and stomped back up the stairs, squeaking as she went.

The two siblings waited until the door slammed to start laughing.

"That was Haylee, by the way," said Maryann. "One 'y' and two 'e's'—and don't ask me where they all go. I'm not sure she knows herself. She moved in with our dad about two months ago. As you can see, she's very affected by his death."

"Obviously," Gertie agreed, though she wondered if Maryann realized the same sarcasm could be applied to all of them.

"Speaking of names, why did you end up with 'Gertie' as your nickname? Why not go with 'Trudy'?" Brian asked.

"There was already a Trudy in my class in third grade," Gertie lied, as usual.

The truth was, as much as she hated her full name, she hated that nickname more. "Trudy" was a name for a pert and perky girl, the type to volunteer for the yearbook and pledge a sorority. Gertie was not that person, and she resented her name for implying she might be. So she chose her alternate nickname in protest—if she was going to be a plain, bad-tempered person with a stupid name, then that's what she would be, and she wouldn't pretend she was anything else.

But that wasn't something to share now.

"Besides Haylee, is anyone else staying here?" Gertie asked.

Maryann shook her head. "Not at the moment, no. None of us live very far away, and it's hard to find bedrooms for everyone here."

"My kids won't even consider it." Brian snorted. "Ariadne says the shower isn't right for her hair, or some bullshit."

Gertie had done some research on the family before coming, and she knew Brian had been twice divorced and had three adult children who occasionally showed up on the fringes of the LA social scene. Maryann's husband was involved with the Glass property business, and all Gertie could find out about their son was that he had some sort of crypto start-up, which was frankly all she wanted to know.

She didn't mind that none of them were there—she was

outnumbered badly enough as it was—but Gertie did wonder about a family that didn't even spend time together when someone died.

Maybe it was a sore subject, because neither Brian nor Maryann continued the conversation. Gertie shouldn't have cared, but she couldn't shake the feeling that the silence her fault. So, trying for another topic, she gestured at the glass walls around them.

"What came first? The family name or the design?"

"You mean all the windows? It is a little on the nose, isn't it? To be honest, we never could get a straight answer from Dad about that," Maryann said in a friendlier tone. "He got a deal on the glass, you know. It came from one of the contractors who was working on a mall he was developing near San Diego. You couldn't just buy that stuff, back in the seventies."

Maryann walked over to one of the walls of windows and wiped off a tiny smudge with a tissue.

"I remember the day they installed it," she said. "I thought Mama was going to have a heart attack, the way she was going on. But all Dad would say was that his guys knew what they were doing. Nothing bothered him."

"Nothing? Remember when Jennifer's friends came over for that party and used one of Mama's rings to scratch dicks on the glass? He wasn't so cool then," said Brian.

Maryann laughed. "He did have his limits," she agreed.

Gertie found herself slipping into the background as they talked about their memories of growing up in this transparent palace, escaping to the mountains or the coast in the heat of summer and having swimming races on Thanksgiving. She didn't think anyone here would be interested in her stories about learning how to dispute eviction notices, or how to cancel someone else's credit card without them finding out, all before she turned ten. They might have thought the child support Arnold had been paying all those years would have been enough to support her in a similar style, but they didn't know about Carla's love of luxuries she couldn't afford or her susceptibility to fake gurus, snake oil sellers, and straight-up con men. The money might have come in, but until Gertie turned eighteen and was given control of her own accounts, it went right out again, without making stops for practical things like groceries or rent, to say nothing of vacations to the South of France.

Gertie might have been born into this world, but she didn't belong here, and the more they talked, the more she felt it.

And yet she couldn't find it in herself to be jealous. As the conversation moved on without her, Gertie's attention wandered to the tall windows and the view beyond. Some people might talk about the stark beauty of the desert, but all Gertie saw in the grays and browns of the landscape was hostility.

5

The conversation behind her moved on to family friends as though Gertie weren't even there. With nothing else to do, she wandered around the room, taking in the dimensions.

The overall shape of the building was a blocky L, with the front door halfway along the short end. The corner under the double-height ceiling was a living room that extended partway down the long arm. Blond wood staircases led up in each arm of the house to what must have been the bedrooms, and at the corner of the L, there was the third set of stairs Gertie had noticed earlier. Made of clear glass, they seemed to float out from the wall to rise up to a landing, but their base was blocked with an awkward collection of houseplants in tall planters. Around the planters, the white marble floor was stained, possibly with water, possibly not.

"What happened—" Gertie began, but they were interrupted again.

"God, it's hot as a witch's asshole out there," said Neil, coming through the door from the courtyard. "Whatever happened to cooling autumn breezes?"

"We don't get those in the desert," Maryann said, sounding mildly amused. "You should know that as well as any of us. Don't you live here? After all, your illustrious husband wouldn't want to fall out of touch with the people he represents."

"Yeah, you spend a lot of time at the beach house, don't you?" Brian had gone over to the bar near the dining table, and he came back, refilled drink in hand. "Is Nestor thinking of changing assembly districts? I'm not sure Dad would have wanted to bankroll that like he did here. Not so much in it for him."

"Nestor is more than capable of fulfilling his residency requirement without me breathing down his neck every minute," Neil replied stiffly. "And what am I supposed to do, spend the rest of my time hanging around Sacramento?"

The way Neil drew out the syllables, he made the state capital sound like a combination of a dentist's office and hell. Gertie had to fight to suppress a laugh—it was exactly how Carla reacted when anyone mentioned Anaheim.

She must not have fought hard enough, because Neil turned on her almost immediately.

"What are you smiling about? I'd better not see any of this turning up in the papers."

"Oh, Neil, relax. I'm sure Gertie has no interest in your minor scandals," said Maryann.

"You're sure? Well, I'm not." Neil waved a hand at Gertie but kept his comments directed to his older siblings. "I ran into

Jennifer upstairs before I went outside. You know what she told me? That as soon as the kid got her alone, she was asking about how Dad died. She came right out and said he was murdered."

Both Maryann and Brian turned to Gertie with accusing looks, and she felt her confidence draining away.

"I didn't say. I asked," she said, and her voice sounded small and lost in the giant room. "I wanted to know why the police weren't letting it be called an accident."

"And what did Jennifer tell you about it?" Brian said in a tone Gertie assumed was supposed to be menacing. She detected a note of worry, though.

Emboldened, she responded. "She didn't tell me anything. Not about what proves it was just an accident or why the police say they're still investigating." Gertie took a deep breath and hoped they couldn't hear her voice shaking. "If you want to fill me in about what really happened, I'm listening."

"I bet you are," Neil sneered, but Gertie wasn't paying attention to him. She was watching Maryann, who had made an involuntary motion when Gertie mentioned the police investigation, turning to look behind her.

She looked away quickly, but not before Gertie had tracked her gaze. Yet there was nothing there, just the front door and the shelf that separated it from the living area, holding what Gertie might call high-end knickknacks—a pair of glass vases, an abstract metal sculpture, and a purple geode as large as her head.

Gertie was trying to figure out what could be important about any of those items when a movement outside the window next to the door caught her eye. She thought at first it might be the shadow of someone arriving—maybe the lawyer, getting there early to start the will reading. But it was just a large black bird, flapping down next to the glass wall to drink out of a dripping sprinkler head.

Now looking firmly away from the door, Maryann didn't seem to notice. "I'm sorry, but frankly, that's none of your business," she said. "You have no standing to come in here and ask us anything, least of all that."

"He was my father," Gertie pointed out. "You may not like it, but this is all the family I have, and I think that makes it my business too."

She wasn't going to tell them about the IOU. Not a chance. Before she had arrived at the house, Gertie had allowed herself the fantasy that she would be welcomed warmly and that the people who had known her father would be able to help her understand what he might have meant by sending it.

She should have known better. They had ignored her for her entire life, and they weren't about to turn into her friends just because the one person who connected them was dead. They had all the family they wanted, and that was never going to include her.

Given that, Gertie didn't see any reason to not try to get her questions answered.

"If it helps, I've got no interest in talking to the media. I know they're nobody's friend when there's a story involved." Gertie had Carla and her life of drama to thank for that. No one could trust the media after the local news ran a story on their mother's boyfriend's Ponzi scheme that heavily implied Carla was luring investors in her own special way.

Gertie went on. "Arnold invited me to be here, so at least he didn't want me completely excluded from his life. At the very least, I deserve to know how he died."

Neither of the men looked convinced, but Maryann just sighed.

"Well, you certainly got some of his determination. Dad would never take no for an answer either."

Neil started to object, but Maryann waved him off.

"Yes, Dad did die here in the house, and the police have been making comments about being unhappy with the circumstances. Obviously, we're confident that there's nothing to it; they're just being exceptionally cautious because he was such an important member of the community."

That was a completely sensible answer, but Gertie remained unsatisfied. "The paper said he fell down some stairs. Did nobody see it happen? How is that possible?"

Maryann sighed, like she had trouble believing they were still having this conversation, but at least she answered. "It was the day of his birthday party, so there were some disruptions. I had actually gone out to run some errands, and even though the others were all here, none of them were in the room at the time."

There was a rebuke in Maryann's tone, but Gertie was more interested in the new information she had just learned.

"You were all here when he died? Had you come over early for the party?" She knew all the siblings had homes of their own, mostly around Southern California, and it hadn't occurred to her that they would have been staying with their father.

"Something like that," Neil said, swallowing whatever he'd been about to say to Maryann. "Dad had us over on Friday for dinner, and we stayed the night, since we would have just had to turn around and come back otherwise. I was the one who found him, since you're so curious. Do you want me to give you a moment-to-moment account of what it's like to find your father dead in a pool of blood on the floor? Obviously, I'd hate to have you miss anything."

Though she was stung by his anger, Gertie held her ground.

"I'm sorry you experienced that," she said, because she wasn't completely heartless. "I didn't know. I didn't know anything, which is why I was asking. It's been pretty much my whole life since I was here or saw my father, and now I've suddenly been invited back, and I'm reading things that say he might have been killed. I just wanted to have an idea of what was going on."

"And now you do," Maryann said. "The media coverage blew everything out of proportion. It's an unfortunate complication to what was already a tragic occurrence, but there's nothing for any of us to be worried about."

"Easy for you to say," Brian interrupted. "You're the only one who wasn't here. How do you think the rest of us felt, having the cops sit there and ask us eight different ways why we killed him?"

"Maybe if you learned how to control your temper, they would have gone easier on all of us," Neil said. "What were you even thinking—"

"Oh God, are we talking about that again?" Jennifer was coming down the stairs from the far side of the house, rubbing her face with one hand as she gripped the railing with the other. Two steps from the bottom, she stopped and glared at Neil. "I thought you said we weren't going to tell her anything."

"Yeah, well, not all of us got that memo," Neil said, glaring in turn at Maryann.

Gertie had the sense that she was the object of everyone's anger, and yet it really wasn't her that anyone was mad at.

"Excuse me." None of them had noticed the young woman come into the room, Gertie included. She was about Gertie's age, white, with an undercut and gauges in both ears, and she was dressed in black chinos and a black polo shirt with "The Glass House" embroidered over her left breast. She must have heard at least some of what had been said, but if it made any impression on her, it didn't show in her face.

"The chef needs to know if there are any dietary requirements for lunch today," she said in an even voice with a hint of a New York accent.

Maryann and Neil both shook their heads, and Brian ignored her, but Jennifer piped up.

"I'm not doing pulses now, and that includes soy. Does he know that?"

"Yes, ma'am." She turned to Gertie with the faintest raising of a pierced eyebrow. "For you?"

Gertie shook her head. "No dietary requirements. I'm just not a fan of cilantro."

To her surprise, that drew a barking laugh from Neil.

"No worries there," he said. "Dad couldn't stand the stuff, wouldn't allow it in the house. Funny thing, because the rest of us love it."

"Really?" said Gertie. "I guess it's weird how stuff works in families, isn't it?"

WEDNESDAY, AUGUST 21

THREE DAYS BEFORE THE DEATH OF ARNOLD GLASS

The moisture from the outside of the water glass left a damp ring on the white tablecloth. Arnold found himself annoyed by the imperfection it introduced, at the same time as he was impressed there was that much humidity in the air at all. But that was Oscar's for you—the staff knew what it took to keep their guests comfortable. Those guests were men and women Arnold's age, people who knew something about comfort.

Well, not quite his age. Arnold doubted there were many people there who would be ninety on Saturday.

Oscar's was a steakhouse in the classic sense, the sort of place you'd expect to find in Palm Springs in the old days. Not like the restaurants they were opening now, where you sat on metal stools and forty dollars got you a plate of leaves and flowers. Oscar's wasn't cheap, but you got what you paid for.

And one of the things you were paying for was the service. The waitress had already taken Arnold's lunch order, and now she came back with the water pitcher to top up his glass. As she leaned over, her tailored white shirt stretched, and Arnold was able to admire the outline of her body.

Not bad, he thought. Breasts a little on the small side, but that could be fixed.

"Is there anything more I can do for you?"

"Not right now," Arnold said with a smile. He had put her age at around thirty, but now that he got a better look, he thought she was more like twenty-five. A little young, but her voice was pleasant.

Arnold always forgot about that sort of thing early on, and once again he was paying for it. Haylee had many qualities he appreciated, but he was at his limit with her high-pitched squeals and baby talk. That was no great tragedy; it was about time he was done with her anyway.

Normally that wouldn't have been a problem, but Arnold had received some information that morning, just before he left for lunch. It had come in an email from a former associate of his—the sort of person you called "a friend" because the other words weren't fit for company. But, while Nigel Olstead might not be Arnold's favorite person, he did have a way of picking up useful bits of gossip. Like the one he had shared in the email, about a how former relationship of Haylee's had ended. Arnold hadn't memorized it, but phrases like "damaging lawsuit" and "physical threats" stuck out in his mind.

He would have to deal with it eventually, but that was a problem for later. Arnold had taken himself out for this lunch because he did his best thinking in public places, and he had a lot to think about.

A busboy silently cleared away his salad plate, and Arnold set his notepad in the empty space. He liked working on paper—you knew where you stood with paper. Plus, when you threw it away or shredded it, it was gone, no worrying about some hidden copy that you missed. That was the sort of certainty that Arnold appreciated.

He wasn't planning to get rid of the notes he was making now, but he wasn't ready to share them yet. Not that he didn't want to. It was all Arnold could do not to tell everyone he saw about the great things the future had in store. But that would have to wait—he had a few more matters to deal with first.

Arnold was still writing when his steak arrived, and the waitress stood silently by until he finished his thought and moved the pad off to the side. She didn't try to read what he had written, which Arnold found annoying. In fact, no one in the restaurant showed much interest in him, which just showed how little they knew.

Even people who recognized Arnold might have overlooked him at this point—an old man in a failing industry. But Arnold didn't feel that way. The oldest man alive was one hundred and twelve—Arnold had looked it up. There was a lot he could do in twenty-two years.

A lot he could do indeed. The waitress was back at a neighboring table, taking dessert orders and laughing at a joke one of the men made. It was a nice laugh, fresh and lively.

Everyone told Arnold he should stop chasing the young women, that he needed someone who would take care of him and he was just embarrassing himself. And sometimes he thought they were right; Arnold longed for a life where no one ever tried to explain another new app to him.

But... Arnold watched the waitress go and chuckled to himself. That was the problem, wasn't it? There was always a butt.

6

It was a tense and awkward group that filed into what must have been Arnold's home office for the reading of the will. The room was on the bottom floor of the house, occupying the short end of the L under what Gertie understood to be the main bedroom suite, but in no other way did it seem like it was part of the same building.

The walls on two sides had tall windows, like the rest of the house, but here the view was blocked—by steel panels with geometric cutouts on the exterior wall and a dense planting of bushy palms on the side that faced the pool. Inside, the white-and-blue color scheme of the main room gave way to a more muted palette of browns, with an occasional touch of mustard yellow, and the furniture was all made of dark wood. Even the floor transitioned from bright marble to thick carpet. Gertie wondered, as she took her seat in one of the straight-backed chairs, which space more truly reflected the tastes of the man for whom both had been built.

The back wall of the room was lined with shelves, all stocked with leather-bound books and expensive decorative items. There were cut-glass decanters and bronze animals, silver-framed pictures, and three globes. But the most interesting to Gertie was a fan on the bottom shelf, looking distinctly functional in its black plastic shell.

There was one new arrival who had joined them, and Gertie recognized him. Jules Rankin had been Arnold's personal lawyer for as long as she could remember, and he was the first person she thought of when she pictured her father. In the extended battles over child support, Jules had been the main point of contact, producing the documents about personal versus corporate funds and signing off on the genetic tests.

Oddly, Gertie had never disliked him. Jules had been the one person in her life who always took her seriously. And his clear level of authority and the respect he commanded had been a factor in her deciding to become a lawyer herself.

It had been several years since she had seen Jules, and Gertie was surprised by how much the time had affected him. She had always thought of him as an old man—in the way any child considers someone with gray hair old—but looking back she realized he must have been only in his fifties when she was born, close to ten years younger than her father. But that would make him around eighty now, and it showed in his face, which was deeply lined and looking more tired than she remembered.

Five chairs had been set up in the office, all but one taken by the family members. Gertie took the last one, in the back row, and noticed that Haylee was sitting in a leather armchair on one side of the room, with a triumphant expression that made Gertie suspect she hadn't been invited to be there, but it hadn't been worth the fight to keep her out.

As soon as Gertie sat down, Jules looked around the room to confirm they were all there, and then opened the leather-bound folder on the desk in front of him and began to speak.

"As you all know, the estate of Arnold Glass Jr. is—"

There was a sickening thump from the courtyard windows, and Gertie turned in time to see a large black bird flop awkwardly to the ground.

"Damn crows," Brian snarled, as Maryann tapped something quickly on her phone. A moment later a member of the staff appeared outside the window and tried to corral the animal, but it hopped away and ultimately took to unsteady flight.

"Dumbass," said Jennifer.

Jules cleared his throat and started again.

"Yes, so the estate is, as I said, complex. Most of the cash value and stocks not related to the business are held in trusts, to be distributed among his children, minus a few charitable bequests."

I wonder if I count with the children, Gertie thought as she listened to his dry, lawyerly voice. *Or maybe charity?*

Jules went on. "As for the company itself, Arnold made some changes to the distribution of his shares not long before his death."

A quiet stirring went around the room. Not enough to indicate this was new information—more like anticipation of an answer they had been waiting for. By Gertie's guess, they knew something had been changed, but they didn't know what.

Jules made no sign of noticing the disturbance. After a pause to turn the page, he continued, looking up only to address his audience.

"As you know, for most of the history of the company, all shares in the Glass Property Group were held solely by Arnold himself. Ten years ago, he distributed 5 percent to each of his four oldest children, so they might have a voting interest in the business, with the understanding that the shares not be sold during his lifetime. Of the remaining shares, another 15 percent goes to each Maryann, Brian, Neil, and Jennifer Glass, bringing their total holdings to 20 percent each. Additionally, 1 percent is to go to each of his six grandchildren. And the final 14 percent is left to his daughter, Gertrude Glass."

Gertie did her best to keep her face impassive as everyone turned to stare at her, but her mind was racing. She had known she was there for a reason, and some version of this outcome had occurred to her, but she couldn't make sense of it. Was this what her father had meant by sending back her IOU? To call her to participate in running a mall-development company with a bunch of people who hated her? Had he held on to that note all these years for that?

The others were still staring, like they expected her to say something, but Gertie wasn't sure what she could, or wanted to, tell them. Finally, Neil broke the silence, laughing and shaking his head.

"Very funny, Dad. You had to have your little joke, didn't you?"

Jules cleared his throat again. "I assure you, Neil, this isn't a joke. Arnold explained his wishes to me very clearly, and the will has been properly signed and witnessed. I have no doubt this is exactly what he intended."

Neil laughed again, louder this time. "Relax, Jules, I wasn't questioning your integrity. I completely believe he did this on purpose. I bet it gave him a lot of pleasure to think of us all sitting here, recalculating our routes now that he's thrown his mini-me in our way."

The analogy might have been a little confused, but Gertie got the general gist.

"Are you saying he made me a part owner of the company to cause trouble for you? Why would he do that?" she said.

"Because he was a mean old bastard, that's why," Brian replied. "Any time he thought he could do something to throw you off, he'd do it, just to see what would happen. Apparently even when he wasn't going to be around for the payoff."

Jennifer sighed dramatically and scowled at the carpet. "I should have known. He was never going to take any of us seriously, even when he was dead."

The idea that maybe Arnold had wanted his legacy shared between all his children didn't seem to have occurred to anybody. And Gertie didn't think much of it herself. He'd had twenty-five years to get in touch with her. Why wait until he was dead to bring her into the family business, if that was what he wanted to do?

"All right," said Maryann, who had been quietly examining Gertie's face. "We know this is what he did. It doesn't matter why.

Let's hear the rest, and then we can discuss what we're going to do next." She inclined her head toward the lawyer. "Please go on."

Jules cleared his throat and adjusted his glasses. "Thank you. We've covered most of the salient points, aside from certain items of memorabilia left to friends and associates. And, of course, the distribution of property."

"Now we're getting to it," Neil said.

The lawyer didn't look up from his papers.

"The two vacation properties, in Vail and in Santa Lucia, are to be sold and the proceeds divided among the legatees as designated above. Should one or more of them wish to keep one or more of the properties, they are to buy out the others at fair market value, to be determined by independent assessment. A similar system is in place for any vehicles that are part of the estate, including cars, boats, et cetera, as well as any pieces of jewelry that are not otherwise designated to individuals."

"And?" said Brian. "What about this house?"

Jules paused, either for dramatic effect or because he was reluctant to say what came next—Gertie wasn't sure.

"The Palm Springs house, along with all its contents and a sum of money in trust to fund its upkeep, are to go to Gertrude Glass."

7

This time, the shocked silence was complete.

Gertie didn't bother trying to control her face. What it registered, she knew, was neither delight or gratitude, but confusion and anger. She had the sensation of being a pawn in someone else's plans, and she didn't like it. She might have said she wasn't going to carry out whatever grudge Arnold had toward his other children, but then they started talking.

"He gave her the house?" Jennifer shrieked. "Our house? The Glass family house, to that whore's brat?"

Neil stood up and advanced toward the desk. "I don't believe it. Let me see that will."

Jules turned the folder around and pushed it across the desk. His expression was blandly amenable, but Gertie noticed he kept his hand on the pages.

Neil studied the text for several minutes, moving his lips as he read through the paragraphs. When he got to the end, he turned away abruptly and returned to his seat.

"This isn't over," he said to Gertie. "We're going to find out how you got around him, and you'll regret what you've done."

The accusation was as stupid as it was toothless, but Gertie still found it unsettling.

"I didn't do anything," she replied. "Whatever Arnold did, it was on his own."

"Do you expect us to believe that?" said Jennifer.

Gertie shrugged. "I don't have any expectations for you. All I can tell you is the truth, which is that I haven't seen Arnold since I was three years old, and my only communications with him have been through Jules or another of his lawyers."

"And after all that, he left you our house?" Jennifer sounded incredulous, and Gertie didn't blame her. But she didn't have anything more to say, so she stayed silent, staring back at Jennifer until the other woman turned away, muttering.

Gertie was unnerved as well. Jules had said Arnold had made changes to his will recently—was this one of them? And if he had been murdered, could it be related? Up until now, Gertie had been thinking about the manner of her father's death as something she felt she ought to know about, but suddenly it became more urgent.

"Anyway," Jennifer said at last, shifting to turn her back to Gertie, "this is shady, and everyone knows it."

"And believe me, we're going to find out how this happened." Brian glared at Gertie and actually shook his finger in her direction. "You may think you're cute, little lady, coming in here and taking what's ours, but you don't know what you're up against."

"I think maybe it's time that we all stop talking, before someone says something unfortunate."

Maryann had looked as shocked as any of them when the will was read, but otherwise she'd been able to contain her reaction. But her tone was suddenly icy, and she gave Brian a look of warning. He started to say something to her when she stood up suddenly, addressing the other two siblings, without a look at him or Gertie.

"Jules has told us what's in the will, and that's all we're going to get out of this today. Lunch should be ready, so let's go and eat, and we can follow up later with our questions."

Maryann started toward the office door, and the others fell in behind, grumbling and casting looks at Gertie as they went.

"Wait! You're not done yet! You haven't read what I get!"

In the excitement, everyone had lost interest in Haylee, but she hadn't forgotten herself. As the others left, she leaped to her feet and pointed at Jules, quivering in outrage.

"You read that again, and this time don't leave out the parts where he left it all to me."

Jules closed the folder, with the faintest hint of a smile playing in the corners of his eyes. "I'm sorry, Ms. Jackson, but you are not mentioned in the will."

"Bullshit! He left it all to me—he told me he was going to!"

"Then he lied," Maryann said. "Or you misunderstood. Either way, there's nothing for you here now, and I think it's time you moved on."

"No! He couldn't have lied to me. He wouldn't do that."

Jennifer snort-laughed and flipped her hair over her shoulder. "Oh, come on. I have trouble believing someone in your line of work could really be that naive."

For a moment, Haylee's confusion overwhelmed her outrage. "What are you talking about? I don't have a job."

"Maybe not, but we all know what you'll do for money," Jennifer said as she pushed aside the curtain and vanished through the door.

As dense as Haylee may have been, that one did finally get through. But by the time she had figured it out, Jennifer was already gone, along with most of the rest of the family, so she focused her wrath on Gertie.

"You think you're so funny, all of you laughing at me. Like you think I'm just dumb and there's nothing I can do about it. But you don't want to mess with me. You don't even know what I can do."

With that, she stormed out, and a few seconds later, Gertie could hear the sound of her heels clacking up the stairs to the bedrooms over the office.

"Well," Jules said once she was gone. "I guess that tells us."

"It does," agreed Gertie. "Though I'm not sure exactly what we've been told."

She kept her tone light, but the confrontation made her uncomfortable. Gertie knew a few things about women like Haylee, and one of them was that you never knew how far they would go if they thought they had a reason.

8

"What the hell is going on?"

Alone with Jules in the office, Gertie had a lot of questions, and she decided to start with the obvious. But instead of answering, the lawyer finished packing the documents back into his case. Only when he was done did he briefly make eye contact.

"I realize this has all come as a shock to you," he said evenly. "I'm sorry your father didn't contact you ahead of time to tell you what he was planning. That wasn't my recommendation."

Gertie wouldn't have said she knew Jules well, but even so she thought he sounded awkward and out of character. She was going to press him for more details—after all, his discomfort was low on Gertie's list of concerns—when she noticed that he was pointedly looking past her, to the office doorway.

The door itself was open, but at some point, a curtain had been added that hung across the space—possibly to deaden the sounds of any conversations the door didn't block. As Gertie turned to follow the lawyer's gaze, she saw the fabric move, like it had been stirred by a nonexistent wind, and she understood.

"I'm sorry too," she said carefully. "This has all come as a big shock to me."

"Of course it has. You're going to need some time to process it, but right now I think we should join the others for lunch. We don't want to keep them waiting."

"Right," Gertie said, smiling and raising her voice just a fraction. "I'm sure they're all sitting at the table right now."

―

By the time Gertie and Jules came out into the main room, the rest of the siblings were, in fact, sitting at the clear rectangular table that took up the area in the long arm of the L. (Neil's chair might have been at an angle, and Jennifer was a little out of breath, but Gertie pretended not to notice.)

Jules had been given a place between Maryann and Brian at the head of the table, and Gertie was seated facing the clear staircase with its cluster of plant pots. Closer up, she could tell from the scuffing that the treads weren't actually glass but plastic, nearly a foot thick. Undoubtedly strong enough to hold a person's weight, but the slick surfaces and lack of railings made Gertie shiver.

The planters obscured but didn't entirely cover a set of marks at the base of the staircase—brownish stains that looked like they had been roughly scrubbed away. But they hadn't come out; Gertie knew from experience that marble was hell for taking stains. The whole area would probably have to be refinished, if they really wanted it to get it out, whatever it was.

Died after a fall in his home.

Jennifer had said that Arnold had fallen down the stairs from his office, but the room they had just come from had been on one level. Gertie looked up, to the landing at the top of the clear staircase with its single white door, and was suddenly certain she needed to see what was behind it.

They had all gotten settled at the table when Haylee tromped down the stairs. She took a look at the full seats around the table, then tossed her hair.

"Get my car," she said to the first staff member she saw, before turning and swaying her way toward the door. She was almost there when she had another thought and turned back. "I'm coming back, and if anybody touches my stuff, I'll call the cops."

With that, Haylee left, slamming the front door behind her. Gertie looked around to see if anyone at the table was concerned, or amused, but they pointedly ignored the disruption.

It took only a few more minutes for Gertie to realize she was also being ignored. She hadn't been expecting a friendly mealtime conversation, even before the scene in the office, but the way no one at the table would look directly at her was more unnerving than Gertie liked to admit.

The food was good, at least. As soon as they were seated, a server came around to place plates of salad silently in front of them—a light dish of mini lettuce leaves dressed with citrus and oil, decorated with toasted pine nuts and tangerine segments.

After her fast-food breakfast, Gertie hadn't expected to be hungry so soon, but the stress of the morning must have done something for her appetite, and she worked her way steadily though the starter.

Without anything else to do, Gertie watched the members of the household staff who circulated around the room. Two were working the table, both of them younger than Gertie—the woman who had asked earlier about food restrictions and a Black man with a shaved head and a serious expression—and she counted another three crossing the patio by the pool, on their way to other tasks. Every one of them was dressed entirely in black, with plain slacks or skirts and matching polos with a stitched-on logo. She wondered how many there were and how much it cost to employ them. Her mother had occasionally hired someone to clean—if the money was there and the latest cleaner hadn't left in a huff—and Gertie had appreciated the days she'd been able to come home to a bathroom she hadn't had to scrub. But that was a long way from embroidered monograms and someone to wipe the water spots off the glasses.

Gertie wondered about the logistics of it. If the house actually was hers, was she supposed to take them all on? What would she do with that many people around? How much money had Arnold left to pay them? Was this the thing he had wanted her to do for him?

Or had it been something else? Gertie thought again about the recent changes to the will and what that might mean. What if Arnold had been trying to put something in motion and had been killed before he could finish it?

CAPTIONS FROM A FIFTY-SEVEN-SECOND VIDEO POSTED ONLINE BY HAYLEE JACKSON (@HONNEEHAYLEE32EE)

Hiiiii everyone

I know you've been waiting to hear from me

So I told you before that my honey died

And that was just, so sad

I really don't know how I am getting through it

But I appreciate all your support

I thought Arnie and I would be together forever

Because he really loved me

And I KNOW he wanted me to be taken care of

So today, they read the will, and all his a-hole children were there, trying to keep me out of the room, but I'm smarter than that

I knew they were going to pull something to keep me from getting what's mine

And I was RIGHT

BECAUSE
The little bitch of a lawyer said he didn't leave me
   anything!
I know that's not true
This is NOT how it is supposed to happen
They're all conspiring against me

And there's some ugly girl, I don't know what her
   deal is
She does look kind of familiar though
Anyway, she's not important
The only thing that matters is I'm not going
   anywhere
This isn't over
They have NO IDEA

9

The lunch party didn't end so much as it dissolved. First Neil got up from the table, saying something about needing to call the nanny to check on his kids, and then Jennifer left, with no explanation at all. Maryann and Brian had Jules cornered at the end of the table, taking turns speaking to him in low, angry tones and making it very clear that Gertie was excluded from the conversation. So, as soon as Gertie finished her dessert, she thanked the waiter who took away the plate and excused herself.

With nowhere to go other than the pool house, which had spent the last two hours baking in the sun, Gertie lingered on her way out, soaking up the air-conditioning. As she hesitated with her hand on the door, she heard Jules speak in a raised voice.

"I can only stay another fifteen minutes, and then I need to get my car from the carport and get on the road," he said. "I know you all have a lot of questions, and there will be plenty of time to go over them with each of you."

It was an awkward way of communicating, especially with the

emphasis he put on "each of you" and the fact that Gertie could see his reflection in the glass door as he turned slightly to look at her, but she got the message.

Would have been easier to text, she thought. But lawyers did hate to put things in writing.

―

The main garage was underground, but it had been full when Gertie arrived. She had been directed to the nearby carport, and apparently Jules had parked there as well.

Gertie waited in the shade of the carport roof, leaning against a post as a hot wind blew in off the driveway. It was early afternoon, with the full heat of the day settled in over the desert, and the hills wavered in the distance. The word "uninhabitable" was floating through Gertie's mind when one of the rocks next to the pavement turned to look at her, blinked, then vanished under a shrub.

"Lizard inhabitable," Gertie amended, out loud.

But that wasn't true, because there were plenty of people who chose to live here, her father being one of them. If she had known him, she might have understood why, but now that was just one of her many questions.

Starting with why she was there. Sending that IOU when she was twelve had been the whim of an overserious child—surely a grown man would have understood that?

Her stepfather, Andy, had been, and still was, the closest thing to a parent Gertie ever had. The time Carla had spent married to him had been a brief interval of stability in Gertie's childhood—after he helped to extract them from the oceanfront hotel of Carla's most recent guru, though not without leaving behind most of their possessions and nearly a year of Gertie's child support money. But it had been worth it, to be able to go back to regular school and wear her own clothes. And Andy, when he wasn't traveling for his work, had remembered things like the deadlines to sign up for school activities and when to make dentist appointments. Gertie suspected he had actually stayed longer than he otherwise would have, for her sake, which made her feel both guilty and grateful.

Honestly, getting Arnold to intervene on his behalf when he was a prisoner was the least she could have done, and Gertie didn't regret it for a moment, even if this was the last outcome she could have imagined. On the rare times she thought about what Arnold might have done with the note, she assumed he'd rolled his eyes and thrown it in the trash.

Obviously she had been wrong. But why had he kept it? Gertie didn't believe the man who hadn't seen or spoken to her since she was three would treasure her note as an adorable keepsake, but she found it equally improbable that he had carefully saved it to use when he needed her help. Much more likely that it had ended up shoved in the back of a drawer somewhere and he had rediscovered it all these years later.

And then what? What had gone through Arnold's mind, that he had decided to take a child's offer and use it to call on the adult? What had he wanted her to do, and why hadn't he told her?

Gertie wasn't sure she would ever have all the answers. But

the man who might be able to get her some of them was coming up the path from the house now.

"Oh good," said Jules. "You understood my message. I thought you would."

Gertie nodded. "Thanks for meeting with me. There are a few things I'm confused about."

"I bet there are," Jules said, smiling grimly. He gestured at a black Mercedes sedan. "Shall we sit in my car to talk? I think the air-conditioning might be beneficial."

The interior of Jules's car was exactly what Gertie expected—spacious, comfortable, and tastefully appointed, with walnut veneer on almost every surface that wasn't upholstered in buttery leather.

Up close, the man himself was less imposing than she remembered. Some of that was that she was no longer a child, worried she was going say something that would deprive Carla of the money that was so important to her. But it wasn't only that; there was a clear diminishment she didn't remember from the last time she had seen him, only a year ago, to discuss the possibility of covering her bar-prep classes as tuition expenses. Then he had been harried but vital, lively in their discussion of what constituted schooling under the terms of the child support document. But now he looked stooped and unhealthily thin, and the hair that she remembered as a well-styled gray swoop was flat and almost entirely white.

This was more than the onset of age she had noticed in the office. There were signs of strain in the lawyer's face and a nervousness in the way he kept glancing at the empty path back to the house.

If Gertie didn't know better, she would say he was afraid of something.

"What's going on?" she asked. "Why did Arnold leave me the house, and what did he want me to do when he invited me here?"

Jules sighed deeply. "I wish I knew. The one thing I wanted to make sure I got through to you is that he was entirely in his right mind when he made the decisions about the will. I know there's going to be a lot of talk, people trying to push the narrative that he had gone soft and sentimental, and you have my word it's all a bunch of nonsense."

Gertie smiled grimly. "Thank you. Though, to be honest, I don't think I ever would have believed he would get sentimental about me."

Jules started to say something, then stopped himself and sighed again.

"At any rate," he said, "you should be prepared to hear some unpleasant things about your father, and some of them won't be true. That unpleasantness is bound to extend to yourself as well. As the executor of his will, it's my responsibility to make sure his wishes are carried out, but if all this is more than you're willing to deal with, you'd be within your rights to make a deal to abandon your claims to your portion of the estate and walk away. I think I should be able get you something, though it will be a lot less than the full inheritance would be worth."

Gertie thought about that. She didn't doubt her half siblings would throw everything they had at her. The legal challenges could take years, and there was a rational argument to be made for taking what she could get now and sparing herself the headache.

That was the sensible option and—aside from Carla, the West Coast champion of greed and spite—no one would blame her for taking it.

But.

The IOU. Gertie was not a romantic or superstitious person, but she had a deep aversion to being in debt, and for nearly two-thirds of her life, she had owed one she had no ability to pay. And she wasn't going to get another chance. So, if she wanted to make good on her childhood promise, Gertie was going to have to at least make an attempt to carry out Arnold's last request, as best as she could interpret it.

The envelope returning the IOU had come around the same time as the invitation to the reading of the will. Logic dictated the two must be connected, and Gertie believed in logic. Arnold had wanted her to do something related to his bequests, and by the disruption the news had caused among his other children, she assumed keeping the house out of their hands was part of that. What she was meant to do with the shares in his company was less apparent, but from the fact that her percentage prevented any two of the siblings from having more than 50 percent of the total, she intuited that his goal was to thwart whatever plans they had.

It would have been nice to have clearer instructions, but Gertie was used to working with what she got.

The message might have been reason enough to influence her

choices, but it wasn't all. Gertie had known the Glass family for less than four hours, and there were few things she would like less than to provide them with another undeserved win in their smug lives. Fighting for her share of the inheritance might leave Gertie with nothing, but she had nothing to begin with, so what was there to lose? It would be worth it to know there was one thing they couldn't take just by being rich enough and mean enough.

Gertie knew a few things about spite herself.

"I intend to pursue my rights under the will," she said to Jules. "After all, it was what my father wanted."

"I thought you would say that. In that case, there are a few things you should know." Gertie must have looked worried, because he smiled at her. "It's not all bad, actually. For one thing, the people you're up against do not, in fact, have unlimited money to spend."

Gertie wasn't impressed. "They're a lot less limited than me."

"Well, yes and no." Jules hesitated, and then went on. "There shouldn't be any trouble with telling you this, since as a shareholder in the company, you're an interested party, but the truth is the Glass Property Group, and by extension the family, is not as flush with cash as you might think."

"Because nobody has gone to a mall since 1998?" Gertie asked.

Jules chuckled. "That's part of it. I don't know if you're familiar with how people like your family practice tax-efficient money management?"

"You mean cheating?"

"Not cheating. Operating fully within the law to minimize their tax burden. Essentially, it boils down to borrowing money against the assets and using that for living expenses, which allows you to write off the interest. There's more to it than that, but you get the idea. But what's important is to borrow only as much as can easily be paid back, without touching the capital."

"I see," said Gertie. "And they weren't doing that?"

"Unfortunately, no. As you said, the shopping mall business has been in decline, which has reduced the income, as well as the value of the shares in the company. But I'm afraid none of the family members, your father included, could be convinced to adjust their spending accordingly, not as long as the banks were happy to lend to them. They're not broke, far from it, but almost every asset in that estate has been leveraged to the hilt, and it's going to take a while to unwind that."

"Almost every asset," Gertie repeated. "Except, I'm guessing, for the house?"

"You guess right. For whatever reason, your father refused to take on any debt for this property or the trust he set up to support it. It could all be sold tomorrow, and you would realize the total value."

"I see." Suddenly, Gertie found the response to her inheritance more understandable. It wasn't just a matter of sentiment; there was also the question of ready cash.

"How badly do they need the money?" she asked.

"I don't know," Jules said. "I'm aware of this much only because I've been going over the financials as the executor, though I had some ideas from things Arnold said over the years. I'm bringing it up because I don't want you to feel like the case is hopeless—aside from having the facts on our side, they simply aren't going to be able to keep fighting forever."

"That is useful to know," Gertie said, then wondered how she could have gone so quickly from never having met her siblings to considering driving them to bankruptcy.

Jules went on. "I'll be in touch once we see what sort of form the challenges take, but one thing I would recommend for the moment is that you stay in the house. I know the family is likely to make it unpleasant for you, but there's a good basis to argue that one of the reasons your father wanted you to be here at this time was to take possession of the property. It's not technically true that possession is nine-tenths of the law, but in practical terms, it can be helpful."

It was something Gertie had been thinking already, but she still cringed at the prospect. Even going back to her mother's condo, with its cycles of aromatherapy products and the constant warnings about "toxins," was more appealing than staying in that baking cottage. To say nothing of the responses she anticipated from the rest of the family. They had their own homes, of course, but she didn't think they would leave her to fight it out with Haylee over who could drive the other away first.

But those weren't the only people in the house.

"What about the staff? Who's in charge of them, and how are they supposed to be paid?"

Jules gave her a look that was both impressed and amused.

"Legally, that's a good question. In practical terms, Mrs. Phan is in charge, and I would strongly encourage you to continue that arrangement. She's the household manager—you'll meet her soon. She's worked here since before you were born."

"Really? I wonder if she remembers me," said Gertie, who really wondered if Mrs. Phan remembered Carla and how much her mother's behavior was going to count against her. She really didn't need to meet another new enemy today.

"Oh, I don't doubt she remembers you" was all Jules had to say about that. "As far as the salaries, the trust will pay the ongoing expenses of the house, for the time being."

The car's air-conditioning was so powerful that Gertie was getting cold, and she was aware that the longer this conversation went on, the more the other people in the house were bound to make of it. But there were a few more things she needed to know.

"Okay, so that takes care of the immediate issues. But I have to ask," she said, twisting in the passenger seat so she could look Jules straight in the eyes, "was my father murdered, or wasn't he?"

10

Jules didn't respond right away, and as the silence stretched out, Gertie wondered if he was mad at her for asking. But when he spoke, Jules didn't sound angry; his voice was tired and worried.

"I don't know. The police certainly seem to think there was something suspicious about his death. But it's hard to imagine how, given the circumstances."

"Which were what? I know he died the day of his ninetieth birthday party, when everyone was visiting, and it had something to do with those glass stairs. So how did it happen?"

Jules fell silent again, but he was fidgeting nervously, and he looked out the car windows and into the mirrors before he spoke.

"You've got it basically right," he said at last. "I can fill in some of the gaps, but not that many, I'm afraid.

"As you say, it was his ninetieth birthday. Arnold had been planning the celebration for a long time—well, he hadn't, but between Mrs. Phan and Maryann, it was being planned for at least the last six months. A big party at the botanical gardens, guests coming from all over, food and music—everything the best it could be. I have to admit, I was rather looking forward to it," Jules said with a sad smile. "Arnold didn't act like he was, though. I'd say he was more irritated by the fuss than anything. But I think that was mostly for show—he always loved being the center of attention."

"Like having his children over the night before?" Gertie asked. "Was that always part of the plan?"

"No, that was a last-minute invitation. Not that they should have anything to complain about. You might hear some of your siblings talking about their jobs, but the truth is, aside from Maryann, none of them do much beyond finding ways to spend Arnold's money. In fact, he said as much to me earlier that week. He was quite animated on the subject, in fact."

"Was that when he changed the will?" Gertie asked.

Jules gave her a significant look. "Yes, it was. I admit, I was concerned at first. I knew Arnold had taken up with this new girlfriend, and you know what they say: there's no fool like an old fool. But when he said he wanted to leave the house and part of the company to you, I didn't know what to think."

"But you did think something. What was it?"

Jules laughed. "Oh dear. You're going to get tired of hearing how much you're like him, but you really are. You're right, I did think some things, but mostly about the other four. Your father wasn't always pleased with the children from his first marriage. He'd had hopes for Brian, as the eldest son, but Arnold found him boorish and unimaginative. Jennifer was the baby of the family, until you, of course. I don't think he ever really expected anything of her, and that's what he got. Maryann was the only one who put any effort into the business, but Arnold didn't respect her contributions very much. And I suspect he never really came to terms with Neil's sexuality, though of course he would never say so to me."

Gertie glanced at the beautifully enameled rainbow tiepin Jules had worn for as long as she could remember him, then nodded. "So you think he changed his will to keep them from having total control of the company?"

"More than that. The house in particular, Arnold saw as his legacy, and he didn't want it handed to someone who wouldn't respect that. And, of course, he wasn't expecting to die so soon. He might have been turning ninety, but Arnold Glass had no plans to leave the stage."

"Right. Speaking of that, when did he give you the letters to send to me? Did he tell you what was in the envelopes?"

"Those were another thing he brought to me the week before he died. He didn't tell me anything about the contents. That was also when he added the instruction that you be invited to come for the will reading, with the specification that you were to stay at the house."

"I see. Were you curious about what was in the letter?"

Jules smiled wryly. "Of course. I didn't ask."

"Of course," Gertie repeated. "But I'm going to tell you anyway."

It wasn't as embarrassing as she had feared, talking about

her desperate childhood plea and the debt it had incurred. Jules listened without interrupting, smiling occasionally and frowning more. When she was done, he looked at her with pity and admiration.

"You took on quite a bit as a child, didn't you?" he asked.

Gertie shrugged. "I did what I had to. And I guess that's what I'm doing here too, but it would help to know what it was. It must have been some sort of sudden idea—I can't imagine Arnold had been saving that IOU for so long in case he wanted to ask me for something."

"I wouldn't be so sure of that." Jules shook his head. "Your father had an amazing way of holding on to things."

"Well, however he had it, he sent it back to me. But there was nothing with it to tell me what it was he thought I owed him."

"I wish I could tell you. Arnold did have a way of believing that people should be able to guess what he wanted, but even for him, that's quite something. There are still some documents I need to go through, so if I find anything that might shed some light, I'll let you know."

"Thank you." Gertie glanced at the clock on the dashboard. She had already been out here for too long, but she still had a lot questions. She wasn't going to get to all of them, so she went back to the other thing that was most on her mind—Arnold's death.

"What do you know about what happened that morning? All four of the children were visiting, plus Haylee was there, right? And the staff? How is it possible no one saw Arnold fall?"

"That is an excellent question. Part of the answer, I think, is that most of the staff members weren't here—they were off at the botanical garden setting up for the party. As far as I know, the children were around, except for Maryann, who had gone off to run some errand. Arnold always spent several hours in the morning up in the tower office, and he liked to work uninterrupted. Neil was the one who found him."

"So why didn't the police think it was an accident? I've seen those stairs; they look pretty dangerous on their own."

Jules nodded. "An absolute death trap. I told Arnold that many times. I have no idea how he was able to get insurance to cover the house. And I'm equally in the dark about what the police were thinking. I know there was some sort of incident when they responded to the nine-one-one call, and the police searched the grounds, but I never heard any of the details. All I know is the body still hasn't been released."

Gertie stared through the windshield at the blank concrete wall of the carport while she thought about that. She didn't know a lot about police procedure or how long it typically took to process a corpse, but two weeks seemed like long enough. Was there something about the body that made the police think Arnold had been murdered?

Jules's phone chimed with an incoming text, and while he answered it, Gertie looked across to the part of the house that was just visible from under the carport roof. The windows of the tower were gleaming in the afternoon sun, like a lighthouse in the desert—and about as practical. She thought about what she had expected her life to be and how she could conceivably fit it into this space, and she could only come up with one thing.

"It would be quite a place to base a law practice."

Jules smiled and followed her line of sight. "That it would. You know, your father practically ran his business out of that house. The downstairs office we were in today was where he took meetings, but the real heart of the place was his office up in the tower. He would go up there every morning at six and have his coffee brought up, and it practically took an act of Congress to get him down before eleven. He told me once that the view over the desert of the city was the thing that inspired him the most. If we could do that, he'd say, then anything must be possible."

Gertie looked up to where the rearview mirror gave a distant glimpse of the shining buildings rising out of the barren landscape.

"That's one way of looking at it," she said.

VOICE MESSAGE LEFT BY NEIL GLASS-ZANES FOR NESTOR ZANES

Hi, babes, it's me. Sorry I missed your call earlier. Anyway, yeah, I guess you saw my message about the house. No idea what Dad was thinking, and I guess we'll never know. Maryann thinks we can get it away from her, but it's going to take some time. I know it's not... I don't know if there's anything else we can do at this point. [sigh] Look, I know this isn't ideal, and I'm doing everything I can. But this is a situation I can't control, and if you could just, you know... if we could find another way, at least for right now. Because, I don't know, Maryann's always been good at handling things, but this kid, she's something different. I thought I'd seen the last of the old man, and now it's like he's back, ready to go another ninety years. I know—save it for therapy. Anyway, call me when you get this. Oh, and we've got the memorial tomorrow and I've been telling everyone you can't make it because you're tied up with committees, so try to stay out of sight, okay? I have enough problems without having to deal with a snarky blind item in the Register. [long sigh] I'm sorry. It's just that I thought we were finally out of it all, and now this. Anyway, take care of yourself. Talk soon. Love you.

11

Gertie was halfway back to the house before she realized she hadn't asked about the other part of her inheritance. What the hell was she supposed to do with 14 percent of a mall-development company?

One thing at a time, Gertie thought. If she got through this fight for the house, then maybe she could find out if the world really needed another food court.

Thinking of food reminded her of another thing. Lunch, for all its discomfort, had been very good, and she wanted to know who had made it. For everything else it was, the Glass House was clearly a functioning machine, its parts whirling away out of sight.

And right now she felt like taking a look under the hood.

There was only one place the kitchen could reasonably be, at the end of the long arm of the L. She didn't think produce deliveries would be getting trucked across the marble floors, so she followed the outside walls around the back corner, where she found another door, set between two small windows.

An old garlic press had been used to prop the door open, so Gertie opened it the rest of the way and went in. The kitchen was only barely air-conditioned, with extra heat from the stoves turning the atmosphere stiflingly hot.

Despite the temperature, the mood in the kitchen was cheerful. A short, heavily-tattooed man with bleached hair dyed pink at the tips was leaning over the stove, stirring a pot of something that smelled richly of onions, while the two members of the staff who had served the lunch were laughing and dipping chips into a bowl of fresh salsa.

When Gertie appeared at the door, the conversation stopped abruptly. The female staffer transitioned smoothly from whatever she had been saying, thanked the chef for his help, and swept a tray off the counter on her way out the door. Her male colleague didn't do quite as well, only managing to stammer something about fish before he shoved a chip into his mouth and fled.

The chef, still in his spot at the stove, looked up at Gertie and smiled. "Welcome," he said. "Anything I can do for you?"

"Sorry, I didn't mean to interrupt." Gertie came the rest of the way into the kitchen and let the door close behind her. As soon as it did, the dry heat of the outdoors was replaced by a damper warmth. "I just wanted to say how much I enjoyed lunch."

The chef's smile grew wider, and he gestured at the bowl of chips. "Glad you liked it. Come on in. I just made pico de gallo. Do you want some?"

Grateful for the welcome, Gertie helped herself to a chip and some salsa, though she was still full from lunch.

"I'm Gertie Glass, by the way," she said, extending her chip-free hand.

"Eduardo Joaquin de Herrera Vasquez, head chef and chief dishwasher of this grand establishment. Call me Eddie," said the chef as he shook it. His palms were as tough and scarred as Gertie would have expected, but his nails were neatly manicured, with each pinkie painted in a sparkly blue. "Glad you liked the food. Usually, for guests, I try to find out about likes and dislikes, but I didn't have a chance today. But Mrs. Phan said you'd be fine with anything as long as it wasn't too salty."

"She did?" It wasn't wrong, but Gertie was stumped how anyone here could know that much about her.

Eddie laughed. "Impressive, isn't she? You don't even know. Anyway, she said it was how you were when you were little, and she guessed some things wouldn't have changed."

"She guessed right," Gertie said, impressed and a little embarrassed to have been so predictable. "I should thank Mrs. Phan for remembering from so long ago. Do you know where she is?"

"She had a vital task to do today, very important, for the memorial service tomorrow. The florist didn't have peonies in the right shade of white, so the family sent her to Carlsbad to pick up replacements." Eddie's tone made it clear what he thought about that job assignment. In case there was any doubt, he went on. "The way they act, you'd think she was some sort of genie—rub the lamp and ask for anything you want. The crazy thing is, she can do it. And if she doesn't, you end up realizing you didn't want it at all."

"I'm going to be interested to meet her. Or meet her again,

I guess. But are you sure you should be talking to me like this?" Gertie thought about how the other staffers had fled at the sight of her; clearly Eddie was not so concerned about her influence.

Eddie shrugged. "I'm not making a career out of being here. Mr. Glass was an okay boss, and the pay's been good, but I've almost got enough saved up to open my own catering company, and anyway, I have a feeling this position was about to turn over no matter what I say."

He smiled again and gave Gertie a wink. "And who knows, maybe there's going to be a change of management, and I'm just getting my points in early."

Gertie laughed, delighted both at his audacity and by the fact there was at least one person who saw her as a potential winner in the fight for the inheritance. Until that moment, she wasn't sure she believed it herself.

Gertie took in the dimensions of the kitchen. It was modest in size and purely functional in its design, with stainless steel countertops and white tiled walls. The space was laid out galley-style, with the stove, oven, and sink lined up against one wall and the refrigerator and counters on the other. The room didn't quite span the width of the house, stopping at a wall with two closed doors.

"Is this all the workspace you have?" she asked. "How many meals can you serve out of here, anyway?"

"As many as you want, madam," said the chef. "Give me a rice cooker and an Easy-Bake Oven, and I can cook a four-course meal for twenty people who've never eaten better in their lives."

"I'll look forward to it." Gertie nodded at the doors at the end of the room. "What's through there?"

"Come and see for yourself."

Eddie turned down the stove under the still-simmering pot and led the way across the kitchen. Behind the first door was a set of stairs going down, the warm, damp air heavy with the scent of dryer sheets.

"Basement," he said. "Laundry, storage, et cetera. There's a wine cellar down there too, but I don't have the keys. Mr. Glass kept them on his key ring and sent Mrs. Phan down any time he wanted something."

Eddie shut that one and opened the second door. "Now, you might think this is a pantry," he said. "You know, to hold all the supplies I need to supply this very professional kitchen I am running here. But you would be wrong."

He switched on the light, and Gertie saw what he meant. The room had clearly been designed to provide kitchen storage, with open shelves over counters that sat on top of plain but well-built cabinets. But instead of dry goods and sheet pans, the space was entirely filled with what could only be described as "mall memorabilia." There were framed newspaper articles, disintegrating architectural models, commemorative wineglasses, and three pairs of giant scissors, their gold paint puffed and flaking. At the far end of the room stood a life-size cardboard cutout of Arnold himself (circa 1970, judging by his suit and amount of hair), holding a sign that read, "Welcome to the Galleria Grande!"

"Wow," said Gertie, which was the best she could do at the moment.

"Yep. He kept every bit of stuff to do with the business. But it didn't suit the decor out in the house, so it all ended up in here, and if I wanted somewhere to put my soup pot, I could go right to hell."

Even with his lack of care for his position, Eddie must have realized he'd overstepped there. He gave Gertie a sideways look to judge her reaction, but she was pretending to be absorbed with the inscription on a commemorative plaque.

"I mean, look, I'm not complaining. He was a cool guy, and hey, it's his house. It's none of my business where he wants to keep his stuff. Wanted, I mean. Anyway, I need to get back to work."

Gertie turned and smiled at him. "Don't worry about it, I understand. Thanks for taking the time to show me around. I should probably—"

But Gertie didn't need to come up with the rest of that excuse, because at that moment the kitchen door opened, and Maryann looked in.

"Ah, Gertie, there you are. Do you have a moment to chat?"

12

Maryann led Gertie back to the office where they had met in the morning. Gertie realized with shock that it had been only three hours since she'd last walked into that room; it seemed like something that had happened years ago, to someone else.

The office had been reset into a normal furniture arrangement, and Gertie chose one of visitors' chairs, while Maryann took the seat behind the desk like she belonged there.

"I understand that these last few hours may have been rather overwhelming for you," Maryann began. "I hope you've had a chance to absorb at least some of it?"

Gertie nodded, still unsure what this was about. She didn't think Maryann just wanted to check on her well-being.

Whatever it was, her oldest half sibling wasn't quick to get to the point.

"You may have found some of the reactions today rather over the top, but I think you should understand we were all under extreme stress. Still, that doesn't excuse some of the things that were said to you."

"I appreciate that," Gertie said, then wondered which ones it did excuse. But if Maryann was feeling like being friendly, Gertie supposed it wouldn't hurt to extend an olive branch of her own.

"It does seem like this entire situation was set up to maximize the drama," she said, being careful to keep her wording passive about who had done the setting up.

But that didn't seem to bother Maryann.

"Yes, well, that was Dad for you. He loved to create a sensation."

Maryann was obviously going out of her way to be nice, presumably to soften Gertie up for whatever she was about to ask, and Gertie decided to take advantage of that.

"By the way, when we were talking earlier, you mentioned you were away from the house when Arnold died. I don't think I caught why you were out?"

From the way she pressed her lips together, it was clear Maryann hadn't intended her to. But she answered anyway. "I left first thing that morning to run some errands. Normally I'd have some help, but the staff were all off setting up for the party. By the time I got back, Dad was dead and the whole place was in chaos. The ambulance was here, and the police, but no one would tell us anything. We're still having trouble getting any information, I'm afraid."

That didn't quite line up with their earlier conversation, but Gertie didn't want to test her luck too far by pressing the question. Instead she asked, "And it was Neil who found him?"

"Yes. He'd been out in the garden, doing his meditation, I think. He uses a recording to guide him, with headphones, so he didn't hear anything. No one did. Brian was out practicing on Dad's putting green, and Jennifer was still sleeping, of course."

Maryann sounded bitter about that, and for once Gertie didn't blame her. Her siblings' failure to take on responsibilities was clearly a sore point, and this must feel like an extreme version.

Unless one of them was responsible in a different way? If the police did believe Arnold had been murdered, then there must have been someone on those stairs with him. And if the staff and Maryann were all away, and assuming no one else had found their way in, then that left only the three remaining siblings and Haylee.

Which meant someone—someone in the house right now—had killed Arnold. But that was more than Gertie could take in right away, so she went with the conventional response.

"I'm sorry you had to go through that. I'm sure it was terrible," she said, then hesitated before going on. "Was that what you wanted to meet with me about?"

Maryann didn't seem bothered by this blunt return to business—if anything, Gertie thought she saw her relax slightly.

"No, it wasn't. I asked you here because I wanted to make a business proposal," Maryann said. "It's simple enough. The will Jules read this morning was very disruptive, for all of us. I don't know what was behind it, and since you seem to be disinclined to enlighten us, I'm afraid it is going to take a lot of time and effort on the part of many lawyers to straighten it out. Which will obviously consume a great deal of money, money that, frankly, you don't have. So I spoke to my siblings, and we thought we would offer you a compromise."

It was so blunt that Gertie was almost impressed. Maryann's plan was to win by outspending Gertie, and she didn't care who knew it. Gertie didn't mention what Jules had told her about the siblings' own finances—as fun as that might be, she didn't see any value in showing her hand yet.

Actually, that Gertie was being offered anything at all might be a clue that their position wasn't as strong as Maryann was claiming. Since when did the avalanche try to make a deal with a tree?

"What sort of compromise?" Gertie asked.

The light filtering through the partially blocked windows in the walls gave the place an underwater dimness, with the occasional flash of reflected sunbeams from the pool outside. One fell across Maryann's face as Gertie asked her question, outlining the creases on the older woman's cheeks. She looked tired, Gertie realized, and in spite of everything, she felt a bit sorry for her half sister, stuck with the dirty work once again while her siblings were off doing whatever they wanted.

Granted, the thing being taken care of right now was an attempt to deprive Gertie of her inheritance, so there was a limit to her sympathy.

The moment passed, and Maryann made firm eye contact with Gertie, any trace of exhaustion gone. "We're offering to buy out your shares in the company at their current market value. As for the house, we've all agreed that you should be given a payment equivalent to one quarter of the assessed price. That's more than the rest of us, after all."

She smiled as she said it, like someone who thought she was being generous to a child.

"We think this is a way to resolve all our problems, and you will still get your share," she finished.

Gertie was almost tempted. As Maryann had said, her problems would be over. No legal battles, no watching her back, no worrying about if somebody in this building had actually killed her father. She'd just take the money and go back to her life. She could do that; she almost did.

But, in the end, that's not who she was.

"My share is what's in the will."

Maryann treated Gertie to almost a full minute of silence before responding. A lesser person would have called it a staring contest, but Gertie felt like they were both above that sort of pettiness. She even made a point of blinking several times, to show she wasn't playing.

"I suppose you think that's your final word on the subject," Maryann said at last, as her phone started buzzing in her pocket. She took it out and looked at it, frowning, then put it away and stood up.

"I have to tell you, you have no idea what you're doing," she said as she passed Gertie on her way to the door. The words sounded like a threat, but her tone was more sad than anything.

Gertie wondered if this wasn't really her choice, serving as the enforcer for her gang of irresponsible siblings. According to Jules,

Maryann was the only one of them who had put in any serious time working in the family business—or anywhere else.

But Maryann wasn't the one here without options, Gertie reminded herself. If she had made the choice to serve ungrateful people, that wasn't Gertie's problem.

So Gertie just shrugged.

"Do any of us?" she said.

13

Gertie lingered in the office after Maryann left, looking through the bookshelves for anything they might tell her about her father, but the knickknacks remained characterless. Still curious, Gertie decided to look in the drawers of the desk. Not that she expected to find any clear answers there—Jules had told her Arnold's real office was in the tower, and if there had been anything important in here, she guessed it would have been cleaned out before she was allowed anywhere near the room. But even unimportant things might be helpful at this point.

Resting her hand on the desk, Gertie thought about her revelation during the talk with Maryann. If her father had been murdered, then someone must have killed him. She couldn't be sure it wasn't a member of the staff—hiding out after everyone else had left to attack for reasons of their own—or even some madman who managed to evade the security systems and get away undetected.

Gertie thought she could set aside the madman theory for

now, but she spent a little longer on the household staff. She had seen at least five or six already, and she was sure there must be more people—a dozen at least. Could one of them be someone Arnold had harmed in the past, here to take revenge on him? Or maybe not so far in the past. Gertie wasn't naive, and she knew plenty about the things powerful men could get away with. There had to be better ways for someone working in a house to kill the owner than to attack him in an open area in broad daylight, but maybe she was missing something.

Or maybe not. The obvious place to look for a murderer was among the people who had been closest to the victim, like his children or his girlfriend. The simple motive for all of them would be the same—the expectation they would get Arnold's money when he died. Haylee hadn't inherited anything, but her behavior at the will reading made it clear she'd thought she would. And the others didn't seem like they'd been short on funds while he was alive, but who knew? One of them might have wanted more than Arnold was willing to give them, or they'd been simply fed up with having the cash under his control.

And why was it any of her business? The question was so absurd at first that Gertie almost dismissed it out of hand, but after another thought, she realized she didn't have a ready answer. It felt important—now that the idea was in her head that Arnold had been murdered, she was uncomfortable with continuing like it didn't matter. She had no clear idea of what she was going to do with any information she did find, but even if she ended up unsatisfied, she couldn't go on without at least knowing she tried.

And right now, the easiest thing to try was to learn as much as she could about her father's life and interests.

She started with the top center drawer of the desk, and she wasn't encouraged. There were some pens—not expensive ones, but the fine-tip roller balls that Gertie preferred. Three pads of Post-it notes in different colors were lined up on one side of the drawer, and a notepad sat precisely aligned in the middle, but all the pages were blank, with no impressions of writing.

Gertie started to open the next drawer when she heard voices from outside the room. The office door was still ajar, with the heavy curtain drawn across it, so the sounds that came through were muffled but distinct. She couldn't quite make out the words, but she recognized Maryann's voice, talking to someone else who spoke in a low mutter. Then Jennifer's voice came through, bright and clear and at least twice as loud as anyone else's.

"Like you guys have done such a good job with your lives! I don't need advice from any of you."

The front door slammed, then opened and closed more gently a few minutes later. Gertie wondered what that had been about and if they realized she was still there.

The building fell silent again, and Gertie resumed her search. There was nothing interesting in the next two drawers, and all she learned was that her father wouldn't have run out of pens if he had lived another decade and that he had sorted his binder clips by size. Gertie was starting to think this office was just a stage set for hosting meetings when she found the file folders.

At first glance they didn't look like much, just a collection of magazine and newspaper articles, but Gertie went through them anyway. Most of the articles dealt with real estate, from trend pieces from mainstream outlets to more in-depth work from business publications. For some of them, the choice was obvious, like the article about the growth of mall traffic in affluent areas or the piece about successful pop-up restaurants in Orange County. Others were less so. Like the entire folder that had been dedicated to the real estate market for biotechnology research facilities: occupancy rates, construction and regulatory challenges, even one printout that went into details about price per square foot in different parts of the country.

The way it was organized looked like something that had been put together to be shared. That made sense, Gertie thought. If this office was where the external meetings had been held, it would be where Arnold might keep the materials he would use to convince people (investors? his family?) of a new plan. And it was no secret the mall business wasn't what it had been.

Gertie looked over the articles again. Together, they painted a rosy picture of the future of the biotech market, but she wasn't so sure about that. Not that she knew anything about that industry, but she was fairly sure Arnold hadn't either, and the occasional quote that brought up things like structural requirements and air handling gave her the impression that it wouldn't be that simple to turn an old JCPenney into a hub of medical innovation.

She closed the folders and stared out at the shadows that fell across the windows. This was interesting, but she didn't see how it got her any closer to understanding what her father had been thinking when he put her in his will or sent his cryptic invitation. What she needed was to get into Arnold's real office, the one in the tower—the place where Jules had said he'd spent hours working every morning. And the place from which he had fallen to his death.

EMAIL EXCHANGE BETWEEN DUNCAN COLEMAN AND MARYANN GLASS-COLEMAN

Hi mom,

What's going on with granddad's will? Dad said someone else got the house? I thought we were supposed to get it? Are you still going to get me the 50k?

duncan

Dear Duncan,

Yes, that's the case. The will that was presented to us had the house going to your grandfather's youngest daughter, from his second marriage. We're going to get it straightened out, but I'm afraid the money won't be available right away.

Love,
Mom

God mom, why do you have to sound like a robot? Just say grandad was up to his old shit. Anyway, the thing is I kind of need the money sooner than that. I got this really great opportunity for my business that's going to pay out huge, but crypto prices have been having a correction and I've got a problem with liquidity right now. Which is going to be totally fine, but there are a couple of customers who were trying to withdraw their money this week, and I don't know how long I can put them off.

dunc

Duncan,

I'll call you.

Mom

14

When Gertie got back to the main room, it was empty, which surprised her at first. But after a few minutes, she started to understand. It was midafternoon, and even though she could feel the breeze from the air-conditioning running at full blast, it was no match for the desert heat that pounded through the giant windows.

As bad as the temperature was, the brightness of the unfiltered sunlight was worse. Every bit of chrome on the furniture reflected it, and the white floor and walls seemed to get closer every time Gertie looked. But she made no attempt to leave. There was nowhere else she could think of to go, and this was her first chance to really explore the space.

Gertie had heard of conversation pits—the sunken seating areas that had been in vogue around the time this house was built, but she had never seen one before. Maybe in a movie? But, as she descended the marble steps, she understood the point of this one. At floor level, anyone in the room was visible through all the windows, and the view was of the landscaping, the front walk, and the garden walls. But sitting on the sofa down in the well, there was an illusion of privacy, and looking up, she only saw the tops of the palm trees against the searingly blue sky.

She spent a moment sitting there, thinking about views, before getting up to continue exploring.

So far, Gertie hadn't been able to find out much about Arnold's death, but everything she did know had to do with this room. She would get to the stairs in a minute—first, she wanted to figure out what Maryann hadn't been able to stop herself from looking at when Gertie asked about the police.

It had been the front door, or something near it, that had drawn Maryann's attention, so Gertie started there. The door itself told her nothing—it was just a door, and if it was someone coming through it that Maryann was remembering, then there would be nothing to learn there now.

But if that was the case, why had her older sister looked away so quickly, like she was trying to cover for a mistake? Leaving the door, Gertie examined the area around it.

The windows on either side looked out to the garden, where clumps of skinny cacti framed the front step. A section of the walk was also visible, and Gertie supposed Maryann might have been thinking about someone coming that way to get into the house. But if the threat had come from outside, then why were the siblings all so determined to call the death an accident?

Abandoning the outdoor angle, Gertie took a closer look at the part of the room that had been in Maryann's line of sight.

Past the door, separating the entrance from the conversation pit, there was a low open set of shelves that displayed a variety of decorative items. Most of them looked like they had been selected by a designer to complement the style of the room, with the exceptions of the beautifully complete fossilized trilobite and the purple geode—egg shaped and the size of Gertie's head—that took pride of place at either end of the top shelf.

The one other outlier in the otherwise pristine selection of mid-century objects was a stylized brass figure of a woman bending to the right, so that it looked like she was throwing up into the short ceramic jar next to her. A visual joke, Gertie wondered, or just an unfortunate combination that no one had caught? She looked inside the jar, yet it held nothing but dust.

Giving up on the vague hint of Maryann's distraction, Gertie turned her attention to the scene of the death.

The plants at the base of the stairs were only a symbolic barrier, and Gertie made her way around them and up the steps. The clear plastic treads were lightly scuffed, but that didn't make them any less slick. As Gertie settled each foot carefully and pressed her hand against the wall where a railing should have been, it was less surprising to her that someone had fallen here than that it had happened only once.

At the top of the stairs, there was a landing, with railings on two sides and a door on the third. Before trying it, Gertie turned and looked back the way she had come.

From above, the stairs looked even more treacherous. The afternoon sun shone through the windows on the far side of the room, catching on the surfaces of the treads and making them a staggered, shimmering surface that dropped away beneath her. Even the polished marble floor lost its definition, turning the whole space into a swimming pool of light.

Gertie tried to imagine standing on this spot with another person, one who might have a reason to place a hand on her arm or back. How much force would it take to send her tumbling down those steps, particularly if she wasn't ready for it? Very little, she decided, and an old man would have no chance.

The lock on the office door was shiny and new, and door was locked tight. Gertie didn't think the basic lock-picking skills she had learned on YouTube were going to get her through this one, so she retreated back down the stairs, being careful not to look down at the steps that seemed to move under her feet.

Safely back on the ground, Gertie wandered over to the windows and held her hand up near the wall of glass to feel the radiating heat. *The electricity bill for air-conditioning this place must be enormous*, she thought, and wondered why there were no blinds.

Standing there, contemplating the battle between the indoors and out, she didn't notice the movement at first. It caught the corner of her eye, one of the palm trees in the side yard waving back and forth like it was in a hurricane, though the rest of the plants were still. Curious, she went to the corner of the room to get a better view, but whatever was happening was being blocked by a row of tall shrubs. She might have given it up as not being interesting enough to be worth going back out into the heat, but then she heard the shouting.

By the time Gertie made it around the house to the tree, most of the action was over. A small group of people gathered around the base of the palm, none of whom she had seen before. They were all dressed in a variation of the uniform she had seen on the house staff—this time the polo shirts were green, and the black slacks had been replaced by cargo pants or shorts—except for one.

The only woman in the group was the shortest by at least six inches, probably the oldest by twenty years, and clearly in charge. Dressed in a T-shirt with a picture of a cactus, chunky short boots, and pants that could only be described as "cargo culottes," with short, spiky gray hair, she was loudly berating a young man.

"You thought it was a good idea? You thought? You don't think, Tim—you're a fucking idiot."

The man dropped his head and shoved his hands in his pockets, looking sullen. "I was just doing my job," he said.

"I'm sorry, did I miss where you got trained as an arborist? Your job is to take care of the garden, not tear it up."

It wasn't hard to identify the source of the conflict. The palm tree had a deep gash in its trunk, freshly cut, and a small hand ax was lying at its base.

"Ms. Jennifer said she wanted it cut down," the unfortunate Tim was explaining. "She said the cicadas in it were right outside her window, and they were bothering her."

It was true—the electric, buzzing noise Gertie had noticed earlier was stronger here, and it sounded like it was hovering above them. The distraction of the argument had kept her from noticing it before, but now she could hardly hear anything else.

Tim's boss was less impressed.

"The bugs were here before we showed up, and they'll be here when we're gone. If anybody doesn't want to listen to them, they can get some headphones." The woman had undoubtedly noticed Gertie, but she was keeping her eyes deliberately averted. "And cutting down trees isn't her business, or yours. You're damn lucky I don't run you off this property right now."

"We're supposed to do what we're told," Tim mumbled, avoiding her eyes.

"You're supposed to do what *I* tell you. Not any of those nimrods. They just own this garden; I'm the one who runs it."

She was definitely aware of Gertie now, and so were the others, who were looking over their boss's shoulder in her direction. Oddly, Gertie found herself unbothered by the open hostility. In a way, it was refreshing to encounter someone who disliked her based on general principles, rather than personal animosity.

Still, she thought it might be time to enter the conversation. Just because she wasn't very bothered by the disrespect didn't mean she had to take it.

"Will the tree survive?" she asked, strolling up to join the group like she had been invited. All three of the men immediately looked at the shorter woman, like they were expecting an explosion, but she merely pursed her lips.

"It depends. Gonna take some work to save it, but this dry air should help. Keeps the fungus spores from settling in. That's the real danger."

Gertie nodded like she knew anything about any of that. "That's good to hear." She looked up at the tree with its crown of fronds and, not able to think of anything else, added, "It's a nice tree."

"And it would be at least two grand to replace, and that's not in the budget," the woman said. In case there was any question she knew who she was talking to, she went on. "I hear you're the new boss."

"That's what I hear too," Gertie replied, then held out her hand. "Gertie Glass."

The other woman looked like she was considering rejecting the gesture, but apparently that was a snub too far.

"Kathy Hammond," she said, taking Gertie's hand briefly in her calloused grip. "I'm the head gardener here. Been working for your father for fifteen years. Anyway, we're kind of busy. Was there something you wanted?"

There wasn't, but Gertie's pride wouldn't allow her to retreat. After all, she was the new boss. So, gritting her teeth against the heat, which felt like it was trying to break into her skull with heavy tools, she said, "I was interested in taking a look at the gardens. I understand they're extensive?"

"Acre and a half. Not counting the bits for the golf nonsense." Kathy obviously had more to say about that, but her attention was divided, and ultimately, it was the damaged tree that won out.

"I'm going to be busy here for a while. Tim, you can show Miss Glass around. Make sure she sees the saguaros. She might also be interested in the roses." She looked at Gertie and nearly smiled. "They were planted by the last Gertrude who lived here. They've got no place in this garden, but your father wouldn't let me touch them."

Based on the attitude Kathy had shown so far, Gertie would have expected disdain in that statement, or at least a little sarcasm, but the head gardener sounded oddly affectionate toward the interloping flowers. *We all contain multitudes,* Gertie thought.

Right now, what Kathy seemed to mostly contain was concern for her tree. Clearly considering the problem of Gertie solved, Kathy began barking orders at the remaining gardeners, demanding a list of things that sounded like supplies for a combination of open-heart surgery and building a shed.

Gertie was curious to see what the rescue operation would involve, and she wanted to stay to watch. Her guide, on the other hand, was eager to get away.

"So, if you'll just come with me, we've got some great plantings here," Tim was saying as he started up the path, all but grabbing Gertie's arm to drag her with him. "Just around the back there's a cactus we think was planted around the time the original house was built, back in the last century."

Gertie wanted to point out that didn't narrow it down much, but her train of thought was interrupted by Kathy, who had a more pertinent message.

"Hey," she shouted after them. "Don't forget to warn her about the agaves. And if you see Ms. Maryann, you can tell her that she can take that guava tree she dumped on me and stick it up her—"

Whatever anatomically improbable act Kathy wanted from the eldest Glass sibling was lost as Tim led Gertie rapidly around the corner of the house.

15

"Everyone thinks about the heat, but it's the UV that gets you." Once they'd gotten out of range of his boss's anger, Tim had been talking nonstop about desert gardening.

"It's because the humidity is so low," he went on, answering a question she hadn't asked. "When there's moisture in the air, it absorbs some of the UV light, but we've got basically none here. So plants you'd think are fine with heat get their poor little leaves scorched to death here."

"Really? I didn't know that." That was mostly because Gertie had never thought about growing plants in the desert, but she was always willing to learn. So she fell in behind the young man as he led her around the garden, listening with half an ear as he told her about spines that were leaves and stems that were storage tanks.

Gertie's first impression of Tim had been of a kid barely out of high school, but closer up she revised her estimate. From the lines and stubble on his boyish face, she thought he must be closer to her own late twenties, or maybe a bit older, and he spoke about the plants with a confidence that suggested many years of experience. And for a guy who had just tried to chop down a tree, Tim was surprisingly sympathetic to the vegetation in his care.

Thinking about the nearly doomed palm reminded Gertie of something she was curious about (and the way she might angle that to some of her real questions).

"I didn't realize there were cicadas in the desert," she said. "Are they always here?"

"No, it's a seasonal thing. And some years are worse than others. They don't do any harm to the plants," he added, with an apparent lack of irony.

"But Jennifer must not be used to them. That's pretty extreme, wanting a tree cut down because of insects."

Tim looked at her with entirely unfeigned surprise.

"The Family wants things when they want them. It's not my business to ask about it."

It was the first time Gertie had heard the word pronounced with a capital "F," and she didn't like it. The Glass business was malls, not Mafia. (At least, as far as she knew. Possibly? But no. People involved in organized crime would have to be more, well, organized.)

"But Jennifer isn't really in charge," she persisted. "Would she have asked for that when Arnold was alive?"

For some reason, that question made Tim as uncomfortable as he had been since they had gotten out of range of his boss. "Well, I don't know. I guess, maybe no." He spotted a thin weed struggling up through the soil and bent to pull it. "Things were different with him around. Mr. Glass didn't want anything changed in the garden until he had a long talk about it, but they still all tried to go around him."

That was interesting and consistent with what Gertie had learned so far about her father's relationship with his other children. She wondered how many other things, besides garden design, they had tried to do without his permission, and what one of them might have done if they were thwarted on something more important.

Tim was unlikely to know anything about that, but there were some things she could ask him.

"I must have been a big disruption when he died. Were you working that day?"

If Tim thought this was a strange way of making small talk, he didn't show it. He just nodded in the direction of a bougainvillea that was draped over the corner of the courtyard wall, looking thoughtful.

"That was too bad. It was going to be a great day, with the party and everyone invited. We even had a cake to have back at the shed, a nice one. We still ate it, but it wasn't the same."

"No point wasting cake," Gertie agreed. "So you were here?"

"Oh yeah. Well, not the whole day, because...there was one thing that came up. But otherwise it was a regular workday." Tim stopped next to a short, scrubby palm and pulled off a couple of brown fronds. "After they found the body, no one knew what to do. The ambulances and the police all came, and we thought they'd close some places off, but nobody said anything. They must have been looking for something in the garden, though, because the mulch was messed up all over the place. But that must have happened after we left. We'd been trying to get on with our work, but then Mr. Brian punched a cop, and Kathy told us all we should just go home."

"He punched a cop?" Tim seemed amused by the story, but Gertie was more unnerved than she liked to admit. If Brian could do that and still be walking around free, what was there that people in this family couldn't get away with?

"That's what I heard," Tim said with relish. For all his deference to their wishes, he clearly didn't mind indulging in a little bit of gossip about his employers. "Or he tried to, anyway. I guess the cop ducked. Anyway, maybe that's why they didn't arrest him. Pretty crazy, right?"

"It sure is," Gertie agreed.

"Not what you expected, right?" Tim was saying.

Gertie wondered for a moment what he was talking about, until she realized he had stopped in front of a bank of rosebushes huddled against a shady wall.

They were low and tough-looking, with small pink flowers that filled the hot air with scent. Looking up, Gertie realized the thick wall behind them was the back of the pool house, and the frosted window at her eye level must be the one in her bathroom.

"They do seem out of place," she said, in answer to Tim's question. "My grandmother planted these?"

"I guess so. That was before my time."

"Mine too." Gertie looked at the flowers and wondered how

much family history she would never know. And why did she care? So she was named after a long-dead woman who had planted roses in the desert. What did that have to do with her today?

And how had her father really died?

She must have been staring for too long, because eventually she noticed the gardener shuffling his feet and clearing his throat to get her attention.

"Hey, so I should probably get back to work," he said. "Are you okay here for now?"

Considering that she was about twenty feet from the gate to the pool, Gertie thought she could find her way back on her own, and she said so. Tim looked relieved.

"Okay, thanks. Hey, I'm really sorry about your dad. I didn't know him very well, but I really liked the way he appreciated the garden. Sometimes he'd come out here in the evenings, walking around and looking at the plants. I think he even talked to them a bit."

"I didn't know that," Gertie said, as if there was any reason that she should.

"Yeah, he was an interesting guy. Anyway, have a good evening." Tim started to go, then turned back. "Oh, and if you're going to be out here on your own, watch out for snakes. We try to keep them out, but sometimes you get a diamondback in here. If you hear something rattling, that's not a baby."

With that surprising burst of humor, he headed back the way they had come, and Gertie was left to wonder if there was anything about this place that wasn't dangerous.

THURSDAY, AUGUST 22

TWO DAYS BEFORE THE DEATH OF ARNOLD GLASS

Arnold steered his car through the downtown tourist traffic, so pleased with himself that he barely paused to swear at the rental SUV that swerved across three lanes to make a left turn. He was coming from his lawyer's office, and the residual glow from Jules's reaction to what he'd done was enough to overcome the effects of a dozen out-of-state drivers.

And Jules didn't even know the half of it! The changes to the will were something Arnold had been contemplating for a long time; he had done it now to get it out of the way before he started his new venture. Not that there was any particular need; he just expected to be busy.

Arnold pulled onto the freeway, still relishing the thought of having something to do for a change. To really do—not just signing the papers that Maryann's husband, Mark, was always giving him. Arnold had been so pleased when Maryann had married Mark, back when he had been a rising manager at the Glass Property Group. It had seemed right, that finally she could have the involvement in the business she'd always wanted, in an appropriate way. But she was still never happy, always putting her nose in places it didn't belong, using her husband's authority to make decisions about things she couldn't possibly understand.

His phone rang, and Arnold grumbled when he saw that it was Neil. Of course, he should have expected this.

"Hello? What's up?"

"Hello, Dad," Neil said, and even through the distortion of the car's audio system, Arnold could tell he was upset. "I just got off the phone with the bank. They said my funds request was declined. Do you know anything about that?"

"Yes, I declined it." Arnold had been anticipating this conversation, but he hadn't been looking forward to it. But some things had to be done.

"What? Why? I thought I told you—"

"You told me a pile of nonsense," Arnold interrupted. "I called the marina—there's nothing wrong with the boat, and they're not raising slip fees until next year. I don't know why you want thirty grand right now, but you aren't getting it by lying to me."

There was silence on the other end of the line, for long enough that Arnold wondered if he had hit a button or something. But eventually he heard Neil sigh, and when his younger son spoke again, his voice was soft and wheedling.

"Look, I'm sorry, but you have to understand. Nestor—"

That was the last straw. Bad enough to hear his son speak like that, but the idea that Arnold was supposed to bail out that simpering husband of his from whatever he had done this time was too much.

"Nestor can find another source of funds. Maybe he can get it from one of those male friends I keep reading about in the papers. But it's not coming from me."

"Oh, come on!" Neil's whining turned into a tantrum, like it always did when he didn't get his way. "What are you getting, holding on to your damn money anyway? Don't you think it's time you let a few things go?"

Arnold barked a laugh. "Let it go into your pockets, you mean? Not a chance. In fact, I have something very different in mind."

That should have been enough warning for Neil to know what was coming, but of course he wasn't listening.

"Dad, Jennifer and I have been talking about the idea of selling the company. I know it's not what you want, but who knows how long the property market is going to be looking like this, and we should get what we can while it's as good as it is. We can't go on like this forever. Something's got to change."

A car blew past him on the right, honking its horn, and Arnold was torn between yelling at the driver and Neil. He usually avoided this route, but it was faster, and Arnold had a lot of things he wanted to get done before the end of the day. And he had just added another one to the list.

"There'll be some changes all right, and they're coming sooner than you know," Arnold said, glaring furiously at the console as if Neil could see him through the screen. "And the first one is that as soon as I get home, I'm calling Harry at the bank to let him know that there are going to be no more cash withdrawals until further notice."

There was some angry babbling on the other end of the line, but Arnold ignored it and kept talking.

"I'm taking the company in a new direction, and that means things can't keep going the way they have been. I'll tell the four of you all about it tomorrow night. You can come down early and have dinner. Just you and your siblings. This is a family matter."

Arnold hit the button to end the call before Neil could come back with any more of his whining, feeling better than he had in a long time. He should have done this long ago, but there was no time like the present. He didn't owe anything to anyone, and it was time his children were reminded of that.

16

It was late in the afternoon, and the sun was getting low, but it was still hot out. Gertie considered returning to the main house, but the rest of the family wasn't going to stay away indefinitely, and she had seen enough of them for one day. She was thinking she could go back to the pool house and stand under the cold shower when she came into the courtyard and had a better idea.

She was staying in the pool house; why not use the pool?

Gertie had packed her swimsuit as a just-in-case afterthought. It took her a few minutes to find it and change, and by the time she got back to the courtyard, it was no longer empty.

Neil was standing in front of a cupboard on the wall, apparently looking for something. He either didn't hear Gertie approaching or didn't care, because she was nearly behind him before he looked up.

"Oh, it's you," he said, holding a box of Band-Aids in one hand. "Going for a swim?"

The way he said it made it sound like Gertie was about to steal all the water from the pool.

"I thought it would be nice to cool off," Gertie replied, trying not to sound defensive. "Are you all right?"

"What? Oh, these." Neil looked down and appeared to notice the box in his hand for the first time. "Yeah, some new shoes giving me blisters. I'll live."

"That's good," said Gertie, too distracted to come up with anything clever. Coming closer, she could see that the cupboard was a fully stocked first aid kit. As well as the supply of bandages Neil was raiding, there were boxes of individually wrapped pills, sunburn lotion, and a variety of supplies for treating more serious injuries that looked like they had been untouched for many years.

And, tidily lined up on the in the middle of the top shelf, was a row of five Narcan boxes.

Neil saw where she was looking and turned away, not meeting her eyes. "Accidents happen. Anyway, enjoy your swim. You might as well get the good out of the pool while you can."

Then he marched back into the house, before Gertie had a chance to ask what he meant by that or how often the accidents around here involved opioid overdoses.

―

He had probably just been needling her about his confidence that Gertie would lose her rights to the house in court, but she couldn't shake the feeling of menace in Neil's words. But even in the shade, the heat remained oppressive, and the seductive shimmer of the pool's surface was too inviting for her to be dissuaded by vague fears. If someone was going to come after her, they could at least do it when she wasn't sweating.

The water was a perfect temperature, of course. Gertie dipped tentative a toe in at first, then felt silly for doing so. There probably was a person who came through twice a day with a thermometer.

It took her a couple of laps to get used to the unfamiliar dimensions of the pool, but eventually she settled into a steady rhythm. Forty minutes later Gertie pulled up on the edge and peeled off her goggles, blinking in the outdoor lights that had turned on while she swam. She hadn't been swimming much lately, because the pool at Carla's new condo was more of the "pose next to" type, and she could feel it in her shoulders. But it was a good ache, and Gertie felt more clearheaded than she had in a while.

"I've got a warm towel here for you if you're ready."

Gertie hadn't noticed the woman standing by the lounge chairs, and she wondered how long she had been there. Gertie had been considering doing another set, but the idea of going back to swimming while someone waited to serve her was too awkward. So she crossed to the ladder and climbed out, taking the towel from the woman's hand.

It was indeed warm—fresh and fluffy, like it had just come out of the dryer. Despite the lingering heat in the early-evening air, the feeling was lovely and familiar in a way that almost wasn't possible. Gertie's life had mostly not been one of prewarmed towels, but both the coziness of the fabric on her skin and the woman who was smiling back at her seemed somehow right.

"I know you," Gertie said, without thinking. She caught herself and corrected, "I'm sorry, I mean, I feel like I recognize you?"

The woman laughed. She was Asian, in her late sixties at least, with short black hair touched with gray and bright pink flower earrings. Unlike the other staff members, she was wearing a blue shirtdress, though it still had the logo embroidered on the breast pocket. "I knew you would remember. He said you'd have forgotten me long ago, but I said no, not her. Are you going to want some dinner?"

"I should probably get dressed first," Gertie said automatically, while she tried to process what she was hearing. "You remember me from before? When I lived here as a baby? Were you working for my father back then?" (*And did he tell you I would be here? Gertie longed to ask. When? What else did he say about it?*)

"Yes, indeed. I've been here all along." She gave Gertie an indulgent look. "You remember, but you don't know my name. I'm Mrs. Phan. I manage the household."

"Mrs. Phan." So this was the woman she had been hearing about. And she had been here since Gertie was a child. Gertie frowned, hoping she could call up something more than the vague sense of recognition she got from the woman's face, but she came up blank. That her mother had never talked about Mrs. Phan was less surprising—wealth and fame were the only things that qualified someone for a mention in Carla's world.

"Your brothers tried to get you to call me 'Phanny,' but you were smarter than that. You always said everyone's whole names. And you loved French toast."

This time Gertie could answer without any reservations. "Well, that part is definitely still true," she said, and a thought struck her. "Did I ever eat it with marmalade? That's always been my favorite, but I never knew why."

Mrs. Phan actually clapped with pleasure. "Yes! We had an English chef, and she said it was what all children liked. We weren't sure, but you ate it right up, and then it was the only thing you would have. I'll have Eddie make you some tomorrow morning. He's not English, but his breakfasts are very good."

"Yes, I've met him," Gertie said. She had no doubt that the man she had encountered in the kitchen would be up to the task of making a child's breakfast for an adult, though she wondered what he would think. But it probably wasn't the strangest thing he had been asked to do, not by a long shot.

Which brought her back to the question of dinner.

"Is there anything planned for tonight? I was thinking I might go out, but nobody has mentioned if I'm expected to be here."

Mrs. Phan laughed in a way that sounded a bit like a snort. "Don't worry about that. Your father liked to have everyone sit down for dinner, but this bunch aren't going to do it on their own. It's restaurants for all of them tonight, and I have to get the reservations. No problem, of course. Is there anywhere in particular you want to go?"

For a moment, Gertie felt a surge of freedom and power. This must be what it was like to belong to a world like this, to go wherever you wanted, whenever you wanted, and someone else took care of the details. Gertie had been taking care of the details, and everything else, for as long as she could remember.

But old habits died hard, and Gertie couldn't stop her brain from generating worst-case scenarios, mostly about who was going to pay for all of it.

Mrs. Phan must have registered her hesitation, because she smiled and patted Gertie's towel-wrapped shoulder.

"But then, you've had a busy day, haven't you? Why don't I have Eddie put something together? He makes very good pizzas. He even built an oven for them out in the garden."

At that point, it became clear to Gertie that she wasn't going to get away with not letting herself be taken care of, and she gave in.

"Pizza would be great, thank you." She thought about the big glass table in the dining room, and the baking-hot air in the pool house and added, "Would it be possible for me to have it out here? The pool house is kind of hot, and the main house... I think it might be nicer to eat outside."

Mrs. Phan smiled like she knew exactly what Gertie meant. "Of course. You go get yourself dressed, and I'll have the food set up on the table."

"Thanks," Gertie said. "When will it be ready?"

Mrs. Phan looked amused by the question. "It will be ready when you want it."

17

She didn't know how Mrs. Phan managed it, but as soon as Gertie was dried, dressed, and sitting at the table by the pool, a staff member emerged from a small door at the back of the courtyard with a tray. By now she wasn't even surprised that the food was as fresh and hot as if it had come straight from the oven (how was it even possible to have a pizza made at a moment's notice?), accompanied by a green salad and light-bodied red wine in a juice glass.

Gertie had wondered if she was going to regret not specifying the pizza toppings—what if Eddie was one of those chefs who put an egg on everything?—but she needn't have worried. All that was on the thin and blistered crust was a layer of homemade tomato sauce, dotted with fresh mozzarella, and basil leaves that were just beginning to wilt on the hot cheese.

"How is everything? It's all right?" Mrs. Phan came back into the courtyard carrying a newspaper, which she set down on the table, before busying herself cleaning nonexistent spots of dirt off the lounge chairs.

"It's perfect. And thank you for the wine. I didn't know how much I needed it until I had some."

The household manager nodded firmly. "I thought since you had been in law school, you must have gotten a taste for it. All lawyers like wine."

Gertie looked up in surprise, less at the assumption about her profession than Mrs. Phan's awareness of it. "You know about me going to law school? How?"

"Your father told me," she said matter-of-factly.

Obviously that was going to be the answer, but it still came as a surprise to Gertie. Arnold would have known about her going to law school; after all, under the terms of the child support arrangement, he was paying for it. But she hadn't expected it to register with him as anything other than another expense.

But Mrs. Phan went on. "He was very proud of how well you were doing. Top 10 percent of your class, every year, and a prize at your graduation. He used to say he could have been a lawyer, if he'd had a different start in life."

It took Gertie a moment to process this new information. Given the child support situation, law school had been the obvious choice. Arnold had been on the hook to pay all her expenses until she turned eighteen and would cover educational costs after that. So Gertie did the math, finished college and a masters in art history, and then started applying to law schools. By the second week of classes, it was clear to Gertie that she was going to hate it, but looking at her options, she decided she didn't have any good ones. If she wanted money, and the security it bought, the path forward was clear.

She had come to see the child support money as a competition between them, Arnold trying to hold on to the cash while she worked to get as much as possible, culminating in Gertie choosing the most expensive law school that would admit her. So it was unnerving to discover he not only hadn't been upset to pay for it but pleased with her success. That wasn't how it was supposed to go.

"I didn't realize," she said weakly. "He never said anything about it. He didn't contact me at all."

Mrs. Phan's expression darkened. "No, and he should have. I told him so, many times. But he was stubborn. When he and your mother separated, he said he would never have anything to do with her again, as long as he lived."

"And here I am," Gertie said.

"Here you are," Mrs. Phan agreed. "And I am glad to see you, but it would have been better for him to bring you here when he was alive. What good is it to either of you now?"

That was something Gertie had been wondering herself.

18

A light came on in the house, and a moment later, Maryann walked by the patio doors. She couldn't have missed seeing Gertie and Mrs. Phan outside, but her gaze passed over them like they were invisible. She kept going, back through the living room toward the staircase that Gertie assumed led to the guest bedrooms. She was almost past the doors when she met Jennifer coming the other way.

The second Glass sister was less subtle in her response to spotting Gertie by the pool. Her mouth fell open, and she turned with a furious expression to say something to Maryann. But her older sister shushed her and pointed Jennifer to the front door without turning her head in Gertie's direction.

It seemed like her refusal of the deal Maryann had offered made Gertie a nonentity within the family. If so, that was fine with her. She considered herself an expert on being ignored.

Mrs. Phan had noticed the behavior too, and she frowned in their direction. Then she picked up the dish towel the server had used to bring out the pizza and carefully folded it, then smoothed it down on the table, all while making her own show of not seeing the act that was going on in the house.

"Of course, your father didn't actually have anything against you," she went on, a shade louder than she had been speaking before. "It was your mother he was thinking about. I tried to tell him you were your own person, and you couldn't be that much like her, with all the things you've done, but he was a stubborn man, and the way she behaved—" Mrs. Phan stopped and looked embarrassed. "I'm sorry. I shouldn't speak of your mother that way."

Gertie laughed. "It's okay, I've met her. I'd be wary of me too."

Mrs. Phan laughed with her and was about to say something when her phone buzzed in her pocket. She took it out to check the screen and nodded with satisfaction.

"Ah good, the flowers are at the church. I didn't want them delivered too early, because they don't keep that place cool enough. They wanted to drop it all off at two p.m. On a day like this!"

The older woman looked scandalized, and Gertie tried to match her concern as she nodded along.

"For the memorial service?" she asked, and Mrs. Phan responded in the affirmative, her attention divided between Gertie and the text she was furiously typing with both thumbs.

"Yes, your father was very traditional. If there was a big event, he wanted lots of flowers, never mind the weather. Not very practical, but he knew what he wanted, and he got it."

That was no surprise to Gertie, and it was the perfect opening to ask one of the main questions that was still bothering her.

"Speaking of things he wanted, do you know why Arnold had us all gather together to read the will? Whatever his reasons for leaving the house and part of the company to me, what was the point of having me here? It could have been an email."

Mrs. Phan lowered her phone and looked up, past the glass walls of the house, at the tower room that sat in the crook of the L.

"Your father loved drama," the household manager said at last. "More than people, sometimes."

Mrs. Phan's explanation was similar to what Neil had said during the meeting, when he laughed and claimed that leaving her part of the company was all a joke. Could that really be it? A rich man who thought it was funny to play with the lives and feelings of the people who should have been closest to him, and she was nothing but a pawn in his posthumous game?

If that was the case, it would be a lot less surprising that someone had pushed him.

Gertie knew Mrs. Phan must have more work to do, and probably a home to get to after a long day, but she couldn't resist asking one more thing. "How did it happen? His death, I mean."

Mrs. Phan pursed her lips. "He fell down the stairs from his office," she said carefully, her eyes returning to the tower. She hesitated before going on.

"He was going to have his birthday party that day, so I was running around like crazy. The last time I saw him, I brought his coffee to the office. He was fine then, pretending he thought all the fuss was silly while he was trying to find out how everything was going. The party was happening at the botanical garden, so I had all the staff over there setting up, from about five in the morning."

"In this weather?" Gertie asked. "That must have been unbearable."

"The party would be in the evening, so it wasn't a problem," Mrs. Phan replied, with barely a hint of irony. "I was going back and forth for the early part of the morning, and I took him the coffee around seven and left not long after that. I didn't find out anything had happened until I got a call at around ten. By the time I got to the house, the ambulance and the police were already there."

From the way she recounted it, Gertie was sure Mrs. Phan had been thinking about that timeline a lot over the last two weeks. If Gertie wanted information about the circumstances around her father's death, she thought, she had found the right person.

"Why did the police come?"

"Because I called them." Mrs. Phan's warm demeanor had turned, not exactly cold, but more businesslike as she spoke. "Your father was an important man, and there were going to be a lot of people affected by him dying. I had to make sure everything was done properly."

"What did the family think of that?" Gertie didn't mention she knew about Brian's run-in with law enforcement, hoping to get another perspective on the events and wondering if there had been any attempt to cover up the embarrassment. But Mrs. Phan didn't hesitate.

"They didn't like it, but they're used to me taking care of

things. Brian took exception to their questions, probably because of his history, but they were mostly asking about the stairs, why there wasn't a railing." Mrs. Phan shook her head. "Of course, your father would never have put one in. It would have spoiled how the whole room looked."

"But it might have saved his life." Gertie wondered what additional history Brian had with the police and why Mrs. Phan hadn't mentioned anything about why the coroner hadn't released the body.

"It might have." The housekeeper's words sounded like she was agreeing with Gertie, but something about how she said it left an open question. Gertie took that as an opportunity to ask about what she really wanted to know.

"Mrs. Phan, what happened? Why won't the police say Arnold's death was an accident?"

"They haven't shared their reasons with any of us, as far as I know," Mrs. Phan said, and this time it was clear that wasn't the end of the sentence.

"But?" Gertie prompted.

"But it was obvious to me they thought there was something wrong with how the body looked," the older woman went on. She spoke with determination now, her mouth set in a grim line. "The paramedics had already arrived by the time I got here, so I didn't see what it looked like when he was found, but the blood—"

She stopped and gave Gertie a concerned look.

"I'm going to say something that will sound bad," said Mrs. Phan.

Gertie met her look of concern with a confident nod. "I can handle it."

"Yes, I think you can. Well, even without his body there, you could see that the blood was everywhere. Not just on the floor where he fell, but the wall and the stairs. I should know, I cleaned it up myself, once the police were done. I didn't want anyone else to have to do that. I'm not one of those crime scene people, but I've cleaned up a lot of spills in my time, and that didn't look right to me."

"What about the actual crime scene people? Did they look at the blood spatter?"

Mrs. Phan sniffed. "Not that much. I mean, they looked, and they took some pictures, but it was nothing like you see on TV. I'm not sure if they would have done much at all if I hadn't told them about the statue being missing."

19

"What statue?" The last piece of pizza was getting cold on her plate, but Gertie ignored it.

Mrs. Phan wiped an invisible crumb off the table and went on. "There was a pair of them on the table near the front door. Solid brass, very heavy, with a square base. And when I got back to the house after your father died, one of them was missing," she said. "The police weren't interested at first, but eventually someone mentioned it to the detective in charge, and he asked me a lot of questions. Mostly about if I was sure it had been there when I left. Of course, I was."

Unlike the police, Gertie didn't feel the need to question Mrs. Phan. A person who would remember a child's favorite foods from twenty-five years ago wasn't going to miss something like that.

Instead, she asked, "What happened to it? Has it been found?"

Mrs. Phan shook her head. "No, and they did look. Brian didn't want to let them, but we convinced him it would be worse if they had to get a warrant. The police made a terrible mess, but they ended up saying it wasn't anywhere in the house. And I didn't find it either. Wherever that statue is, it isn't here."

"So it disappeared sometime between when you left to set up for the party and when Arnold's body was found," Gertie said, thinking about the possibilities. "I guess it could have been taken before he fell for some other reason?"

"That's possible," said Mrs. Phan, though it was clear from her expression that she wasn't impressed by the idea.

Gertie didn't like it very much either, but the other options weren't much better.

"Otherwise, if someone used it to hit him, they would have had to get it out and away before anyone saw them," Gertie went on.

"Or they put it somewhere for a while and then moved it," said Mrs. Phan, who must have already given it some thought. "The police searched the house and some of the garden, but they didn't do much outside until they came back later with a team. There was nothing there by then, but it might have been."

"I guess so. Did they find anywhere where the ground was disturbed?"

"No, but the dirt here is so sandy, it would be hard to tell."

"I see." It occurred to Gertie that this was a very strange conversation for her to be having. However well Mrs. Phan might remember her as a toddler, the woman was essentially a stranger to Gertie, and yet here she was, talking about the details of Arnold's death with her, like they were about to roll out a whiteboard and start drawing lines between names.

Not that Gertie minded. She had showed up at this house wondering about what had happened when her father died, and up to this point, she had been frustrated at every turn. So the fact the household manager was willing to fill her in on the details was welcome.

And maybe not that surprising—the questions had clearly been on Mrs. Phan's mind, and why wouldn't they be? Gertie had been uncomfortable enough with the idea that one of these people she had known for less than a day might have killed someone she didn't remember meeting—how much worse would it be to wonder if someone you had known for years had murdered your employer?

That was, assuming there were no other options.

"Who was here when Arnold died?" Gertie asked. "Did all the employees come with you to the party venue?"

Mrs. Phan nodded definitively. "Yes. We had rented vans to get everyone there, and I did a count when we arrived, because they were getting time and a half for the work."

"And no one could have left after that?"

"Maybe, but it wouldn't have been easy. The botanical garden isn't close to much, and you need a parking pass for the lot. That's why we had the vans. I'm not saying someone couldn't have slipped away from what they were assigned to do without anyone noticing and had somebody come pick them up and bring them back, but it wouldn't be easy. And why?"

That was a good question. Gertie could imagine reasons that might motivate someone to want to kill their employer—from the pedestrian to the outrageous. But she could also think of about a hundred ways to do it that would be easier and less risky. Still, there was at least one other option.

"What about someone breaking in from outside? I haven't seen any security cameras, but—"

"And you won't," Mrs. Phan interrupted. "Mr. Glass hated those things. He said they let anyone on the internet spy on you, and he refused to have anything like that around. But I can tell you that all the gates were locked, and anyone who tried to climb over one of the walls would find some very nasty plants on the other side."

She pointed to a cluster of agaves next to the table where they were sitting, with every one of their sturdy leaves ending in a vicious point. "Mr. Glass was generally happy to let Kathy do what she wanted with the garden, but he did insist on things like this around the edges. It was better than a guard dog, he would say, and cheaper to feed."

"I see. So the only people who would have been in the house when Arnold died were Haylee and his children. Or most of them, anyway. Maryann said she was out when it happened?"

"Yes, she arrived right behind me. All the cars have transmitters in them, to get through the gate, so I looked, and she'd left just before eight that morning. Mr. Glass would have been still alive then—both Brian and Neil came through the main room after that and didn't see anything."

There was no point asking why Mrs. Phan had found it necessary to do that research. She must have known since the moment she saw the missing statue that there was something wrong about her employer's death, and she wasn't the kind of person to ignore questions like that.

And neither was Gertie.

"So four people then," she said. "Haylee and Jennifer in their rooms, and Brian and Neil out in the gardens. And nobody saw anything?"

"That seems to be correct. I haven't talked to any of them about it directly, though."

"No, I can see how that would be tricky for you. But I'm going to try." Gertie smiled at the other woman's look of shock and concern. "Why not? They can hardly like me less than they do already. And I think I deserve to know what happened to my father."

"The police..." Mrs. Phan began, but she let the thought trail off.

Gertie picked it up. "The police might solve it, or they might not. But I'm here, and I have an interest. And also..." she said, then took a deep breath. "As part of the letter that summoned me here, Arnold included something I gave him a long time ago. When I was a child, he did something for me. I couldn't pay him back, so I sent an IOU. He had it sent back to me after his death, and I'm starting to wonder if he had an idea that something like this might happen."

For as wild as the suggestion was, it didn't get much of a reaction from Mrs. Phan. The household manager contemplated it quietly for a moment, then shook her head.

"That man. He always had to do things his own way, no matter what they were."

"So you think it's possible? Arnold might have known someone in the house wanted to kill him, and he assigned me to solve it? Why would he do that? What did he think was going on?"

The older woman looked up sharply and studied her face for a minute before relaxing a little. "You really are so much like him," she said. "I think he saw that. If only he had been able to get over his pride, you might not have to ask these questions."

She hesitated, looking like she was about to say something more, but then shook her head. "I hope you have some nice clothes for tomorrow. He would have liked that. Not black, though."

"Mrs. Phan—" Gertie began, but the other woman interrupted her.

"Later. I need to think. You are—maybe you're not wrong. But it's not that simple."

"I didn't expect it to be," Gertie said. "Nothing ever is."

#GLASSHOUSESENIOREMPLOYEES SLACK CHANNEL, FRIDAY, SEPTEMBER 13

Jean Phan 9:32 p.m.
Checking in about the schedule tomorrow. The memorial is at 11 am, and the family invited a small group to a reception at the downtown office directly after. **@eddie.vasquez** is everything ready for the food?

Eddie Vasquez 9:36 p.m.
On it. Any changes in numbers since yesterday?

Jean Phan 9:37 p.m.
Not that I am aware of. Jennifer hasn't responded if she has any guests.

Eddie Vasquez 9:42 p.m.
I've got enough for twenty over, so we should be okay. Btw I met the young one today. Damn, she looks like her dad. Anyway, seems like a nice kid.

Kathy Hammond 9:52 p.m.

No worse than any of them. She turned up in the garden too, looking at her new place I guess. What's going on there anyway?

Jean Phan 9:53 p.m.

I don't know. Mr. Glass's will left the house to his daughter Gertrude, but it appears that the other heirs are planning to dispute it.

Kathy Hammond 10:05 p.m.

He didn't tell you anything about what he was doing?

Jean Phan 10:06 p.m.

No. He should have. I think it might have saved us all a lot of trouble.

20

After dinner, Gertie retreated to the pool house, which had cooled down enough that the air inside was almost bearable. She had meant to spend some time online, trying to learn more about the people in the house, but though it was early, she was exhausted. *Maybe I'll just lie down for a twenty-minute nap*, she thought, and then she would be able to think clearly and be more productive.

When Gertie woke up, the lights around the pool had been turned off and the house was dark and silent. She groped around for her phone, and when she found it, on the table in the living room, it told her it was just past two in the morning. She knew she needed more sleep, but as she changed and brushed her teeth, Gertie was aware the night was still uncomfortably warm.

Back in bed, the temperature was even more oppressive. Even the breeze that had given some relief earlier had died off, so the air was completely still. Gertie could feel the sweat beading on her face, and she knew she would never get back to sleep like this. Even a fan would have helped, but she wasn't desperate enough to risk the ancient one she had found in the pool house.

She had seen another fan somewhere, though, hadn't she? Where was that? She let her mind float over the places she had been that day—the kitchen, maybe? No, the office. Gertie remembered it clearly now, on the shelf behind the desk.

It felt outrageous for her to even consider sneaking into the house in the middle of the night, to take something without asking. But she had been left to bake in this heat on purpose, and Gertie decided the usual rules of hospitality didn't apply.

The pool house, with its thick walls and small windows, had been stuffy and nearly pitch-black; in contrast, the main building seemed to float in the moonlight. The glass walls nearly vanished, opening the space up to the desert and its great expanse of sky.

It was beautiful, in a stark way, and Gertie stopped next to the windows to admire the view. As she watched, a small owl glided out of one of the trees and dove to the ground. A minute later it lifted back into the air with something wriggling in its beak. *After the heat of the day, the night must be time for life in the desert*, Gertie thought. *And death.*

Gertie stayed by the window long after the owl had vanished, trying to pull herself together. Normally she loved this time of night, and she would have relished a chance to spend it alone in the darkness. But there was nothing calming about where she was, and when she placed her hand on the cool glass of the window, she could feel her pulse throbbing in her palm.

Because, of course, she wasn't alone at all. Somewhere in this dark, quiet house, there might be a person who had killed a man to get what they wanted, and now Gertie may have taken his place in their way.

She was foolish to think she was any less safe here than she was in the pool house, of course. It was only because she was so exposed in this open space that Gertie felt like she was in danger. That was what she told herself as she turned toward the office to complete her mission, walking a little faster than normal.

As well as the illusion of emptiness, she had been thinking of the house as silent, but that wasn't true either. From the moment Gertie had come inside, she had been aware of a muffled, repetitive noise that she had put down to the laboring of something mechanical. But as she got closer to her destination, she became aware that the sound was coming from the office. Gertie was starting to suspect she was not going to end up getting that fan, but curiosity drove her forward. She had come this far, after all. If she was going to leave empty-handed, she wanted to know why.

The door to the office was in the darkest part of the room, shaded by the overhanging story above it. Gertie approached slowly, her bare feet silent on the marble floor. The curtain hanging over the doorway moved slightly, like it had been disturbed by a breeze. There was no question now that the noises were coming from there, and as they grew more distinct, Gertie thought she had a good idea what they were. She should have turned around and gone back to her overheated bedroom, but something made her reach up and lift the edge of the curtain.

The chairs in front of the desk had been pushed back to make space on the floor. That was where the noises were coming from, courtesy of Haylee, biting down on a piece of fabric with her eyes squeezed shut. She was naked—a filmy nightdress to one side of her and a pair of thong panties on the other—and Brian was on top of her, gripping her nipples as he pumped away with his shorts pooled around his knees.

Gertie let the curtain fall into place and fled back to the patio doors.

What kind of place is this? she thought madly. *What am I doing here?*

21

Just before dawn, Gertie woke again, to the sound of nearby voices. It took her a moment to remember where she was, and another to figure out that the voices were coming through one of the windows she had left open to let in any nighttime breezes. Now it was admitting a conversation between two men—gardeners, probably getting started on their work before the day got too hot.

"Where are we taking this?"

"'Round the front, next to the big palm. Kathy wants it to keep animals off the cut while it's healing. If this fucker doesn't, nothing will."

"Wasn't Tim supposed to do this?"

"He no-showed. Asshole."

"Yeah, well, I hope he enjoys the new one Kathy's gonna tear him."

Both men laughed, and their conversation lapsed into grunts and occasional instructions. Curious, Gertie risked a peek through the crack between the curtains to see what they were doing.

The men didn't notice her—they were too busy trying to dig up a short barrel-shaped cactus that was so covered with spines, they looked like fur. She watched until they loaded it into a wheelbarrow—swearing at the pain, the absent Tim, and the entire concept of gardens—and hauled it away out of sight.

With them gone, Gertie contemplated what she was going to do with the morning. It was barely six, and there was no sign of stirring from the main house. She could have gone back to bed, but she was fully awake, and for the first time since she had been in the desert, the temperature was actually pleasant.

Unlike her mother, who was always tired, Gertie had found she could get by on four or five hours of sleep a night for up to a week before she needed to shut down for a day or two. It was a talent that had been useful in law school, and she decided to use it now.

Another thing that had helped in law school was starting the day with a workout, especially when she was under stress. The question was, what to do?

She could go back to the pool, but several of the bedroom windows in the main house overlooked it, and the staff would be getting started soon. Gertie wasn't self-conscious about her swimming, but she didn't like the idea of that much attention.

Yet there was another option. The house was surrounded by a state park, and Gertie's research showed there was a trail that passed close to the edge of the property.

The sun was just rising over the edge of the mountains when Gertie stepped out into the courtyard to do her stretches. The early-morning air still had some of its overnight cool, but she knew that wouldn't last, and running in the desert heat wasn't smart. But the route she had mapped out—down the trail to the park's visitor center and then back along the road—was only a little over four miles total, and Gertie was confident she would be back before the conditions became hazardous.

And if not, she could always call a cab. Wasn't that what a person who lived in a house like this would do?

As soon as she passed through the gate in the garden wall, it was like all the color had drained out of the scenery. The dark greens and dusty blues of the cultivated succulents in the garden, and the occasional bright pops from their flowers, were replaced by a landscape of pale dirt and scrub brush with tiny leaves.

The trail started out uneven, like it had washed out in a storm and never been repaired. But after about a quarter of a mile, it smoothed out, and Gertie was able to save her attention for watching for snakes that might be using the open ground to warm up for the day.

Gertie settled into a steady rhythm, taking care not to push her pace. There would be time for that on the way back, if the temperature hadn't risen too much. For the first part of her run, she was content to take in the scenery and wonder at the series of choices that had led to her being there.

To begin with, there were the choices Arnold Glass had made long before she was born. It wasn't surprising that a rich man who made his money in the middle of the twentieth century would have built a trophy house in the Southern California desert; plenty of them had. What Gertie couldn't understand, among other things, was why he had settled there year-round. Why not spend the summers at the coast and leave this place to the lizards?

As if in agreement with her, a small four-legged something skittered away from Gertie's foot as she sped up down a slight incline in the path. For all the attention she thought she was paying, it still startled her, and she nearly lost her footing.

Gertie let loose with a burst of obscenities and pinwheeled her arms, and somehow the combination kept her from hitting the ground face-first. She stumbled to a stop and stood for a moment, catching her breath and hoping no one had seen. It had been stupid of her, running along too fast, wasting all her attention on trying to understand a dead man's real estate decisions.

Particularly when the much more interesting question was how he'd died.

Her own stumble fresh in her mind, Gertie restarted her run with more caution, wondering what her father had felt in those seconds when he was falling down the stairs. Terror, obviously. And panic, and every other impulse the body put out when it knew it was about to die. But had he been surprised? Had he been angry? Was Gertie right about him having summoned her because he suspected something like this might happen, or was he caught completely off guard?

Gertie wasn't sure how many of those questions she would ever be able to answer, but she knew she had to try. If not her, then who? There were the police, but Gertie didn't have a lot of faith in them. She'd had a few encounters with law enforcement when the scams that trapped Carla would fall apart, and her opinion was that if it looked like it was going to take more than twenty minutes to get an arrest, the cops weren't interested.

It had been two weeks now, so Gertie figured that finding the answers was probably up to her.

How she was going to do that would be a question for when she got back to the house. She came around a curve and saw she was nearly at the visitor center—a modest single-story building that blended into the bare hills behind it. As she got closer, she could see that the front door was open, and there was a rack of maps next to the sign warning about poisonous animals and heatstroke.

Gertie slowed to a jog and trotted around to the back of the center, where she found a water fountain between the bathroom doors. She took a long drink, and as she wiped the lingering drops from her lips, she heard boots crunching on gravel.

"Good morning. Getting an early start?"

The young man who approached was a park ranger, easily identifiable by his olive-colored uniform, complete with a flat-brimmed hat that sat on top of long white-blond hair pulled into a ponytail. The embroidered name tag over his breast pocket identified him as Ranger Boyd, and the tattoos that wound around his wiry arms suggested he was a fan of desert reptiles.

"Just out for a short run," Gertie said, in answer to his implied question. "I thought I had better do it before it got too hot."

"Good thinking." He looked up to where the sun had crested the mountains behind them and then back to Gertie, giving her a once-over she thought might have been appreciation before she realized he was looking for a water bottle. "Were you planning to go far? You might be surprised how fast the days can heat up around here."

"I can believe it. Actually, I just came from the house up the trail. I was planning to go back by the road—it shouldn't take more than about twenty minutes. I know enough not to overdo it."

Gertie wasn't sure why it was suddenly so important for her to convince this guy that she was knowledgeable about a place she had never been, but she suspected it had something to do with the way he was still looking at her with those blue eyes.

At least, he had been. As Gertie spoke, his expression went from interested and mildly concerned, to confusion, then understanding, followed by a look of suspicion and judgment

"Oh, that house. Yeah, sure you should be fine to make it back there."

Gertie wasn't sure what the family had done to make a negative impression on their nearest neighbors, but she could imagine some possibilities.

"Gertie Glass," she said, smiling and extending her hand. "Thanks for the tips. I haven't spent much time around here, and I have to admit, I really wasn't prepared."

Whatever was annoying him, it couldn't have been that bad, because the ranger's expression thawed as he shook her hand with his heavily callused one.

"Herman Boyd," he said. "I see we have parents with equally charming senses of humor."

Gertie laughed. "The curse of the family name. Do you go by 'Harry' or something?"

"No, most people just call me 'Boyd.'" He gestured at his name tag. "It's what it says on the shirt."

"Well, it's nice to meet you, Boyd. I'm planning to stay around for a while, and I'd like to get to know the park. Maybe I'll run into you again?" Gertie wouldn't have minded staying and chatting with him, but she was acutely aware of the rising sun that had now entirely cleared the mountain ridge. It was bizarre, but oddly exhilarating, to be so afraid of the air around her.

"Sure thing," Boyd said, falling into step behind her as she started toward the road. "I'm here most days, or someone will be."

"Great, well, I'll see you around then." Gertie did a couple of quick stretches and was about to take off when Boyd held up a hand.

"Hey, at your house, the staff uniforms—" he began, and then stopped. The ranger clearly had something he wanted to say, but at the last minute, he checked himself.

"Yes?" said Gertie. "What about them?"

"Oh, nothing. Never mind. Anyway, be careful on that trail in the evening, by the way—mountain lions are most active around that time," he said at last. "We caught one on the trail camera just last week. They've been coming in closer lately. No attacks around here yet, but a cat's a cat. They see something running, they're going to chase it."

"No sunset jogging then," Gertie said, though she would have to admit that at the moment, her number one concern was more prosaic. "So, you have trail cameras?"

"Sure, all over the park. Why?"

Gertie was aware she was blushing; she hoped Ranger Boyd thought it was sunburn.

"Well, I had kind of a moment back on the trail there with an unexpected lizard. No harm done, but if you're putting together a blooper reel of best spontaneous dances, I think I might be a contender."

"No worries," Boyd said, laughing. "The competition there is stiff. You would be amazed at what the jackrabbits get up to. Anyway, you'd better get going. Sorry for holding you up."

"No problem. See you around."

Gertie started up the visitor center's driveway, running slowly at first to let her stiffening muscles warm up. As she turned onto the road, something made her look back, toward the building. Boyd was still standing there, watching her go with an expression she couldn't quite place.

EMAIL FROM ANDY BURNETT TO GERTIE GLASS

Hey kiddo,

Just wanted to check in and see how you were doing, waiting for your ship to come in out there in the desert. (Did you get that reference?) I know today is the memorial for your father and from what I saw on the internet it looks like it's going to be quite the shindig.

I hope your dad's other kids are treating you okay. The stories your mom told me about them made it sound like they're a real bunch of loons, even accounting for the effect she has on people. There was even one time when one of them locked the others out or something? Not sure how that worked, but make sure you get your own set of keys.

Your mom called me yesterday; she wanted me to get you to hire this new lawyer she's been talking to. I told her I'd tell you, so consider that done. She wouldn't tell me if she's paying him for anything, but it sounded like he has her hooked pretty good. You might want to do the thing with her bank account like you did that time with the psychic, just to be safe.

I'm heading out next week in your direction to go take some pictures of the Playa after the Burning Man cleanup—it's for a project a friend of mine is putting together on nature and art. Should be pretty cool, and maybe I can stop by on the way back and see you if you're still in the area. Your mom said she wasn't sure when you were coming back to her place?

I'd tell you to take care of yourself, but I know you will.

Your pal,
Andy

22

The ranger was probably going to tell her about the harm the house was doing to the park environment or something, Gertie thought. She was lucky to have gotten away with just a warning about mountain lions. As she ran, Gertie wondered if all her interactions around here were going to be like that. She was used to being prejudged—for her entire life, she had dealt with expectations people carried over from meeting Carla. No one ever bothered having an opinion about Gertie herself; she was Carla's daughter, and that meant whatever it meant to them.

And now she was one of the Glass family, according to everyone but them. Of course, she didn't have to be. She could finish this run, change her clothes and pack her bag, and be back on the coast by lunchtime. Easy enough to decide that she had paid her debt by coming here in the first place—if Arnold had wanted more from her, he could have taken the time to explain it.

As she was thinking it, Gertie came over a rise in the road and saw the house ahead of her. The east-facing windows flashed in the morning sun, like they were winking at her indecision.

You could leave, the house seemed to be saying. *But we both know you won't.*

The house—or the part of her subconscious it was representing—was right, of course. If Gertie were going to leave, she would have done it by now. And, of all the things that might have driven her off, an uncomfortable interaction with a park ranger wasn't going to do it, no matter how intriguing his tattoos looked.

So she was staying. But what was she going to do next?

The immediate answer was that she was going to change into her nice outfit and attend the memorial service. It would be interesting, at least, to see how the people there reacted to her publicly appearing as Arnold's daughter. She wondered how many of them even knew she existed.

Some were bound to, of course. Gertie had noticed older people didn't measure time the same way she did. Twenty-five years wasn't much when you were seventy, and it was possible there would be guests who still thought of her as a toddler.

There was no sidewalk on this stretch of road, so Gertie ran on the pavement, facing where the oncoming traffic would be if there were any. There wasn't—the road that led to the house didn't go anywhere else, at least not for a while. Which was why Gertie was surprised to hear a car approaching from behind her—coming fast, by the sound of it. It was in the opposite lane, but to be safe, she moved onto the narrow dirt shoulder

Slowing down, she turned to see who was coming and stopped running as a police car, lights off and sirens silent, flew past.

23

It took another fifteen minutes for Gertie to make it to the house. She expected to find the place in chaos, but besides the police cars parked in the driveway, there was no sign anything was going on at all.

"Oh, you were out for a run? We were wondering where you had gone." Maryann was sitting at the dining table, a cup of coffee and a folded newspaper in front of her, and Brian was at the other end of the table, working through a plate of eggs. No one else was there, but there were three more coffee mugs scattered around the room.

Gertie glanced at the stairs that led up to the room where Haylee was supposed to have been sleeping, but whether she was there or not, the two doors were firmly closed.

"You can talk to Eddie if you want breakfast," Maryann went on. "He'll need to get started on the food for the reception soon, though. We're having a gathering of few of Father's business associates after the memorial."

Gertie caught the snub, but she couldn't even begin to process it under the circumstances.

"What are the police doing here?" she asked. "Where did they go?"

"Fuckin' cops," said Brian, who was gripping his coffee mug like it might try to escape. But he didn't go on, so Maryann did.

"It was one of the gardeners, I'm afraid. He was hit by a car last night. Killed him instantly. His name was Tim, I think."

Still dressed in her running clothes, Gertie made her way out into the garden, where the temperature was starting to rise. Maryann had told her that Tim's death was a tragic accident, with the heavy implication that it was just the sort of thing that happened to people who rode bicycles at night. But Gertie didn't think you got this many police officers for an ordinary accident, and when the detective's car pulled into the driveway, she was sure of it.

She had expected to find the cops outside, talking to the other gardeners who would have been the ones to know Tim best. But the paths were empty, and the only sign of life was a hummingbird working its way through a bright pink cactus flower and a faint beeping sound in the distance.

Confused, Gertie wandered deeper into the garden until she could hear voices coming from the far corner. She was heading toward them when one of the policemen appeared from behind a clump of short palms.

"Can I help you?" he asked, in a tone that said, *You aren't going any farther.*

Gertie didn't mind; she was looking for a person who knew something, and she had found one. "I heard there had been a death," she said. "I wanted to find out what happened."

"Um, yes, but—I'm sorry, who are you?"

"Gertie Glass. Arnold Glass's daughter." The officer didn't look convinced, so Gertie added, "I was out for a run, and I saw the cars arrive. Is everything okay? Why are all these people here?"

She felt like she was laying the dumb act on too thick, but growing up with Carla had taught her that wasn't possible. She even tried a little simpering, which must have been convincing enough, because the cop dropped his look of suspicion and smiled indulgently at her.

"Yes, ma'am. One of the landscaping employees here was killed last night by a hit-and-run driver. It happened as he was biking home from a night out at a bar. He didn't have any family in the area, so we came by to see if any of the people who worked with him might know who he could have been out with. They might be a witness."

The policeman might have believed that, but Gertie didn't. There were easier ways to find out who a guy was hanging out with on a Friday night than going to his workplace, like talking to the people who had been at the bar. And if they wanted to ask other landscapers about Tim's social life, the police had phones.

But she saw no benefit in challenging him. Instead, Gertie nodded sympathetically.

"I wish I could help you," she said. "I met him for the first time yesterday, and he seemed nice. We didn't talk about anything he was planning to do, though; he just told me about the plants."

The policeman showed no interest in her interactions with the dead gardener. He kept looking over his shoulder, in the direction Gertie had heard the voices coming from earlier.

"If you wouldn't mind going back to the house, we'll be in touch if we have any more information to share," he said, and before Gertie could ask another question, the officer turned away from her and mumbled into his radio. A staticky answer came back, and he nodded and then glanced at Gertie.

"I need to go. Have a nice day, ma'am," he said, then left in the opposite direction from which she had come. In the silence that followed, the beeping sound Gertie had heard earlier was clearer, and she was finally able to identify it. Gertie had spent long enough living near the coast to know a metal detector when she heard one.

Gertie had wanted to ask about what time to leave for the service, but when she came back into the main house, there was no one there but Haylee, standing at the bottom of the staircase and looking mad.

"Hey, you," she snapped at Gertie, in a voice that had lost all its babyish affectation. "What do you mean I can't have breakfast in bed?"

"I'm sorry?" said Gertie.

"You'd better be! When I'm in charge here, you're gonna be fired so fast, girlie. And why are you out of your uniform? What is this, casual...?" she trailed off, and Gertie took the opportunity to correct her.

"I don't work here, I'm Arnold's daughter," she said mildly. "And it's Saturday."

"Whatever." Neither Gertie's identity nor the concept of time must have been very interesting to Haylee, who proceeded to descend into the conversation pit and start pulling cushions off the chairs. From this angle, Gertie could tell her outfit was a romper—tiny silk shorts sewn directly to the blouse in a way that caused them to ride up every time Haylee raised her arms. She demonstrated the effect as she threw one of the pillows across the room in frustration.

"Where are all the workers, anyway? I want coffee, and I think one of them stole my phone."

"They may be getting ready for some events to do with the memorial service. You could try the kitchen. For the coffee, I mean," Gertie said. In fact, she had been wondering something similar, about her own breakfast. (As for the phone, it was probably where Haylee had left it, and there would be no apologies once it was found even if the woman managed to accuse every member of the staff.) But Gertie did wonder at the lack of anyone around. Had Maryann's pettiness extended to making sure Gertie would have to go into the day uncaffeinated?

That, Gertie decided, would mean war. Haylee might want her coffee, but Gertie needed it.

She was about to take her own advice to check the kitchen, but Haylee looked horrified at the suggestion.

"Like I'm going to go poking around in that filthy place? No way. You can bring me a latte."

"I can," Gertie agreed. "But I won't. See you at the church." She started toward the back of the house and glanced back at where Haylee was pulling down the shorts that had crept up again. "You might want to think about changing."

Gertie expected she would find the kitchen empty too, and she was prepared to do whatever it took to get her own coffee, but this time she was lucky. Eddie was there, directing traffic as young people in chef's whites stacked hotel trays onto carts and wheeled them out the door, and he gave Gertie a wave as soon as he spotted her.

"Oh, hey," he said. "Sorry I didn't catch you earlier. We're just about to head out—was there anything more you needed?"

He seemed so cheerful and genuine that Gertie felt bad for thinking he would conspire with Maryann to cut her out of breakfast.

"I was just hoping to get some coffee," she said. "If you're busy, you can point me in the direction of the machine, and I'll make my own."

Eddie grinned at her. "See, this is what you get for being so crazy about exercising. If you'd stayed in bed instead of running around the desert like a nutcase, you would know that there was a whole breakfast all set up in the pool house for you."

"Oh! Wow, thanks. I'll go back there then. I should really take a shower anyway."

"Yeah, I wasn't going to say anything." Eddie laughed. "And don't thank me—it was Mrs. Phan's idea. She figured you might want to have some time to yourself to get ready for the day. The coffee is in a thermos, so it should be hot."

"I won't risk it. Heading that way now." Gertie started to go but stopped at the door.

"Hey, I heard about what happened to Tim. I'm really sorry. I met him yesterday, he seemed like a nice guy," she said.

Eddie's expression clouded over. "He was. I didn't know him well, but I saw him around, you know? It's a bad business."

"No kidding." The other chefs had left with the pans, and Eddie clearly wanted to follow them, but Gertie had one more question she had to ask. "The number of police who came here when he was killed somewhere else is surprising to me. What's going on here?"

Now it was Eddie's turn to head for the door.

"What isn't? Look, I've got to go. Enjoy your breakfast, and take care of yourself."

JENNIFER GLASS ONLINE THERAPY JOURNAL ENTRY

Okay, so it's been a few weeks since I wrote here, but things have been really crazy. After Daddy died (RIP Daddy) I had some setbacks but I can handle it. I'm back at our house and everything is going wrong. Maryann acts like I can't do anything right and Brian is so mean. And Neil is all like his life is so perfect, like we don't know. But the worst thing is the stupid lawyer read the stupid will and now we don't even get the house! I don't know what I'm going to do. I wasn't expecting this.

    I know I need to learn to move on and not focus on assigning blame, but it's really all his fault. It was Daddy having his midlife crisis that made everything start to go wrong. If he hadn't been so obvious about how he was cheating with that skinny bitch, Mama never would have left him, and she wouldn't have needed to get that plastic surgery that killed her. And we wouldn't be stuck with this other girl claiming she gets to keep the house. Like really? Really? I don't care what the will says, this house is ours and we get to have it.

And this couldn't be at a worse time. Maryann's going on about how there isn't so much money in the business, but we can't sell it or whatever, but she doesn't understand how much I need it. Everything is easy for the rest of them. I'm the one who's all on my own.

It was bad enough coming back here after what happened last time. I'm going to need some help to get through the memorial. I won't overdo it this time.

I don't know what I'm going to do if we can't keep the house. I thought everything was finally going to be fixed but now it's worse than it was.

24

Gertie left the kitchen wondering about the chef's answer, but eager for her breakfast. Wanting to avoid Haylee, she went out through the small door that led from the kitchen to the patio and nearly collided with Jennifer, who was sitting at a small café table that hadn't been there before. She was positioned behind a clump of cacti with paddle-shaped stems, drinking something green in a tall glass and blocking the entire path.

When the door opened, she jumped like she was about to come out of her skin. She relaxed only slightly when she saw Gertie.

"Oh, it's you," she said. Her voice was shaking, but it also had an edge of anger.

"I get that a lot lately," Gertie replied. "What are you doing back here?"

Jennifer glared at her. "Minding my own business. You should try it."

"Happy to. Mind letting me by?"

Jennifer would have had to move her chair only about six inches to let Gertie pass, but she clearly had no intention of doing it.

"Forget it," she said. "You're good at getting around things."

Gertie looked at the spines on the cactus, thought about Haylee back in the house with her equally prickly attitude, and decided on the third option.

"No thanks," she said. "I'll just stay here and chat. I guess you heard about Tim, the gardener who was killed last night?"

This was obviously not an outcome Jennifer had considered, because she reacted first with surprise, then annoyance. Finally, she answered the question.

"I saw the cops were here. Doesn't have anything to do with me. I never met the guy."

"Yes you did," Gertie said helpfully. "He was the one you told to cut down the palm tree outside your window yesterday, because the cicadas were bothering you."

"No I didn't."

Jennifer said it so automatically that Gertie assumed she was lying, but the apparently genuine confusion on the other woman's face made her wonder.

"Anyway," Jennifer went on. "Why do you care? You're leaving today anyway."

"Am I?" said Gertie. "That's the first I've heard of it. Actually, I'm planning on staying a while."

"The hell you are!" In her anger, Jennifer twisted her chair to face Gertie, unaware that as she did, she opened up a gap on the path wide enough to get around her. "You think you can just invite yourself in here and stay as long as you want? You've got no right!"

"Arnold invited me. And he also willed me the house. So I'd say I have at least as much right to be here as anyone." Gertie maintained steady eye contact as she moved forward, and Jennifer shrank back like she thought Gertie was going to attack.

"I'm staying," she repeated, with a bravado she absolutely did not feel. "And the sooner you all accept that, the better. Now, if you'll excuse me, I've got to get changed for my father's memorial service."

With that, Gertie nimbly stepped around Jennifer's chair before the other woman had a chance to block her. Not that she didn't try—in her lunging attempt to move her chair back across the path, Jennifer nearly tipped over into the cacti and did spill her green drink across her lap. The sound of her cursing followed Gertie across the patio and into the pool house, where Gertie gratefully shut the door.

The breakfast was on the table, under a silver cover, with the thermos of coffee next to it. Gertie didn't even bother thinking about what it meant to be served like this—the food was good and the coffee was hot, and she could wonder about where her life was going later.

Gertie was so absorbed in her meal, it took her several minutes to notice that she wasn't sweating. It was midmorning, and the sun was streaming through the pool house windows, but the temperature inside remained tolerable.

Leaving her breakfast, Gertie investigated the cottage. She found the answer in the bedroom window, where a small, brand-new air-conditioning unit had been set up, and the cool air it produced flowed sluggishly through the building.

"Mrs. Phan," Gertie murmured appreciatively. She took a moment to bask in the temperature, then went back to finish her meal.

Forty-five minutes later—caffeinated, fed, showered, and dressed—Gertie sat down at the table and took out the leather-bound notebook she had bought when she started prepping for the bar. It was over two hours until the service, too early to think about leaving. With the windows closed to keep in the cold, she couldn't hear if anything was going on in the main house, and if she was being honest, she didn't want to.

Feeling trapped, a bird in a stucco cage, Gertie turned to a fresh page and thought about the questions that had been piling up since she had arrived back at her first home.

Less than twenty-four hours earlier, those had been about why Arnold invited her here, to say nothing of his bizarre bequests to her. At the time, they had been confusing—unnerving, even, but now, with another man dead, they became more sinister.

The statue had gone missing in the same window of time when Arnold died, she was sure of that. It was the sort of thing Mrs. Phan wouldn't get wrong, and Gertie couldn't see any reason for her to lie about it. A coincidence was possible, but so unlikely that Gertie didn't waste her time thinking about how it could have happened. The obvious answer was that the statue had been used to hit Arnold while he was lying on the floor, leaving the spray of blood that Mrs. Phan noticed at the base of the stairs.

It was a terrible thought. Gertie hadn't known her father enough to care about him, but the idea of anyone battering an incapacitated elderly man's skull made her shiver.

And now a second man was dead—as far as she knew, a perfectly nice man with no obvious faults beyond being too eager to please his employers. It might have been nothing to do with the house, of course. People got hit by cars every day for no reason other than the drivers weren't paying attention. But those people hadn't been employed at a place where someone had been killed two weeks earlier.

So she put Tim's name at the top of the next page, facing the one where she had already written Arnold's. On her father's page, she wrote down what she knew about his death so far—that he usually spent the mornings in the tower office, which was where he had been on the morning of his birthday. He had been alive there at seven in the morning, when Mrs. Phan brought his coffee, and the household manager had said she got the call about Arnold's death at ten.

Gertie wrote those times down and tried to remember what else she had learned in that conversation by the pool. Mrs. Phan had mentioned Maryann was gone during the critical time, so Gertie made a note of that. Then she though a moment longer and added another one, to ask Mrs. Phan for the gate logs, covering the time between when the staff left that morning and when Arnold's body was found.

Assuming Mrs. Phan's information was correct, that left Gertie with the three remaining siblings and Haylee. Gertie put their names in order down the page, with what she knew about where they had been at the time of Arnold's death—outside for Neil and Brian, and both of the women presumably still sleeping in their rooms. As far as she knew, none of them had an alibi from any of the others—that was another thing she was going to need to find out.

That, and why any of them might want to kill Arnold Glass.

She had been distracting herself with the technicalities, but that was what it was all about, wasn't it really? It wasn't enough to say they were all terrible people and so it could be any of them— this was murder. The murder of an old man who couldn't have had that many years left in him anyway. So what was it that made someone decide Arnold needed to die now?

The money was the first thing Gertie thought of, of course. From what Jules had told her, her father's wealth had been the only source of income for all the siblings except Maryann, and probably most of hers as well. (And if Haylee had any other way of making a living, Gertie would eat any hat available.) They all seemed to be living well off it, but appearances could be deceiving, particularly with what she knew about how much debt they had taken on. What if one of them needed more and Arnold wasn't willing to give it to them? It wouldn't be out of character—after all, he had tried to do it to Gertie for most of her life.

But even that, on its own, wouldn't be enough to drive most people to kill. There had to be another reason, something that might convince a person take the most extreme action possible.

Desperation? Betrayal? Gertie thought about Haylee's conviction that she was going to be the sole benefactor of the estate—what if she was right about that and Arnold had been killed to stop him from changing his will again? Or what if she had been wrong but killed him anyway, to ensure he didn't survive for long enough to get tired of her?

There were more questions than Gertie could fit on her page, and she wasn't sure how she would answer most of them. But one more occurred to her, one she felt confident she would be able to track down. She picked up her pen again, skipped a line, and made a new bullet point.

- *What was the dinner about?*

Of course, Arnold's death wasn't the only one with questions around it. Gertie's eyes drifted over to the other page, the one with Tim's name. The second death, she thought, and not just in terms of time. If the two were connected, the only way that made sense was that Tim's death was caused by Arnold's. Could he have been involved in the murder somehow? Or known something that made him a danger to the killer? Two weeks was a long time to not tell anyone something that important, but maybe he hadn't known the meaning of what he knew, or the amenable, plant-focused young man had decided that making himself a bit of money from blackmail was more important than seeing justice done.

And then there was the question of the statue. The minimalist interior of the house would have made for a bad place to hide things, but the grounds were much larger and wilder. But they were also well-maintained, and someone using the garden as a hiding place might not realize how soon a disruption would be noticed. Gertie wasn't sure how many people knew about the importance of the missing item—Tim could have found it and had no idea what he had. The obvious thing for him to do would have been to tell his boss, but Gertie had already seen his willingness to go around her if it meant gaining favor with a member of the family. And if he had told the wrong person...

It was all pure guessing, of course. The only thing Gertie really knew about Tim's death that made it suspicious was how soon it had happened after her father's. There was more to it, she was sure of that, but she was going to be on her own in figuring it out.

That was okay with her. Doing things on her own was what Gertie was best at.

25

The church was an aggressively modern building on the outskirts of Palm Springs proper. Built like an upside-down funnel, it had as few windows as the Glass house was dominated by them. Gertie was met in the foyer by an usher who handed her a program and left her on her own to decide where in the cavernous interior she was going to sit.

She found a pew in the middle of the sanctuary and chose a spot in the center. No one paid much attention to her, though she did get a double take from an older woman who saw her in profile. Gertie watched her out of the corner of her eye as she went to join a man of the same age who had been chatting with another couple, then lost track of both of them as they headed toward the back of the church.

Gertie flipped through the program and glanced over the bio. It mentioned Arnold's four older children and his first wife, but left Carla and Gertie out entirely. Reading it, a person might think Arnold had died a grieving widower, alone since the death of his first and only love.

There was a group of three men next to Gertie, and from their chat, Gertie gathered that they worked for Glass Development. She would have liked a chance to eavesdrop, to learn more about the company in which she was suddenly a part owner, but an opening chord from the church organ ended the conversation.

The lights dimmed, like a play was about to start, and Gertie had a sudden mad thought that someone else with suspicions about Arnold's death was about to pull a *Hamlet* and reenact the fatal fall. But, of course, that didn't happen, and the organ music gave way to a string quartet playing "My Way."

As the song reached the first chorus, the doors at the back of the sanctuary opened, and six pallbearers entered carrying a gleaming black coffin.

They should have put some weights in it, Gertie thought as she watched the light steps of the men coming down the aisle.

The coffin was closely followed by the minister, and then, in a staggered line, came the rest of the dead man's children. All four of them were on their own—Gertie saw no spouses or children—and Gertie wondered about that. What kind of person wouldn't show up for their father-in-law's funeral? For their grandfather's?

That might have been something for Gertie to think about, but then Jennifer spotted her.

The obvious thing for Jennifer to do would be to smirk, perhaps raise an eyebrow over their obviously different status. It made no sense for her to burst into laughter, hooting away as tears ran down her face. None of the attempts of her siblings had much effect on her, but eventually she was able to get herself under control and continue down the aisle, hiccupping occasionally.

The older gentleman sitting to Gertie's right sighed and shook his head. "Grief's a funny thing," he murmured to the woman next to him, who nodded and patted his arm.

There was some sort of hurried conference once the family was seated, and Jennifer was placed at the end of the pew with ushers on either side of her. She was clearly agitated and tried to stand several times, but firm hands kept her in her seat.

That might have been enough to make her the biggest story of the day, but Jennifer had some competition there.

No sooner had the quartet finished playing and the minister stepped behind the lectern than the main doors opened for a second time. There were sounds of a scuffle, and then Haylee appeared in the doorway.

She was dressed in a black gown with a deep neckline and a hat the size of a deli platter. Close behind her were two of the ushers, trying without success to guide her away. One of them looked over to where Maryann was sitting, and Gertie turned in time to see the oldest Glass sibling sigh and give a quick shake of her head.

Unimpeded, Haylee proceeded down the center aisle, occasionally dabbing her eyes with tissues she pulled from a sequined packet. She paused for a moment next to the pew where the family was sitting, then crossed to the other side and moved a flower arrangement so she could take its spot.

After all that, the service itself was something of a letdown.

Gertie learned some things about her father that she didn't believe, like that he had been a passionate supporter of environmental causes (based on donations to various well-connected charities) and he had enjoyed baking.

There were a few more songs and a moment the guests were asked to spend in silent contemplation of what Arnold had meant in their lives. Then the quartet came back out, played a few bars of "We Are Family," and Maryann took the podium.

"Thank you all for coming," she began, before stopping to take a breath. "It is so comforting for all of us in the family to see how many people valued our father, and I know he would all offer you a warm welcome if he were here."

Someone behind Gertie chuckled, quickly followed by some vigorous shushing.

Maryann went on. "Arnold Glass was a great man, a visionary, and an inspiration to everyone who knew him. But he was also a man of profound personal passions. His house, his garden, and of course his family were every bit as important to him as any professional achievement, even if he didn't always show it in the ways the world would generally recognize. We are here to acknowledge the passing of a successful businessman, but more than that, we celebrate a life lived well in every way."

Gertie listened to the eulogy with extreme cynicism, wondering if Maryann had turned to some AI program to generate her platitudes or if she had simply assigned the job to an underling from the office. Nothing she had seen or heard made her think Arnold had given more than a passing thought to his children, herself most definitely included, and as far as she could tell, the lack of feeling was mutual.

She was so wrapped up in her analysis of the speech, Gertie stopped fully listening to what was being said. But something caught her attention, and against her will, she found herself staring at Maryann's face as her half sister spoke.

"When Father first invited me to join the company, I knew that he wasn't just giving me a job, he was passing on his legacy. That was how he communicated, not in words but in actions, and he expected us all to do the same."

Her voice had a strangled tone, and Gertie realized to her shock that Maryann was crying. She felt embarrassed, like she was witnessing a private moment, but of course everyone else in the church could see it too. She wondered if it was a performance—the perfect older daughter playing her role—but for once Gertie wasn't very sure of herself.

The service was over, and Gertie stood in front of the church, watching the other guests as they flowed by. She wondered what they were thinking—about the family and, most of all, about Arnold's death.

She had chosen a spot by the corner of the stairs to the church, in the meager shade provided by a short palm tree. Maryann, Brian, and Neil were at the base of the stairs, accepting condolences, while Jennifer hung back, looking like she wasn't sure where she was. None of them were facing the door, so they had no time to prepare when Haylee stepped out into the sunshine.

"Well," she said in a loud, bright voice. "Wasn't that a beautiful service, for a wonderful man?"

She paused, turning her head so her hat rotated like a satellite dish. A smile played over her pursed lips, and she placed a hand on her hip, though her eyes remained as blank as ever. Two ushers and one of the pallbearers emerged from the church and huddled in the door, as though their jurisdiction ended at the threshold. Belatedly, the siblings realized what was going on and that trying to intervene would only make it worse. Everyone else just waited to see what would happen next.

They didn't have to wait long. Arnold's girlfriend tilted her head back and lifted her hands to the sky. "If only—" she began, intoning the words with a drama her thin voice couldn't quite support.

"Excuse me, Miss Jackson?"

"Yes? What?" If Haylee had expected to be interrupted, it wasn't by a tired-looking man in a suit, who had somehow quietly worked his way up the stairs while two uniformed policemen waited below.

"You're under arrest. For the murders of Tim Martin and Arnold Glass," said the cop. "Would you please come with me?"

GATE LOG FOR THE GLASS HOUSE, 24 OF AUGUST, 5:00 A.M. TO 12:00 P.M.

5:03 a.m. Jean Phan entry

5:28 a.m. Kathy Hammond entry

6:39 a.m. Manual Entry, 2 vehicles [US Van Rental]

7:02 a.m. Manual Exit, 2 vehicles [US Van Rental]

7:18 a.m. Kathy Hammond exit

7:46 a.m. Maryann Glass exit

8:01 a.m. Jean Phan exit

10:03 a.m. Kathy Hammond entry

10:26 a.m. Emergency Services Entry, [Paramedics, Palm Springs Fire Department]

10:45 a.m. Emergency Services Entry, 3 vehicles [Palm Springs Police]

10:52 a.m. Jean Phan entry

10:58 a.m. Maryann Glass entry

11:26 a.m. Manual Entry, [Riverside County Coroner]

26

The post-memorial party must have been canceled. Gertie didn't know how it was decided, but when she got back to the house, most of the others were already gathered in the living room.

Though "gathered" was the wrong word to describe them. Each person was lost in their own world, scattered around the open space. Brian was glaring out the window toward the front gate, while Neil hovered in the doorway that led to the patio and spoke in urgent hushed tones into his phone, and Jennifer sat on the sofa in the conversation pit, staring into nothing.

None of them paid any attention to Gertie. She crossed, ghostlike, to a strange decorative chair in the corner and sat there while she thought about what had just happened.

Haylee had gone without putting up a fight, staring slack-jawed at the police as they led her away. The only time she protested was when an officer tried to take off her hat to fit her into the patrol car.

That surprised Gertie less as she thought about it. She knew well enough that there were people who had never faced a problem someone else wouldn't solve for them, and the idea of being in trouble that wasn't going to just go away was beyond their understanding. Which was unfortunate because, in Gertie's experience, that was something everyone ran into eventually.

Though being accused of murdering two people was a new one.

"Does anyone know what happened?" she asked at last, when the silence started to get to her.

"Nobody's told us anything," Neil said. With his call finished, he carefully buckled the embossed leather case over his phone and came to the edge of the conversation pit. "But Maryann went to find out. She'll get some answers out of those assholes."

"She had better," said Brian. "Not that I have any issue with them nailing that bitch, but why the hell did they pick that time to do it?"

"I think they wanted to arrest her as soon as they could. They went straight there as soon as they finished here."

Mrs. Phan came in from the kitchen, her handbag looped over her arm. She was dressed entirely in black—from her knee-length dress and lightweight blazer to her tinted nylons and low-heeled shoes—aside from the bright white scarf that sat folded sharply in her breast pocket. She must have been at the service, Gertie realized, but she had no memory of seeing her there.

"You let them in here?" Neil approached her, enraged. "What the hell were you thinking?"

Mrs. Phan held her ground. "I wasn't here; they were let in by the other staff. And what they were thinking was that the police had a warrant."

"Where did they search?" Gertie asked Mrs. Phan.

"Mostly out in the garage. They took her car with them, and they looked around where it was parked," the household manager said. "I believe they also went up into her room. And they took the remaining bronze."

She gestured at the table by the front door, where there was a gap in the array of decorative items. That was where the pair to the missing statue had been, Gertie realized. Why hadn't the police taken it sooner?

Some people had other questions.

"So, you talked so much about the damn thing being missing that they finally came and took the other one?" Brian sneered at Mrs. Phan. "We'll be sure to remember it in your Christmas bonus. Why did they need to take it now? What difference does it make?"

"Because they found the other one in Haylee's car. Covered with Dad's blood," said Maryann.

27

Maryann had entered through the patio doors, and she went straight to the conversation pit and took the chair across from Jennifer. Her sister lifted her head and looked at her, frowning in confusion.

"How did his blood get on the statue? The stairs he fell down are all the way across the room."

Neil was quicker on the uptake. "Because, dear Sister, Dad's latest in his series of charming whores used it to smash his head in."

"Neil!" said Maryann, and Brian just laughed. But Jennifer, who was still on her way back from wherever she had been, remained confused.

"Why would she do that?" she asked. "He didn't hurt her, did he?"

Neil snorted. "Of course not. She must have thought she was going to inherit. Remember how shocked she was yesterday when she found out she wasn't getting anything? She probably figured she had better get it while she could, before he got sick of her like all the others."

Nobody was paying any attention to Gertie. Aside from Neil's comment that she recognized as being at least partially aimed at her mother, none of the siblings seemed to even be aware that she was sitting in on the discussion of their shared father's death.

And since her revelation about the police search, Mrs. Phan went equally ignored. She moved quietly around the edges of the room, picking up some bits of paper and a discarded coffee cup, like no one else was there.

From her spot in the lone chair by the window, Gertie caught Mrs. Phan's eye and gave her a quizzical look. The other woman responded with a barely perceptible shake of her head.

"What I want to know is what made her so sure she was in for the money?" Brian said. "I know Dad would tell those dumb bitches anything they wanted to hear, but I'd think even silicone-for-brains there would want more than a man's word for it before she got herself sent up for murder one."

Maryann rubbed her temples. "Can you say a single thing without being maximally offensive, Brian? I have no idea what Haylee was thinking. I don't think we ever will. All I know is the police found the statue in her car, covered in his blood and wrapped in one of her scarves. That, plus something about what she did last night, was enough for them, and it's enough for me."

It wasn't enough for the rest of them, though.

"What if he hadn't been lying to her, though?" Brian went on, like he was thinking out loud. "Dad wasn't exactly as sharp as he used to be, and we all had our moments of annoying him. Look at the will he did make, leaving just enough to young Gertrude to give the rest of us nothing but headaches. Are we so sure he wasn't going through with it?"

Surprised as she was by the sound of her name, the main thing on Gertie's mind was if Brian realized where this line of reasoning might be leading him.

Apparently, Neil hadn't thought of it either, because he picked up where Brian left off.

"Didn't he have a meeting with Jules that week? God, that would be ironic. What if he really was going to write her into the will and she offed him before he could go through with it?"

"Would you all just stop it!" Jennifer jumped up from the sofa and turned on Neil and Brian. "Can't you hear what you're saying? Daddy is dead, and you're just making your same old jokes. He knew about you; he knew about all of us! And now there's nothing any of us can do about it."

With that, she stomped away toward the patio, stumbling on the steps out of the conversation pit as she went. Maryann reached out a hand—to restrain or to help her, it wasn't clear—but Jennifer flapped her hands like she was shooing away a bug and made her way out of the room on her own.

"Well, I did my best." Maryann stood up, without looking in the direction of either of her brothers. "I thought I would put the effort into going to the police for the facts about Haylee's arrest so I could share it with all of you, but I can see I might as well have saved my breath. If no one else has anything useful to add, I'm going to go lie down for a bit."

"Actually, there was one thing I'd like to know." After Brian's reference to her inheritance, the siblings had gone back to pretending Gertie didn't exist, and they all looked surprised when she spoke.

"Yes?" said Maryann. "What is it?"

"What time was Tim killed?" Gertie asked. A thought had just occurred to her, one that was probably nothing, probably easily explained. But if it wasn't...

"Who?"

"Tim. The gardener who died last night. Does anyone know what time he was hit?"

Maryann stopped at the base of the stairs to the bedrooms and stared back at her blankly. "I don't know. Sometime after the bars closed, I imagine. Why do you care?"

"No reason," said Gertie.

28

"Can I talk to you for a minute?"

It was two hours later, and Gertie had been busy. Leaving her half siblings to their arguing, she had gone back to the pool house and settled herself in front of her laptop, trying to learn as much as she could about Tim's death. The official statement from the police was thin on details, but between what she could glean from it and the additional information Maryann had shared, Gertie was able to put together what she thought was a pretty complete picture of what had happened.

Which was why she had tracked Brian down in a far corner of the garden, where he was practicing his putting on a patch of grass that was shaded by a stand of trees. It was midafternoon, and the heat was almost unbearably oppressive, but small nozzles sprayed a fine mist over the space to cool it.

The cicadas were particularly active in this part of the garden, and their noise must have covered Gertie's approach because Brian jumped at the sound of her voice.

The ball missed the hole and rolled off into the shrubs around the green.

"Fuck. What the hell do you want?"

It wasn't a great opening, but Gertie had given up on pleasantries. "I need to talk to you," she repeated. "It's about Haylee and what she was doing last night."

That got his attention. Brian turned and looked at her, still leaning on his putter. "Since when is that any of your business?"

"Since never, but it is the police's. I was able to find out when Tim died. He left the bar just before two in the morning, and he was killed two blocks away."

"So?"

"So I happened to come into the house around then. I was looking for an electric fan, thanks to your very generous placement of me in the pool house. I thought I might find one in the office."

Gertie paused to give Brian a chance to put the pieces together. Which didn't take long, by the way his expression melted into shock and anger. She guessed he hadn't registered the precise time of his encounter with Haylee, but Gertie didn't think she needed to spell out why she was talking about seeing something in the office.

"What the hell were you doing sneaking around in the middle of the night? You may think that will means you can do whatever you want around here, but you can't."

Gertie stared at him in disbelief. "What I think is that if Haylee was in the office with you, she couldn't have been driving her car into a man on the street. And I'm also thinking that if Haylee didn't kill Tim, then someone else did."

"I guess you've been doing a lot of thinking then," Brian sneered. "But you had better keep your nosy nose to yourself if you know what's good for you. We have enough trouble around here without you trying to stir up more."

Gertie wanted to shake him or slap his giant baby face. Two people murdered, including his own father, and he treated it like just another opportunity to condescend to her. For a mad moment, she was grateful to Carla for being so unbearable—their life might have had its troubles, but at least Gertie hadn't had to grow up with these people.

But this was something bigger than her disgust or irritation, and Gertie couldn't leave it at that. She tried again.

"Look, I don't give a damn what, or who, you do with your free time. But you know as well as I do that Haylee wasn't running Tim the gardener down with her car at two this morning. You need to tell the police they have the wrong person."

"You don't tell me what to do!" Brian turned on her with a shocking fury, spitting the words as his face turned bright red. "And you don't need to tell anyone else either. Because if you do, I'm going to make sure everyone knows about the lies you're spreading, as part of your scam to try and take our house. You think that's going to work out well for you?"

Gertie had thought of Brian as a blowhard and a buffoon, but in that moment, she found herself honestly afraid. Not just of his anger, but his confidence. And what made it more frightening was that it wasn't unearned. This was a man who could punch a police officer and get away with it—why shouldn't he think he would be able to do whatever he wanted to someone like her?

Almost worse was what he was threatening her over. Brian knew she was telling the truth, and instead of acknowledging it, he was calling her a liar. He was honestly going to deny he had been with Haylee, to let her be prosecuted for a murder she couldn't have committed, in order to protect himself and try to gain an advantage in the fight over the house. As little as she had thought of the man before, this was a low Gertie couldn't even comprehend.

Apparently taking her silence as a victory, Brian went on.

"I thought so. And now I think it's time you packed your little bags and got out of our house. As you've seen, this can be a dangerous place for people who don't belong here."

EVENTS AROUND TOWN COLUMN, *PALM SPRINGS DESERT COURIER*, MARCH 10, 2019

LOCAL NOTABLE IN SCUFFLE WITH LAW ENFORCEMENT

I'll say this for the new owners of the Arcadia Hotel and its famous Dive In pool bar—their opening party certainly made a splash. After all, what could be a better way to make your name as the place to swim and be seen than to have one of your VIP guests get so carried away with the festivities that he nearly drowns himself in the pool and tries to bite the cops who pull him out? Bartender, I'll have what he's having.

The guest in question was one Brian Glass, known for his contentious divorce last year from a former Miss Nevada runner-up—one that included accusations of violence and fraud from both parties—and not much else. Reports are conflicting about what led to the incident, but we do know that Glass, 54, was seen arguing with a female companion who attempted to leave the party with him in pursuit. And when a chivalrous bystander tried to intervene, Glass took a swing at him, and that's how he ended up in the water.

Fortunately, an off-duty police officer was on hand to help pull him out; unfortunately the thanks he got was Glass biting him on the leg. Glass was arrested on charges of public drunkenness and assault, then was released from custody the following morning.

Brian's father, the legendary mall baron Arnold Glass, could not be reached for comment.

29

Gertie didn't leave. She considered it, after Brian had stalked away into the garden, swiping at the plants with his golf club. There was nothing here she needed, nothing she couldn't live without. Gertie had her wits, her health, and a debt-free law degree; if she came out of this weekend with no more than she'd arrived with, she would be fine.

But Tim wouldn't. Or Arnold. Of course, they would be no better if she stayed, but at least she could try to get them some sort of justice.

And if she didn't, who was to say they would be the last?

Gertie sat under the cooling spray of the misters and thought about the two deaths. One of the things Gertie had done after she got the information about when Tim had left the bar was to find out as much as she could about what had led the police to arrest Haylee. Maryann had said the police were able to place Haylee's car at the site of the crash that killed Tim, and from Mrs. Phan, Gertie learned that they were seen examining the front bumper when they came with their warrant. Not only that, but one enterprising staffer managed to get a photo while the vehicle was being towed away.

Haylee had been driving an enormous white SUV, which was useful when it came to seeing the fresh damage to the paint, with dark red smudges on it.

So Haylee's car might have been the killer's vehicle, but she hadn't been in it. Which raised the question about the second piece of evidence Maryann had mentioned: the missing statue found in the back of the same car.

Haylee only had an alibi for Tim's death, of course. But what were the chances she was being framed for that one when she had actually killed Arnold? Not high, Gertie thought. To her, it was more likely that someone had done both, killing Tim with Haylee's car and planting the weapon used in the other murder on her at the same time.

That would mean one person, or group of people, had killed them both, connecting the two deaths in a way Gertie couldn't imagine yet.

Which made Brian's furious denial that much harder to understand. Gertie fished his ball out of the shrub where he had left it and tossed it in her hands while she thought about that. As the other half of Haylee's alibi, he couldn't have killed Tim either, but unlike Haylee, Gertie wasn't willing to write Brian off entirely. The only reason that made sense for him to have denied being in the office—aside from general cussedness, which was a possibility—was that he knew or suspected someone else had been driving

Haylee's car and Haylee was supposed to take the fall for it. That might even have been the plan all along—for him to make sure Haylee wasn't somewhere else, establishing a more believable alibi.

Gertie tucked the golf ball into her pocket and started down the path back to the house. Just that morning she had decided one or more of her half siblings could be murders. Haylee had been on the list in her notebook as well, and Gertie mentally put a line through her name. Brian might have conspired with one of the other people in the house, but Gertie couldn't believe any of them would have worked with Haylee.

So it hadn't been Haylee driving the SUV that knocked Tim off his bike and into a light pole on a quiet back street, where his body had lain until a passing motorist spotted him about twenty minutes later. But it had been her car, and the missing statue had been hidden in it.

Maryann hadn't said when or how the statue was found, but there would have been plenty of places in a car like that to hide it. And most of those would be places Haylee would have been very unlikely to notice it if it had been planted ahead of time.

So, who could have put it there? Leaving Brian aside for the moment, Gertie had the three other siblings to consider.

Of the three of them, Maryann was the one Gertie could most easily see pulling off a successful murder, but the fact she had been away from the house at the time of Arnold's death put her out of it. And actually, Gertie felt like Maryann's efficiency counted against her. The crimes weren't well thought out, with too many points where bad luck could unwind everything. There had been people in and around the house when Arnold had fallen—in a room surrounded by windows, with no hiding places. And finding a lone cyclist on an empty back street would be hard enough, never mind the chance that someone would get a good enough look at the driver to be able to say it wasn't Haylee.

Put together, it gave the impression of a killer, or killers, willing to take risks they hadn't thought all the way through. That sounded most like Jennifer to Gertie, though she didn't necessarily believe that the younger of her half sisters had the focus to carry it off. Neil, on the other hand, struck her as being far more cautious, but probably with more follow-through.

Could they have worked together? All of them, or some subset? Or what if the conspirator was in on only part of the plot, rather than the whole thing? Could Brian have been convinced that Haylee and Tim were somehow the real killers and his cooperation was needed to bring them both to justice? Gertie had him pegged as the stupidest of the bunch, and from the way he talked about Carla, she had a pretty good idea of his views on women.

Too many possibilities, too little solid information. The only things Gertie was sure of were that two men were dead and whoever had done it was not some kind of criminal genius.

Although, so far their plans had worked out fairly well, with a few key exceptions. That the police hadn't simply accepted Arnold's death as an accident was one. And her own interruption of Haylee and Brian's assignation might count as another.

Gertie wondered how worried she should be about that. She

had become a fly in this particular ointment in more ways than one, and she was up against someone who had already turned twice to violence to solve their problems.

Because, after all, why kill Tim? Gertie could think of plenty of motives for Arnold's death, mostly financial. But unless the gardener was going to turn out to be yet another sibling vying for the inheritance, those reasons wouldn't apply to him. The most obvious answer was that he had seen something on the day of Arnold's death and needed to be gotten out of the way before he talked.

Why he hadn't said anything in the last two weeks was another question, but Gertie wasn't sure it mattered. Maybe Tim hadn't understood the importance of what he had witnessed, or maybe he'd been paid off until he could be silenced more permanently—either way, the thing that mattered was that he hadn't told anyone whatever it was he knew, and Gertie wasn't about to repeat that mistake.

And she had a clear first option of who to turn to. Gertie might not be Haylee's favorite person, but she thought her father's last girlfriend was going to be interested in what she had to say.

30

"I don't know what you're talking about."

It hadn't been easy for Gertie to get to Haylee. It had taken calls to some of her law school classmates who knew people who knew people, plus a long time waiting in the lobby of the county jail and three statements that technically were not lies. And thanks to all that work, she was sitting in a small, cold interview room with Haylee sulking on the other side of the unsteady metal table.

Haylee had changed out of her black dress into a jail jumpsuit (which still looked pretty good on her, Gertie noticed with annoyance), and a rubber band held back her extensions. She hadn't recognized her visitor at first, and once she was convinced Gertie hadn't been sent by someone named Carlos, she'd lost interest.

That was okay; Gertie hadn't been expecting a warm welcome. What she had been expecting was that Haylee would see the value in having someone who was willing to vouch for the fact she hadn't been driving the car that ran down one of the two people she was accused of killing.

Above them, a camera sat prominently in the corner of the room. Haylee didn't seem to notice it, but Gertie certainly had. She wasn't bothered—that they were being recorded was the least of Gertie's worries. She had nothing to say that she didn't want the police to hear. In fact, if things went well, she would expect them to take an official statement from her soon.

Things were not going well.

Gertie had put her story to Haylee in plain language, not wanting to confuse her with subtlety. There was no question her message had been understood—the way recognition, suspicion, and then a sort of pride had passed over Haylee's face made Gertie sure of that.

There was a moment when Gertie had been sure the other woman was about to confirm her story and they might be able to make some progress. But then Haylee got a glint in her eye, one that Gertie recognized. It was the way Carla looked whenever she believed she had thought of something clever. That look had cost Gertie more sleepless nights than she could count.

"The hell you don't," Gertie said. "I didn't come all the way over here because I love the smell of linoleum. You're currently accused of hitting a guy with your car at two a.m. this morning, but I know you didn't, because at that moment I saw you faking an orgasm for Brian Glass. And I get that he might have some reasons to deny that he was there, but he isn't the one who's accused of two murders."

"He denies it?" Haylee asked, and Gertie knew she had made a tactical mistake. She watched Haylee's face as her brain worked through the calculations, and two plus two turned into twenty to life.

"Like I said, I don't know what you're talking about," Haylee repeated, pronouncing each word like it was the first time she had heard them. "As you know, the Glass family has a very important reputation to protect. A valuable reputation. And I think they should talk with my lawyer if that's something they care about."

She didn't actually say the word "blackmail," but Haylee couldn't have been more obvious if she had. Gertie suspected this wasn't the first time Haylee had gone down this path—the easy way she had slid into the threat and the sudden change in her tone were the first clues. The problem (or, at least, *a* problem) was the same thing Gertie had noted earlier—the idea that she might be in danger from the murder charges was simply too alien to Haylee's thinking for her to take it seriously. Collecting hush money from a man she had slept with, on the other hand, was right up her alley.

And that was bad news for Gertie. She had considered going straight to the police with her information; now she was glad she hadn't. Unlike his other threats, she thought Brian's claim that he was going to accuse her of lying had teeth, and the police were even more likely to believe that if the person with the best motive to agree with her account refused to.

After all, who would reject an alibi for murder because they thought they were onto an opportunity to scam some money?

Gertie suppressed the urge to sigh, then tried a different approach.

First, she started with the basics. "You do deny you committed the murders, right?"

It took Haylee a minute to parse that question, frowning as she worked through it. "I do—don't—I didn't do it," she said at last.

"Okay, I'm glad we've got that settled. So, what can you tell me about the day Arnold died? Were you in the house then?"

If Haylee had a lawyer, they would almost certainly have told her not to answer, but that wasn't Gertie's problem.

"I was still in bed. Arnie was a morning person, but not me. Actually, I don't know if he slept much at all. He didn't when I was around." She smirked and preened as she said it, and Gertie wondered if Haylee had already forgotten again who she was talking to.

"So you didn't see or hear anything?" Gertie asked, aware that the time she had for the visit was limited. She doubted she was going to get anything useful out of it, but she was determined to try.

"Nothing interesting." Haylee looked like she was actually thinking about that, scrunching up her face in a parody of concentration. "There was one of the servant guys out in the courtyard, but they were going the other way, out into the garden. I remember because I'd been trying to get someone to bring me my smoothie, and they said no one was around to do it, but there's this guy right there. So I was calling them some more to make him come back, but then Jessica or whatever her name is started screaming. For a junkie, she sure gets excited about stuff."

"A what?"

Haylee looked surprised. "She's high like half the time. Pills, I guess. You didn't notice?"

"I've only been here for a little over a day," Gertie said weakly.

"Arnie didn't believe it either. But that Chinese lady knows. She went out and got a bunch of Narcan, which is smart. I was at a party once where a girl OD'd, and it was super gross."

Gertie would have liked to pursue the subject of Jennifer's alleged addiction, but the clock was ticking, and that was something she could look into later. "So you came out of your room and Jennifer was there. Was anyone else?"

Haylee hesitated before answering, and Gertie wondered if she realized she shouldn't be talking so much. But that didn't seem to be the thing on her mind.

"I didn't come out right away," she said. "You know, there's always some sort of drama when those people are around, and I'm not going to jump every time one of them screams. But they kept getting louder, so I did go and see when I was ready."

Reading between the lines, Gertie gathered that she hadn't wanted to appear until she had done her hair and makeup.

"And when you did get downstairs?" Gertie prompted. "What did you see there?"

If she had been expecting a show of emotion from Haylee on recalling her lover's violent death, Gertie would have been disappointed.

"I don't know; it was all just crazy. Someone was crying, and Brian was standing there shouting, and Neil was on his phone.

"And Arnold? Did you see his body?"

"His what? Oh yeah, that." Haylee made a face. "So gross. It was lying over by the bottom of the steps to his little office in the tower. It was really bad. There was blood all over the floor, and nobody was doing anything about it."

"Did anyone say anything?" Gertie asked. "About what had happened or if they had seen something?"

"I don't know. Maybe? There was a lot of shouting. I didn't want to go down and stand on the floor because I didn't know how much the blood and stuff was going to spread, so I went back to my room until the cops came to talk to me."

And that was all Haylee claimed to know about the day her boyfriend had died. Frustrated, Gertie turned her attention to more recent events.

"And last night? Had you met Tim in the time you've been living at the house?"

"Who?"

Haylee might have been playing dumb, but Gertie doubted it. Some people just had a natural ability.

"Tim Martin," she repeated. "The gardener you're accused of killing last night. With your car."

"I wasn't even there!" The exasperation in Haylee's voice was the most emotion she had shown so far, and Gertie hoped it might lead to Haylee admitting where she had been at the time. But the accused woman had something else on her mind. "The police keep saying my cell phone was tracked right to that spot, and they even showed me something they said proved it, but that's dumb because why would I take my cell phone there? I couldn't even find it this morning."

That was interesting. Gertie knew the police were allowed to lie to suspects in interrogations, but remembering Haylee's search of the living room, she had another idea.

"When was the last time you saw your phone?" she asked.

Haylee frowned again, attempting to think. "I'd had it earlier because before I went to bed, I was texting Harry, my stylist, about if I could do bangs. But later, I woke up and it wasn't there. So I went downstairs to look for it and—"

Just then, Haylee must have remembered her clever plan to let herself be framed for two murders in order to make some money off a hypothetical blackmail scheme, and she stopped herself.

"I mean," she went on with exaggerated caution. "I went downstairs to look for it, and I couldn't find it. So I went back to bed."

And that was all Gertie could get out of her. Haylee hadn't seen anything or anyone while she was downstairs, hadn't gone to look for her phone in her car, and didn't remember meeting Tim or any of the other gardeners.

She also had no idea how the statue might have ended up in the back of her car. And when Gertie tried asking about the dinner the night before Arnold's death, all Haylee remembered was that there had been a lot of business talk, which clearly bored her, and she had been served dessert last.

Gertie had hoped that eventually Haylee would absorb the seriousness of her situation. But reality had nothing on Haylee's bulletproof belief that things would always turn out well for her, and by the time Gertie was ready to leave, she was convinced Haylee wouldn't understand the danger she was in until it was too late.

That was what she was thinking as the officer came to the door of the interview room to tell her that her time was up, and Gertie turned to leave with more frustration than regret. But she glanced back to where Haylee was still sitting behind the metal table, looking confused, and some hopeless impulse kicked in.

"I know you didn't do it," Gertie said. "If you can help me figure out who did, we'll all be a lot better off."

It wasn't the sort of sincerity that Gertie expected would carry weight with someone like Haylee, but for once the other woman surprised her. Instead of the obvious disdainful or ignorant reply, she looked for a moment at her interwoven fingers, then back up at Gertie.

"Why are you doing this for me?" she asked.

Gertie looked back at her with a brief, sad smile. "I guess you remind me of my mother."

FRIDAY, AUGUST 23

THIRTEEN HOURS BEFORE THE DEATH OF ARNOLD GLASS

"What is everyone drinking? Brian, I see you've already helped yourself."

Three of his four children were in the living room when Arnold came down from his office. Neil and Maryann were sitting in the conversation pit, and Brian was over by the bar, of course.

"White wine," Arnold said to the server who was waiting at the bottom of the stairs, then sent her off to take orders from the other two. Nobody could say he wasn't a good host.

"Where's Jennifer?" he asked.

"I texted her; she said she would be running late," Maryann said.

Arnold grunted. "She should make more of an effort. It's not like she's got anything else to do."

Maryann gave him one of those looks like her mother used to, when she thought he was being unreasonable. "It was a very short-notice invitation," she said. "I think you could give her a little grace."

"Why not? I've given her just about everything else."

The server returned with Arnold's wine, and he looked around in irritation for somewhere to sit with it. That was the problem with this room: not enough chairs. They'd be setting the dining table soon, and he didn't like the idea of trying to get down into the conversation pit with everyone watching. He'd felt shaky coming down the stairs, and he was sure they had noticed.

"Will Haylee be joining us?" Neil asked.

"Of course. She lives here, doesn't she?" Arnold looked up to where Haylee's bedroom adjoined his own and regretted giving her access to his bathroom. The last time she'd been in there, she'd left hairs everywhere, and the whole place smelled like a cathouse.

"Anyway, you don't need to worry about her. I invited you all tonight because I wanted to tell you about some important changes that are going to be made."

Maryann got up and came out of the conversation pit. "Does this have to do with Haylee?"

"No, it does not have to do with her," Arnold said, his irritation boiling over. "Would you all just listen to me?"

"We're listening, all right." Brian had come up behind Arnold, and now he was standing uncomfortably close, gripping a highball glass in his beefy fist. "What the hell is this deal about telling the bank to cut us off? I've got a project I'm about to get off the ground that I need to fund now, or I'm going to miss an opportunity."

"Well, maybe you can draw yourself up a business plan and see if you can get a bank to lend to you," said Arnold. "That's what I did, when I was starting out. Unless this project is just another friend of yours opening another overpriced bar where you can go and drink the profits."

For a moment, Arnold thought Brian was going to take a swing at him, but even his stupidest child wasn't that brain-dead.

"Okay, so Brian's made some bad investments. Is that any reason to punish the rest of us?" said Neil.

Distracted by Brian, Arnold hadn't noticed that the other two had come up to surround him. With Neil on one side and Maryann on the other, and Brian blocking his path to the courtyard, Arnold found himself trapped in a circle of angry faces.

Of course, they weren't just mad at him.

"My bad investments? How about all the money that got poured into Nestor's campaign to be a House rep? Where'd all that go? 'Cause it sure didn't get him a win," Brian said, waving his glass so the brown liquid sloshed over the side. "At least my cash is doing something useful."

"Like usefully covering child support payments," Maryann snapped. "Honestly, if Dad's experience didn't teach you anything, you'd think you would have figured it out for yourself after the first two."

"Enough!" Their voices were like hammers, hitting Arnold's head from all sides. He wanted to throw them all out of his house, right there and then, but there were some things that needed to be said first.

"I don't care what any of you want to spend my money on; the point is you're not going to get it. I have plans for my business, real plans—none of your half-baked nonsense. Truly visionary work takes sacrifices, and maybe if you'd gotten your brains from me, instead of that dumb cow who whelped you, you'd have a shot at understanding what that means."

"Dad!"

That was Maryann, ready as usual to defend Doreen. But Arnold had no time for that today.

"I've already made up my mind," he went on. "You can get on board, or you can be left behind; that's up to you. But either way, it's time to get used to the idea that you aren't going to be spending the way you're used to."

"What are you talking about? Are you saying there's no more money?" Jennifer had come in while they were talking, and she was standing by the front door, looking confused.

"There's plenty of money," Arnold snapped. "I'm just done wasting it on all of you."

The babble of voices that rose up around him was almost unbearable, to the point that it was actually a relief when Haylee's shrill tone cut through the noise.

"Ar-neee, the outlet by the sink is broken again. I can't finish doing my hair."

She came slowly down the stairs, teetering in one of her dozens of hideous shoes, apparently too caught up in her own idiotic concerns to notice what was going on.

Arnold was grateful for that.

"I'll have someone reset the breaker. What do you want to drink?" he asked, as he tried to regain his composure. But his children weren't done with him yet.

"Wait a minute," Maryann said, grabbing his elbow while he headed toward the bar. "What are these plans you're talking about?"

Arnold smiled and patted her hand. "Let's sit down for dinner, and I'll tell you all about it."

31

Gertie hadn't been allowed to take her phone into the interview room, and when she got it back, she found a missed text from Jules, asking her to stop by his office. Gertie wrote back to say she was free now and asked for the address.

The GPS suggested the freeway as the fastest route, but Gertie opted for surface streets. She had meant to spend the drive getting a better sense of the city, but she kept being distracted—first by the struggles of her elderly hatchback's air-conditioning to do anything against the almost-unbearable heat in the car, then by an awkwardness in the steering that made Gertie worry about repair bills.

But that was a problem for another day. And who knew? Maybe after this week she would have enough money to get herself a new car—or at least something made in this decade.

Or not. The car wobbled toward the center line of the road, and Gertie made a mental note to learn what she could about the local bus system.

Jules's office was in a mid-century building, a modernist structure with a roof that extended out on all sides, providing shade to the picture windows and bright red door. The garden in front was minimal, with a handful of slim cacti planted in a landscape of decorative gravel.

A sign next to the door listed the building's tenants—mostly lawyers, with a sprinkling of CPAs and one dentist. Jules had included the suite number in his text, so Gertie went there directly, noticing as she did the building's smell of old carpets and fresh cleaning solution.

The door to Jules's office was standing open, and the gray-haired woman behind the desk in the outer room was unsurprised when Gertie came through it.

"Good afternoon, Miss Glass," she said, with a smile of recognition Gertie wished she could share.

Fortunately, the woman went on.

"I'm Helen Mariscal, Mr. Rankin's office manager. I'm sure you won't remember me, but when you were little, your father brought you with him when he came to meet Jules. We had a fine time playing with the date stamper while they were talking. I understand you're going to law school now?"

"I just graduated," Gertie said. And she might have been fooling herself, but now that she thought about it, she did have a vague memory of a smooth wooden handle and the satisfying *kerchunk* it made when someone helped her push it down.

"See, I'm going to take credit for that. And when it's time for you to set up your practice, you go ahead and give me a call. If there's anything I don't know about staffing a law office, it isn't worth knowing," she said. "But here, I can't keep you chatting. Jules is expecting you, so go right in."

Helen waved at the door behind her, and Gertie dutifully went through it.

As soon as she did, Gertie felt like she had stepped back in time. The outer office had been ordinary enough, furnished in the sleek-but-comfortable way of a business balancing style and practicality. But Jules's office was something else, a meticulously curated collection of furniture that perfectly matched the building it was in.

Jules was seated behind the desk—a spare, lightly built table with a single block of drawers and no panel to block the view underneath. Gertie took a seat in the chrome-and-black-leather chair in front of it and tried not to stare at his socks.

"Thank you for coming by," Jules said, after Gertie had gotten settled. "I meant to catch up with you after the service but, well…"

"Events transpired," Gertie agreed. She had some things she wanted to talk to the lawyer about, but first things first. "What did you want to see me for?"

Jules pushed a folder and a set of keys across the desk.

"Your father's key ring for the house," he said as she took it. "It was passed to me, as the executor, and I thought it would be prudent for you to have it. I'm afraid we may be in for a bit of a fight. The folder has the initial court filing by your four half siblings, declaring their intention to dispute the will. I'm afraid they've already tried to get you evicted, which I managed to block, but there are some complications."

That was no surprise to Gertie, though she did wonder when they had found the time to do it. Had the process already been underway when Maryann made her offer?

"What complications?" she asked.

"Well, I'm afraid whoever went to the sheriff with the request didn't really think it through," Jules said, sounding rueful and a little amused. "We had some back-and-forth, and the upshot is, since the court isn't ready to rule on who owns the property, no one is allowed to remain in the house after Monday."

Two days. That was how long Gertie had to figure out who had killed her father and another man, and why. Not long ago she had been trying to think her way into leaving; now she was determined to stay. There was some comfort in the fact that her half siblings had accidentally revoked their own access to the same place, but they all had their own homes to go back to. All Gertie had was Carla's condo, where her every move would be questioned and her options for tracking down more information about what had happened to Arnold and Tim were much more limited.

"What time on Monday?"

Jules gave her an appraising look. "It wasn't specified. Presumably at midnight, local time."

Gertie nodded. "Okay. And the keys in here, they should get me into every part of the house?"

"Yes. You also have the codes for the gates, at least as of now. I'm assuming those won't be changed right away, since the staff still need to come and go, but you never know."

"I've been noticing that." Gertie gave the contents of the folder a glance, then looked up at Jules. "Speaking of which, there's something I need to tell you. Haylee didn't kill them. Definitely not Tim, and probably not Arnold either."

She filled him in about everything she knew, starting with her search for a fan, through some euphemisms about what she had witnessed, to the timing of the gardener's death, and finally the refusal of either participant to support her story. Jules listened, first with apparent skepticism, then increasing concern, and finally horror. When she got to the part about Haylee not wanting to accept her own defense, he put his head in his hands and sighed.

"Oh dear. Arnold really could pick them, couldn't he?" Jules must have realized what he was saying, because he looked up and added, "Of course, I didn't mean—"

"It's okay," Gertie interrupted, waving him off. "It's not like I don't know where I come from. Though I'll say, I don't have a lot of illusions about Carla, but I think she has more sense than this."

"Yes, I'd say Miss Haylee is in a league of her own here. But if what you're saying is right, and I don't see how it couldn't be, then she can't be a murderer, at least in the case of the gardener," said Jules, sounding disappointed by the revelation.

"Which means someone else is," Gertie reminded him. "Someone who's currently staying in the house I'm about to go back to."

It was obvious enough to her, but Jules balked at the statement, frowning and stammering. "W-well, I don't know…"

"I do. It might not have been Haylee driving it, but it was her car that hit Tim, and the statue in the back that had Arnold's blood on it came from the house. There's no way an outsider could have gotten those things."

"Not an outsider, but does it have to be one of your family?" Jules argued weakly. "The staff—"

"Would have no reason to want to kill either of them," Gertie finished with certainty, but as soon as she said it, doubt crept in. What had Haylee said, about seeing someone on the patio before the body was discovered? Haylee was anything but reliable, but if she had the timing right, that person might at least have seen something. Why hadn't they raised the alarm? Could it be that Gertie was letting her animus toward her siblings cloud her judgment? What if the real danger was from some lunatic Arnold had hired or even a person he had wronged who had joined the household to get their revenge? What Mrs. Phan had told her about the arrangements that morning made it hard to see how it would have worked, but maybe even the household manager didn't know everything.

It was crazy, but she had to admit it wasn't impossible.

"I don't think it would have been a member of the staff," she amended. "But I'll talk to Mrs. Phan about it again. If Haylee was right about someone being there, there must have been some way for them to get away from the party prep."

Jules shook his head. "I understand what you're saying, but I have a hard time believing it. The idea that someone in the house could have actually killed Arnold..."

"But someone definitely killed Tim," Gertie pointed out. "And they would have to have been in the house to frame Haylee and put the statue in her car."

Thinking about that reminded Gertie of another question.

"Do you know anything about the dinner Arnold invited the children to the night before he died? I know it had something to do with the business, but I haven't been able to find out more than that."

"No, I don't know anything about that. I wasn't even aware that he had invited them until after the fact. Though I will say, when I saw him earlier that week, I had a sense he was up to something, and it wasn't just to do with changing the will. When Arnold had an idea he was excited about, he liked to drop little hints about it, and I remember him asking me something like what I thought about modern medicine."

"Do you think he was getting into herbal remedies?" Gertie asked, thinking about the various bottles that cluttered Carla's counters and the corresponding charges on her credit cards.

"Arnold? Never. Not unless he thought he could make a profit selling them. He had no patience for anything he called 'crunchy granola woo.' And anyway, I didn't get the impression he was concerned about his health. When he brought his new ideas for the will to me, I asked, and he made it clear he was planning to live pretty much indefinitely."

"So much for plans," said Gertie. "Wasn't there a poem about that?"

"Something along those lines," Jules agreed. "It sounds like you're making some plans yourself. Are you really going to keep looking into your father's death?"

"Somebody has to, don't they? The police are satisfied that

Haylee killed them both, and as long as I can't convince her to say what she was really doing last night, there's not much I can do about that. So, other than me, who is there to do it?"

Jules looked like he regretted bringing up the question, but he didn't say anything other than "Be careful."

"I will," Gertie assured him. Mindful of the time she had spent there and the rate Jules was probably billing at, she tucked the keys and the folder into her tote bag. "Was there anything else you wanted to talk to me about?"

Jules started to say something, then stopped and shook his head.

"No, nothing right now." He hesitated again and then went on. "I know you have only two days left in the house, but I'm not so sure staying there is a good idea anymore. Your mother doesn't live very far away, right? We can fight to get what's rightfully yours wherever you are."

Gertie stood up and shook her head firmly. "Not a chance. I'm here and I'm staying."

32

Gertie got back in her car with her mind full of what she knew and what she had to do. She only had two days left on the property, thanks to her half siblings' work, and she needed to make the most of the time. Once she was out of the house, it was going to be a lot more difficult to get her questions answered, like who could have been the staff member Haylee saw and what had been discussed at the dinner. And it would be impossible for her to do other things, like search for clues to where the statue had been between the time it disappeared from the living room and when it turned up in the back of Haylee's SUV.

What to do first was a question for when she was back at the house, but unfortunately, that meant getting back into her car. The only parking spot she had found near the office had no shade, and the interior felt like it had been parked on the surface of the sun. So there was nothing to do but roll down all the windows and crank the AC, and this time when her phone directions said to use the freeway, she didn't look for other options.

As she drove, Gertie thought about what she was going to do first when she got back to the house. It would depend on who was there, she decided—she would like to take advantage of the keys Jules had given her, particularly while there was a chance that no one else knew she had them yet. But that would only work if she had the place to herself, and the open plan of the main room made that unlikely.

Again, Gertie wondered at the fact that no one had seen Arnold's death. Maybe she was making a mistake, thinking about the people who might have killed him individually, rather than as a group. Maybe the reason no one admitted to having been there was that they all were.

Of course, in that case, Gertie would have thought they would have worked together to give each other alibis, instead of leaving only Maryann with one. And her conversation with Haylee had made her even more confident that no one in their right mind would have involved that woman in a complex conspiracy.

That left her with Brian, Neil, and Jennifer working together, and Gertie struggled to imagine that. She didn't know them well, but her sense was that what she had seen so far wasn't out of character. Could those three really have stopped sniping at each other for long enough to plan a murder, let alone carry it out? And why? What could Arnold have done, or been planning to do, that would have driven that kind of conspiracy?

The Saturday-afternoon traffic was light, and as she was thinking about what she was going to do, Gertie unconsciously pressed her foot down on the gas pedal until she was going over eighty.

That was when the first tire blew out.

The front of the car dipped and swerved suddenly to the right. Gertie struggled to keep control, fighting both the weight of the car and her own impulse to stomp on the brakes. She had almost managed it when there was another explosion, from behind her, and the car began to spin.

Gertie held the wheel as the landscape flashed by. A crunch of gravel under the remaining tires told her she had made it to the shoulder, which slowed her down and stopped the spinning. But there was only a narrow space before the flat dirt dropped off to the open desert, and even stomping on the brakes as hard as she could, Gertie knew she wasn't going to stop in time.

Somehow the little hatchback stayed upright and finished its run at the bottom of the slope, its front bumper buried in a tangle of spiky shrubs. Slowly, Gertie unclenched her hands from the steering wheel and brushed aside the deflated airbag.

She checked herself and was surprised to find nothing worse than a red mark where the seat belt had dug into her neck. The driver's side door was blocked by some loose rocks, but Gertie was able to push past them and climb unsteadily out.

The gas tank didn't look damaged, and there was no smell of smoke, but Gertie still backed away from the damaged car while she thought about what to do next. The berm she had come down was only about fifteen feet high, and she thought she could climb it, but she wasn't sure if she was supposed to leave the car. Not that it would be going anywhere—the right front and left rear tires were almost completely gone, with only strips of rubber left on the rims.

She had her phone out and was about to call for help when a voice came from above.

"Hey! Are you all right?" A man appeared at the top of the rise, looking down at her with his hands on his hips. "I saw what happened—that was a crazy ride! I think there might be something wrong with your tires."

EMAILS FROM NEIL GLASS TO HARRISON HENNING, LICENSED PRIVATE INVESTIGATOR

Hi Harrison,

Thanks for getting back to me. Nestor and I appreciated the work you did around the campaign last year and I'm hoping you can work your magic again.

I assume you heard about my father's recent death. Since then, it has come to light that he changed his will not long before he died, to benefit his daughter by his second wife. As I'm sure you can imagine, this has been very distressing for my family. We would like to learn as much as we can about this girl, and her mother, and any way they might have gotten to Dad to corrupt him. We're particularly interested in any communications there may have been between either of them and my father—if there's anything we can do to help you with that part, don't hesitate to ask.

The daughter's name is Gertrude Glass. I think she's lived most of her life in California but she went to college and law school on the East Coast somewhere. I don't have her social security number right now but I might be able to get it. The mother is Carla Glass, nee Di Luca. She was married to Arnold from 1996 to 2000—we had an investigator look into her background then, so I can forward you that. For both of them, aside from the communication thing, we're interested in anything you can get. Police records, finances, other people they may have been involved with, all the usual stuff. Obviously, if there's anything that's not public knowledge, that the daughter wouldn't want to be shared, that's going to be very interesting. (I have a feeling the mother is going to be a better source for that, but you never know, right?)

Anyway, thanks for taking this on. Nestor and I have a lot of faith in your abilities.

Best,
Neil Glass

33

It was the tow truck driver who figured out what had happened.

"Overinflated your tires, huh? You thought it would get you better mileage, right? You know that doesn't even work," he said once the car was loaded onto the truck.

"I didn't know that," Gertie said. She also didn't overinflate them. Gertie had always made car maintenance a priority, ever since she was old enough to get her license and realized Carla's regular disasters that left them with major bills and no transportation could largely be avoided by doing things like learning to change the oil and checking the tires.

But she could tell from the way the man was looking at her—a little bit pitying, a little bit of a sneer—that he wasn't going to believe her. So she kept quiet and let him go on.

"Yeah, and normally it's not going to do you much damage except reduce the lifetime of the tires. But that's a thing people from other places don't get about the desert: things are different here. A full day in this heat, under that kind of pressure… Well, you see what can happen."

"I do," Gertie agreed. "So I guess that's something someone from here would know?"

"Oh yeah, or they should anyway. It's not any kind of secret. But we get so many folks visiting and moving to the valley from all over, you wouldn't believe how little they know about how things can be different from what they're used to. And that's how I end up meeting them and setting them straight."

"I appreciate it," Gertie said. "I'll know better next time."

The driver laughed. "I bet you will!"

When Gertie finally got back to the house, she didn't pull up to the front gate. Instead, she followed the road around to the back of the property, where she found the staff lot—a patch of bare dirt that was screened from the house by a dense stand of scruffy palms. There was no shade, and she had to walk all the way back around to the gate, but her rental subcompact sat anonymously in between the pickups and the sedans. Someone might guess she had parked there, but Gertie would bet money that none of her siblings knew what cars their employees drove.

She didn't know how all four of her tires had gotten so badly overinflated that the two remaining ones measured at the limit of the truck driver's gauge, but she was sure they hadn't been when she gave the car its usual checkup two weeks ago. Tires didn't inflate themselves, and the truck driver's words echoed in her mind, that anyone who had spent time in the area was likely to know the danger of raising the pressure so much.

Of course, there was nothing she could prove. She had no direct evidence that she hadn't been driving around like that for months, and Gertie could just imagine what the police response would be if she tried to tell them that the accident that looked like her carelessness was actually part of a conspiracy that had already killed two other people.

She needed to know more before she could get anyone to listen to her, and now that she had the set of keys, Gertie had an opportunity to look for some of that information. As soon as she stopped by the pool house to get herself cleaned up after her adventure, she would be on her way.

But something was wrong. Gertie knew it the minute she opened the door and was hit by an overpowering smell of bleach.

It was a minute before she could even go inside, and when she did, she moved quickly, opening every window she could reach and trying not to breathe in too deeply. The source of the smell wasn't clear, not until she got to the bathroom and found all her things in the tub—her clothes, her laptop, even Andy's old duffel bag, all piled together and soaked, with the empty bleach bottle taunting her from the middle of the floor.

Gertie shut the bathroom door and slowly turned away. So this was it then. First her car, now her possessions. She was being sent a message, one that was probably supposed to scare her, that she wasn't safe as long as she stayed where they could get at her.

And Gertie was scared. But she was also was mad.

She didn't know if the attack on her had to do with the questions she had been asking about Arnold's death or if it was just another attempt to separate her from her inheritance, but it didn't matter. These were the actions of a person or people who couldn't accept anything but their own absolute victory, and they would do whatever it took to get it. But it was going to take more than this.

"There you are. I didn't see you come back. What's that smell? Has someone been cleaning in here?" Mrs. Phan came bustling in through the open door, sniffing the air and looking concerned.

"Not exactly," Gertie said, then gestured toward the bathroom. "More of an attempt to take out the trash."

Mrs. Phan opened the bathroom door and looked in, then closed it again and turned away, her lips pressed into a thin line.

"I see," she said. "I'll get some fresh clothes for you by tonight, and I'll have the computer taken for repairs. You need a new toothbrush as well."

Gertie hadn't noticed that part, but she took her word for it. She could imagine what the person who'd done this would think to do with a toothbrush.

"Thanks. The laptop should be backed up anyway. Do you need my clothing size? And the money…"

"Is not your concern," said Mrs. Phan, waving away both questions. "Why don't you go in the house where it's cool, and I'll get this cleaned up."

She hesitated, then went on. "Unless you would rather not stay here? I can have the things delivered to you."

Mrs. Phan was only being considerate—why wouldn't a person consider leaving the place where someone had just vandalized their possessions?—but at that moment it was exactly the wrong thing to say to Gertie.

"I'm staying," she said curtly. "Thanks for asking."

Mrs. Phan looked concerned, and Gertie knew she was being rude. But as the first flush of anger started to ebb, fear and uncertainty took hold, and suddenly Gertie didn't want to trust anyone or share anything that might make her more vulnerable.

There was one question she had to ask, though.

"Is there anything here that could be used to inflate tires?"

Mrs. Phan was clearly surprised by the question. "Yes, there's an air compressor in the garage. Do you want me to have someone bring your car over and fill them?"

"Not right now," Gertie said, and she left to go into the main house.

34

Gertie stalked into the house, her fear still fighting with her anger. What had been done to her tires was obviously the worse thing, but in spite of that, or maybe because of it, the bleach attack was mostly on her mind. It was the breathtaking pettiness of it—whoever had done it had to know they weren't going to do anything more than inconvenience her. Obviously, Gertie had other clothes, and computers could be fixed or replaced. And still they went out of their way to cause as much damage as possible, just to make sure she knew how much she was disliked.

As much damage as possible without harming anything else on the property, Gertie amended. There was already no question in her mind that the vandal had been a member of the family, but this proved it.

And now she had something else to prove, and not a lot of time to do it. It was nearly sunset. If she had to be out of the house on Monday, that only left her forty-eight hours at the most to search for anything that could help her find her father's killer.

For that reason, she was glad there was no one in the main room when she got there. Gertie still had some questions to ask her half siblings, but she wasn't sure she trusted herself to confront any of them at the moment, not after what had been done to her.

She didn't think the reason no one was there had anything to do with her, though. The same as it had been the day before, the afternoon sun slanting through the walls of glass made the room almost unbearable.

As she stood there blinking, Gertie wondered again how anyone could have killed a man in this wide-open glass-walled box and expected to get away with it. That was what made her think the murder had been a sudden impulse. If a person were going to plan a crime, almost anywhere else would be better.

So a crime of the moment, not careful planning. But what if it had been more than that—a crime of opportunity? Gertie didn't doubt Arnold had been hit over the head after he fell down the stairs, not with the way Mrs. Phan had described the scene, but what if only the second part was intentional? It had never been hard to believe a ninety-year-old man might have slipped on an unsafe staircase—what if someone had heard him fall, or just happened upon him there, alive but defenseless, and decided this was their chance to kill him and get away with it?

It was an appalling thought, imagining one of the people she had met coming up on an old man lying on the floor, calmly selecting a statue, and using it to smash his head in. What could possibly drive a person to do that? Did Gertie even really want to know?

As she was thinking, Gertie reached into her bag and found

the key ring Jules had given her. There were at least a dozen keys on it, in a variety of sizes and ages, and as her fingers coiled around them, they spoke of opportunity.

Gertie glanced up at the stairs to the office. She could think about the risks later—right now she wanted to take a look around.

This time, when Gertie went up the stairs, she was ready for the disorientation of the clear treads, and she found that the best approach was look straight ahead, while listening for anyone coming up behind her. When Gertie reached the landing, she risked a look back and found she was still alone. Feeling more relief than she'd like to admit, she turned her attention to the office door.

She had no trouble finding the keys for the lock and the dead bolt, noticing as she did that the dead bolt key was clearly marked "do not duplicate."

Inside the door there was another set of stairs, just high enough so the floor of the office was in line with the roof of the rest of the house. Despite being barely higher than Gertie's head, this flight had a sturdy railing and strips of anti-slip tape on the steps. Here, at least, Arnold must have cared more about safety than appearances.

She wondered if that was because he didn't expect anyone to see it. As Gertie climbed the stairs into the office itself, it was clear the cleaning staff didn't get into this room very often. It wasn't dirty, exactly, but there was a level of disarray Gertie hadn't seen anywhere else in the house. Papers were stacked on top of books, which were on top of more papers, which were on top of old cardboard banker's boxes, and no book or binder on the bookshelves was aligned with the one next to it.

There was even a coffee cup left sitting on the desk, next to the computer. It was slightly askew in its saucer, like it had been set down hastily, and there was still about an inch of coffee at the bottom.

That surprised Gertie. Was it possible that it had been left there the last time Arnold was in the room? Was she the first person to be in here since his death?

Gertie looked down at the key she was still holding. DO NOT DUPLICATE. Did that mean it was the only one? A thought struck her, and she went back down to check the door—sure, enough, it had locked behind her. So Arnold would have had to take his keys with him to keep from locking himself out, and they would have been on his body when he died. From there it had passed through who knew what process until Jules had given them to her.

If that was true, then she had an opportunity to find out what her father had been doing right up to the moment of his death. She sat in the desk chair, with the cup of stone-cold coffee resting next to her right hand, and turned on the computer.

35

There was no password. Arnold must have had enough faith in the lock on the door that he didn't feel the need to bother.

He had been careful enough to close whatever he was working on when he left his seat, leaving an empty desktop on the screen. But he hadn't cleared his history of recently used applications or documents, so Gertie started there.

The first place she went was the web browser, hesitating only a moment before she restored the most recent session. There was definitely a chance she was about to find out about Arnold's OnlyFans subscriptions, or worse, but Gertie decided she was going to take that risk. She had never had any illusions about her father, and she didn't think there could be much in an old man's browser history that would shock her.

Fortunately, she didn't have to find out. There had only been one tab open when Arnold closed the program, for a bank's web portal. He hadn't stored the password in the browser, though, so Gertie didn't have that interesting avenue of research open to her.

That would have been too easy, Gertie reasoned as she dove deeper into his browsing history. She couldn't expect to have that kind of information just handed to her.

What she did have was a lot less informative, at least on the surface. Arnold had read some stories in the local and national news, checked the weather, and played a word game. There were a few pages that were less understandable, like one for the permit office in a small city in Arizona and three different companies that installed industrial-scale air handling.

Gertie went back to the desktop and looked at the other items in the Recent list. One was an email client, which also needed a password Gertie didn't have. She spent a few minutes hunting around the desk, in case Arnold had been careless enough to keep them written down nearby, but came up empty. So she moved on to the files in the list: two spreadsheets and a document, all saved last at 8:12 a.m. on August 24.

Gertie was prepared for more disappointment. So when she opened the first document and saw the title "GLASS PROPERTY GROUP BIOTECH CONVERSION PROJECT" marching across the top, she blinked a few times before she was sure it was real.

But it was. The document had the form of a list, with details filled in under some of the bullet points. Halfway between a set of notes to self and a formal presentation, it had sections for costs, risks, and timelines, as well as parenthetical questions like "sewage requirements for laboratories?" and "occupancy rates upper Midwest?"

The document covered more than two pages, and Gertie took her time reading through it. The impression she got was that this was a big project, and Arnold was completely serious about it. He clearly thought the time for shopping malls was finished, and the future for the company was in converting the buildings that had housed them into research centers for biotech and pharmaceutical companies, with Arnold including quotes about occupancy rates and per-square-foot prices as justification. The last section of lists had projections for eventual profits, with numbers that struck Gertie as highly optimistic, despite how little she knew about the field.

That led her to look at the spreadsheets, and Gertie understood why Arnold needed to depend on so much upside. The first file was labeled "pilot site" and had a breakdown of the costs of converting a mall outside of Ventura, and Gertie was struck by both how high the estimated numbers were and the fact they were clearly incomplete, with line items like "electrical upgrade" left blank. The other spreadsheet was even more ambitious, with costs for converting the rest of the properties in the portfolio and notes on how much the early conversions would need to be earning in order to finance the expansion.

Gertie marveled at the plans, trying and failing to get her head around what they would involve. What Arnold had outlined here was an enormous undertaking, something that would take years if not decades to achieve. How did a ninety-year-old man think he was going to do it? And why? What good would it do him to start a project he couldn't possibly live to see finished?

And where was the money supposed to come from? Gertie thought she found part of that answer in the Calendar app, which showed a meeting with a banker scheduled for the Wednesday after Arnold's birthday. The woman he was planning to meet with was listed on the bank's website as a specialist in corporate loans, which made sense with everything else Gertie had seen so far.

Whether it made sense in general was another question. If Jules was right, the family had been borrowing against the value of the company for a long time, using that money to live off. If Arnold had gone ahead with this, at the very least, that cash was going to dry up for the foreseeable future, and then some.

That would be motive enough for any of the children. It was probably what Arnold had invited them to dinner to discuss, and Gertie would very much like to know how that conversation had gone.

Not well, she suspected.

36

Gertie spent some more time going through what she could find on the computer, but nothing caught her attention. She did log into her own email account and send herself what she had found, in case there was more there that she hadn't picked up on, but she didn't have high hopes. She might have discovered a plausible motive for her father's murder, but that wasn't proof of anything. What she needed was evidence, and there was none of that here.

So Gertie sat there at the desk, turning her mind away from her father's death to think about his life. She'd been told he spent a lot of time in this room, and she could understand why.

The tower office sat above the flat roof of the house, with windows on all sides. One looked back at the mountains that rose behind the property, two over the park—to the visitor center in one direction and open desert in the other—and the last across the valley toward where the lights of the city were starting to sparkle. It was a position of power, of dominance over the landscape.

Gertie watched for a while as the sun sank behind the mountains and the first stars began to appear. She wondered if Arnold had still looked at the view after all these years or if it had faded into the background for him—just another luxury to be taken for granted. She was also curious about what he had thought about the changes that had come through the valley since the house went up, and if he had ever considered moving somewhere closer to other people or less hot.

And why had he left it to her?

Gertie knew sitting here wasn't going to get her the answers to any of those questions, but she couldn't bring herself to go back downstairs. She had a feeling the room wasn't done with her yet.

Without thinking about it, she found herself turning the chair back and forth, and then, on a sudden impulse, she spun it. She stopped herself by grabbing the edge of the desk, her dizziness overwhelmed by a sudden, powerful sense of déjà vu.

Gertie had been here before; she was sure of it. And why wouldn't she have been? She had lived in this house for the first three years of her life—it made sense that she would have spent at least a little time in all its rooms. What was surprising was this was the only one she remembered.

Except it wasn't remembering, not exactly. It was the feeling of the leather on the chair, the way the windows looked as she was spinning past them, the smell of old paper and air-conditioning. Not memories but impressions, things experienced by a different version of herself.

When would she have been in here? Not by herself, obviously. Only a lunatic would let a toddler up those stairs alone. Either Carla or Arnold must have brought Gertie up for a visit—to "see Daddy's very important work" or something. She would have been put on the chair, maybe allowed to briefly touch some of the less important items on the desk. And what else?

Gertie looked down at the carpet and felt another wave of recognition. She knew that pattern, remembered tracing it with her fingers. It had been bigger then, and there was something else. Trouble, something that was wrong. A green pen, Gertie thought, and the memory became clearer. She dropped to her knees and searched around the desk until she found it, faded but still visible—a blob of green ink that had settled into the carpet fibers, disfiguring the pattern.

That had been when it went wrong, Gertie thought, though she wasn't sure what she meant by that. Staying on her knees, she closed her eyes, trying to let the sounds and images come to her. Angry voices, and not just at her, not just for the pen. That made sense—for her to remember even as much as she did, she must have been here later in her time in the house. That would put it near the end of her parents' marriage, when the shine of Carla's looks had worn off and Arnold was ready to find someone else to lie to him about how youthful and attractive he was.

So tiny Gertie had been left alone to play on the floor while they argued, and she had done the sort of thing unattended children did. It wasn't her fault, but even now looking at that stain sent a shudder of shame through her.

Coming here had been a dumb idea, Gertie decided as she started to pull herself back to her feet. She wanted to know who had killed her father and his gardener, and rehashing childhood hurts wasn't going to get her any closer to that. Determined to do something more useful with her time, she was almost back on her feet when something else caught her eye.

It was a floor-level power outlet, completely normal, except something told her it wasn't. This was a different kind of memory, not angry or shameful—a feeling of wonder. But why? What could possibly thrill a child about a power outlet?

Gertie dropped back into a crouch to examine it more carefully. Up close, it was clear there was something off about the fixture. It was made of the same kind of dull, off-white plastic as every other outlet in the room, but the color was slightly wrong, yellower than the one a few feet away. And where there should have been two screws, top and bottom, to attach it to the wall, there were merely molded lumps in the plastic, imitating screwheads.

Barely aware of what she was doing, Gertie caught her fingernail under the top edge of the plate, pulling it toward her. It slid open to reveal a compartment, just like Gertie knew it would.

THREAD SUMMARY
FROM R/TRUECRIMETOPICS

r/truecrimetopics

lost_coaster_5682: Arnold Glass and his gardener killed weeks apart, Glass's girlfriend arrested for the crimes.

Comments

    lost_coaster_5682: Crazy one here. Rich old guy falls down the stairs on the day of his ninetieth birthday, then two weeks later his gardener gets run down in the street. The police arrest old guy's girlfriend for both, but I don't know, this one smells.

    hansonaceventurasing: Bitches be crazy.

    wldrouycend34: Maybe she was having an affair with the gardener, and they killed the guy together, and then he got cold feet so she took him out too?

polar_flying_insect: I'm not buying it. Four other people in that house, and none of them noticed her killing him? And it doesn't look like she gets any of his money. I think there has to be more here.

jgtimonstar-1967: Of course she did it, why are you being so dense? She's a totally evil woman, and plus, they found the weapon in her car.

wldrouycend34: What weapon? I don't remember seeing anything about a weapon.

DCM-HCM: I thought the gardener was just hit by the car? Where did you hear something about a weapon?

jgtimonstar-1967: I don't know, I just saw it somewhere. Anyway, the point is that Haylee totally killed him. She's crazy and dumb and she never should have been in the house in the first place. None of you people who are sitting here making things up know anything about it. Why don't you all just go and get a life?

lost_coaster_5682: So, it looks like that account has previously been used to post on r/privatetravel about the private terminal at the Palm Springs airport, where jgtimonstar-1967 describes herself as having lived in the area since the late seventies, at her father's house. Ever heard of a throwaway account, Ms. Glass?

37

There was a hinge on the bottom of the fake outlet, and it swung open in a semicircular wedge. In Gertie's memory, the space had been empty, but it wasn't now. Where she might have put one of her toys, there was a single old-fashioned computer disk.

The disk was made of hard gray plastic, with "records" written in cursive on the label—it looked like someone had 3D printed the Save icon. She had encountered them a few times as a kid; now she didn't even know where she would find a computer that could read it. But someone would; she was sure of that. And Gertie was going to find them, because she had a very strong feeling the disk had been hidden to keep it safe from someone in the house. She put it in her pocket and turned to leave.

She paused at the tower door, her hand on the handle, and looked back into the room. Thanks to her half siblings, she might not have a chance to be in there again for a long time—or possibly ever. The setting sun cast a golden glow through the windows and illuminated the motes of dust she had disturbed. She watched them for a moment, and then her gaze dropped to the coffee cup, still sitting on the desk where Arnold had left it when he had walked out of this room for the last time.

Gertie was going to find out what was on the disk. And if it didn't tell her what she needed to know, she would keep looking until she found something that did.

Gertie emerged from the tower to find that she was not alone in the main room. Jennifer was sitting at the dining room table, and she jumped at the sound of the door, then stared at Gertie with undisguised shock.

"How did you get up there?" she asked as Gertie reached the ground floor.

"Same way I got down," Gertie said. "How would you do it?"

Jennifer was either confused or unamused by the joke, because she ignored it and stuck to her original point. "Dad never let anyone up there. It should have been locked."

"It was," Gertie said. "I have a key. I did inherit the house, after all."

Jennifer gripped the edge of the table and almost snarled at her. "Like hell you did," she said. "You've got a hell of a lot of nerve, hanging around here. Don't you think you've done enough harm?"

"I haven't harmed anything," Gertie said, noticing as she came closer that there was a constellation of white spots on the sleeves of Jennifer's blue silk shirt. "Unlike some people."

Her half sister followed her gaze and recoiled when she saw the damage. Before she could respond, Gertie went on.

"You should be more careful when you use bleach. At some point you might wreck something valuable."

"You little bitch!" Jennifer jumped to her feet and slapped her hands on the table. "Why can't you take a goddamn hint! This isn't your house, and it never will be, and I don't care what that stupid will says. You can't just come here and take things from us!"

Inside Gertie, something snapped. She had been insulted, threatened, sabotaged, and vandalized, all on the day of her father's funeral. She would have been justified in ripping into Jennifer for all that and then some, to let her know she had them all figured out from the moment she had come through that door, and even if they managed to kill her, they would never impress her.

Instead, she laughed.

"I think you'll be surprised at what I can do."

Back in the pool house, Gertie was relieved but not surprised to discover that all evidence of the attack had been eliminated, with only a lingering smell of bleach remaining. She realized she was already taking it for granted that she had only to present a problem and Mrs. Phan would magically make it go away, and that was a very appealing notion.

Except it wasn't magic, Gertie reminded herself. It was skill and effort, and living a life where you never had to acknowledge that was how you ended up like Jennifer.

Of course it had been Jennifer who had ruined Gertie's things. It was the perfect combination of pettiness, laziness, and pointless cruelty, executed with a total lack of imagination. The bleach had been under the sink—Gertie remembered seeing it there when she'd been exploring the house after she arrived. So Jennifer had simply grabbed the first thing at hand, done as much damage as she could, and considered the job done. A high school bully would have been more creative.

The trick with Gertie's tires was another matter. Whoever had done that must have known it had the potential to put her in danger; they might have even been counting on it. That didn't leave Jennifer out, but the amount of foresight and automotive knowledge required probably did.

The other three were still on the list. Brian had been open with his threats to her, particularly after she revealed she had seen him with Haylee, but they all would be happy to have her out of the way, and she thought any of the oldest three siblings were at least competent enough to operate an air pump.

But was there any reason to believe whoever had done it had also killed Arnold or Tim? Like Arnold's death, whoever had sabotaged Gertie's tires had relied on luck—that her car wouldn't have a sensor to tell her something was wrong, or she wouldn't just suffer a slow leak instead of a dramatic blowout, or any of the other things that would have made it more of an annoyance than a hazard. And even so, she had been lucky that the damage had been extensive but not fatal. Did the attacker not care?

Gertie looked up at the front door to the pool house and was surprised to notice something that hadn't been there before. Two brand-new sliding bolts, carefully color matched to the wood, had been installed at the top and bottom of the door. She tested them a couple of times and thought about what it meant. There wouldn't have been time to install an entirely new lock on the door, so Mrs. Phan had done the best she could for the moment. Gertie's things wouldn't be protected, but she could be.

It was comforting, both that the locks were there and that Mrs. Phan was looking out for her, but frightening as well. Here was a physical reminder she was in danger, and she wasn't the only one who saw it. And in the end, how much could a couple of bolts do? There were still windows, and things could be done to a building without ever going inside.

But that was a risk she would face later, because Gertie's next task was going to take her away from the house. She had spent a lot of time looking at the place where Arnold had died, but she had only a vague idea of where Haylee's car allegedly had run Tim down on his bike. She wasn't sure if the site itself was going to be accessible, but she was also interested in where he had come from before it happened. If the gardener really had been specifically targeted, whoever did it must have known how to find him, and in doing so, they might have left some trace of themselves there. It wasn't much of a chance, but Gertie was determined to follow every thread she could pick up until one of them led her somewhere. And the place she was going to look for this one was at the bar where Tim had had his last drinks.

38

The Yuppie Bar didn't look like the sort of place any yuppie Gertie had met would drink, except ironically. The facade was plain brick, the windows were smudged, and a neon sign flickered half-heartedly over the door. But no one paid her much attention when she came in, even though she was still dressed in her professional clothes from the jail visit, and the bartender gave her a welcoming nod as she sat down.

"What'll it be?" she asked.

"Rum and coke," Gertie replied. "And a glass of water."

As the woman poured her drink, Gertie took in the room. One side was occupied by the bar itself, its battered wooden sides almost completely covered with stickers—advertising bands, alcohol labels, and skateboard brands. The seating at the bar was standard stools, bolted to the floor, their upholstery repaired with duct tape. For the rest of the room, the seating choice was a selection of office chairs, some in better shape than others.

The same could probably be said of the patrons.

Three other seats at the bar were taken—two by men in chef's whites and the other by an old woman wearing pajamas and nursing a tall glass of something brown. At the tables a group of people in hotel uniforms laughed and ribbed each other, two men held hands and spoke quietly, and one woman with short hair was drinking alone. There was something familiar about her, and from the way she was staring at Gertie, it was clear the impression was shared.

She was on the verge of figuring it out when the woman got up and came over to the bar. She set her nearly empty drink down next to Gertie's and gave her a look that wasn't entirely friendly.

"A little bit outside your part of town, aren't you?" she asked, as Gertie managed to place her.

"I thought I'd try a change of scenery," she said. "Kathy, right? Can I buy you a drink? I really admire the garden you've created."

"Hmph." The Glass House's head gardener was clearly neither fooled nor flattered, but she didn't argue when Gertie put a pint of IPA on her tab.

"So, what's the story?" Kathy asked once it was served. "You here for any reason, or do you just go around buying ladies drinks?"

There was no point in Gertie lying now. She had come to the bar looking for information, and Tim's boss would be a good person to provide it.

"I was wondering," she said. "From what I can tell, this is the place Tim was drinking before he died. I wanted to see it."

"Why?" Kathy looked genuinely confounded, and Gertie didn't blame her. It was a strange thing to do, particularly with the alleged killer locked up.

Not ready to show her hand, Gertie temporized.

"I thought it was strange, how his death could have been connected to my father's. Tim didn't seem like the sort of person who would be involved in something like that, when I met him. I thought maybe if I came here, I could learn more about him."

"You met Tim? When?"

"Yesterday. I was there when he tried to cut down the palm tree, and he gave me a tour of the garden."

"That's right, the palm tree. Jesus Christ, was that yesterday?" Kathy took a long sip from her beer and stared into the glass. "I was going to give him hell for that today when he got in. The tree probably isn't going to make it."

Her voice cracked, and Gertie focused on her own glass while Kathy collected herself.

"Anyway, I was never sure about having a tall tree there. It disrupted the rhythm of the bed. Maybe replace it with a grouping of euphorbias or something."

Gertie nodded along. They weren't really talking about the garden, anyway.

"What was Tim like? I didn't get much of a sense of the guy," she said.

Kathy took another swig that left only about two inches of beer in the bottom of her glass. "Honestly, there wasn't much to know. He was a decent enough gardener, even if I never could really get the design principles through to him. The only thing he really cared about was that bike of his. Or bikes—I don't even know how many he had. But they were his whole life, outside of work. If it had more or less than two wheels, Tim didn't care about it."

That was interesting. Tim had been hit riding a bicycle home from the bar, and the killer must have known he would be—it would have been a lot harder and riskier to kill him if he'd been in a car.

"Did he always ride?" Gertie asked.

"Always. Didn't matter the weather, if it was a hundred twenty in the shade or monsoon flooding, Tim was on a mission to convince the world that no one needed any other way to get around, and he was out to lead by example. Also, he had one of those apps that tracks where you ride and how fast, and he was always looking for ways to log more miles on it. I had to send a couple of guys out for him one day when he went to pick up some compost in the middle of July and tried to bring it in on his cargo bike. Idiot collapsed in the middle of Dinah Shore Drive. After that I made him use the truck for work stuff."

Kathy finished her beer and turned her attention on Gertie. "So, what is this, anyway? Are you doing a school project? 'Murdered guys I met on my summer vacation'?"

Gertie contemplated the head gardener. If she was going to get more information out of Kathy, she was going to need to convince her it was worth her time.

Her rum and coke was only half-empty, so Gertie ordered another beer for her guest and a refill on water for herself.

"I don't think Haylee killed Tim," she said. "Let's leave aside why I think that for now or why I'm not taking it up with the police.

Maybe I'm just nuts. But because I'm so crazy, I don't think she killed Arnold either, but I do think whoever did it killed both of them. So I think if we can find Arnold's killer, we'll have Tim's too."

"That's not how most people would put it," said Kathy. "Most people would have them in the other order, with the rich guy first. Especially if he was their father."

"Yeah, well, I knew Tim better. Besides, the way the police are treating it, I don't get the sense they're putting that much effort into investigating his death, not now that they've got Haylee in custody. I thought I might be able to push them a bit, if I knew more."

"I see. A bit of, what do you call it, noblesse appliqué?"

"Something like that." Gertie took in the design on the other woman's T-shirt, a faded image of a slug perched on top of a Greek column. "With a classics degree from UC Santa Cruz, I'm guessing you know better than I would."

Kathy looked down at her shirt and gave a brief snorting laugh. "Okay, fine, you caught me. Just another overeducated lawn jockey trying to sell the world on the concept of low-water desert gardening."

"Ah, yes. That old story." Maybe it was the rum, but Gertie was enjoying this more than she had expected. She hadn't lost sight of the fact that two men had been killed, and that unless she was able to pull off something like a miracle, an innocent(ish) woman would take the fall for both deaths while the guilty person went free. But it had been a rough couple of days, and trading banter with someone while "Piano Man" played over a terrible sound system almost counted as a break.

Kathy had thawed as well. Already well into her second beer (11 percent ABV, according to the blackboard behind the bar), she was regarding Gertie with something like friendliness.

"Okay," Kathy said. "Let's say I believe you. What would you want to know?"

"Mostly, where Tim was and what he was doing on the day Arnold died. Because unless you can think of someone who wanted to kill Tim and had to take out my father to get to him, I think the best explanation is that he saw or knew something that made him dangerous to the killer."

Kathy nodded. "That makes sense. Let me think for a minute. Things got kind of crazy that day."

"It was the day of Arnold's birthday party," Gertie added helpfully. "Mrs. Phan said she had all the staff at the site, helping to set up."

"That's right. She had most of my guys pulled in too, for the heavy lifting. The household staff, they're not hired for their muscle, you know? I didn't mind. The summer isn't our busiest time, in this climate. It's mostly just trying to keep the plants alive."

"Were you there helping?" It occurred to Gertie that her only source of information about the staff being away from the house was Mrs. Phan. Who was someone she wanted to trust, but wanting things wasn't enough.

"I was there, though I don't know how much help I was. We were in the middle of getting some of the drip irrigation redone, so I just set up in the same corner where Mrs. Phan was directing the operation, on my phone most of the time. I did manage to tell her to warn her people about the cholla cacti—we don't have any at the house, but they have a gorgeous collection at the botanical garden. They look all sweet and fluffy, but they have some of the nastiest spines there are."

Ignoring that probably useful advice, Gertie stuck to what she wanted to know. "So Mrs. Phan was there the whole time?"

"For as long as I was," Kathy confirmed. "I left a little before ten, and I'd say there wasn't ten minutes when I didn't see or hear her nearby."

That was more of a relief than Gertie wanted to admit. So much of what Gertie knew about what happened that day relied on Mrs. Phan having been honest with her; it was vital to know that at least about that part, she hadn't been deceived.

That settled, Gertie got back to her original question.

"And Tim? Did he also help with the party?" That would have put a serious dent in Gertie's theory, but Kathy shook her head.

"No, he volunteered to stay behind and take care of the hand watering. Like I said, we're upgrading the irrigation, but in the meantime, there are a few new plants that need some extra support, and they can't take a day off. Thinking about it now, it does seem kind of weird. Everybody helping with the setup got lunch from the caterers, and Tim wasn't a guy to miss out on free food."

Gertie thought about the staffer Haylee had seen. Could it have been Tim crossing the courtyard? The uniforms the gardeners wore were different from the household staff, but Gertie was positive Haylee had never noticed that.

"So he was in the garden for the whole morning? Do you know if he ever came into the house?"

Kathy took another drink of her beer. "He didn't go into the house, as far as I know. But I think..." She frowned, like she was trying to remember. "Yeah, it must have been that day. Anyway, he wasn't in the garden for the whole time either. I had to come back early from the party setup to get some measurements for the irrigation people, and when I got there, he wasn't around, and his bike was gone. I was going to give him hell for it, but that's when the commotion in the house started, and everything else got a lot less important."

"Obviously," Gertie said, abstracted. She was thinking about coincidences and how much she didn't believe in them. Under normal circumstances, a young guy skipping out on his work task because he wanted to ride his bike would be completely uninteresting. But these circumstances were as far from normal as Gertie could think of.

"Did you ever find out where he was?" she asked, without much hope.

"No, it kind of slipped my mind." Kathy looked regretful, but not terribly embarrassed. And why should she be? She'd had no reason to believe a missing gardener would have had anything to do with her employer's murder. Even now, it was hard to imagine how they could be connected. But, considering all that had happened, it was even harder to imagine they weren't.

"What was he...?" Gertie began, then paused, trying to think of how to phrase her next question delicately. "Did Tim ever have anything to do with members of the family? Anything more than just dealing with things in the garden?"

"Like, was he having an affair with one of them and so in love he'd help them kill their father? Not that I ever noticed." Kathy's words were sarcastic, but her tone was just tired. "But what the hell do I know? Maybe he was masterminding the whole thing, in between making his seaweed shakes and posting pictures of himself on trail rides."

"I guess it's possible," Gertie agreed, though she didn't think it was any more likely than Kathy did. The impression she had of Tim was a young man of simple interests and focused passions. Not someone who was likely to have engaged in intrigue, at least not knowingly.

"Did he seem at all different since Arnold's death?" she asked. "Like he was preoccupied or worried about anything?"

Kathy frowned into her glass. "I've been thinking about that, since they arrested that lady. Honestly? I don't know. After Mr. Glass died, we were all feeling pretty unsettled. Nobody had any idea of what was going to happen with the house or if we'd have jobs in another month. I don't mean to be insensitive, but I'd be lying if I said it wasn't the first thing on my mind. I liked your father just fine, and I was sorry he died, but I've had a lot of bosses in my time, and I don't get attached."

She looked at Gertie and, seeing no judgment, went on. "So I'd been giving my guys a little more leeway than usual. I figured they'd be stressing too, probably looking for new jobs. Now I wish I'd paid more attention."

"You couldn't possibly have known that this would happen," said Gertie, knowing that it was both true and completely unhelpful. She had wondered why Kathy hadn't pressed her on why she didn't think Haylee was the killer, but now Gertie suspected it was because she didn't care. Kathy was interested in her plants and her people, and that was it.

Which brought Gertie to her next question.

"I was wondering," she said. "Tim was here last night; you're here tonight—is this bar a regular hangout for you and your staff?"

"No, this is the first time I've been. Tim lived nearby, so I think he was here pretty often, but I'm over on the other side of the city, past the airport. I just wanted..." Kathy's voice caught, and she took a moment to stare at the bottles behind the bar. "I don't know what I wanted. To make sense of it? I wish I could say I was like you, out to get the truth, on a mission for justice. Not sure I believe in that stuff anymore, to be honest. I guess it didn't feel right, that someone like Tim could get dragged into all this. He was just out for a drink at his local bar, going for a ride on his bike. How could that get him killed?"

The drinks must have been starting to kick in, but Kathy's speech remained clear and her hands steady. Only the unguarded emotion in her voice gave her away.

"What now?" Gertie asked. "Are you going to keep working at the house?"

"I don't know. That's a question for later, I guess. I've got tomorrow off, so..." She raised her beer. "For tonight, here's to Tim. God damn it."

#GLASSHOUSESENIOREMPLOYEES SLACK CHANNEL, SATURDAY

Jean Phan 1:04 p.m.
Hello, checking in. How are all your people doing?

Eddie Vasquez 1:06 p.m.
Freaked out but okay. I've seen some crazy stuff in the kitchens where I've worked, but this takes the cake.

Jean Phan 1:07 p.m.
I understand. You have told them not to talk to the press?

Eddie Vasquez 1:12 p.m.
I can tell them, but I can't say they'll listen. Crazy former nudie model kills two is the kind of thing that can get a lot of drinks bought for you, if you know what I mean.

Jean Phan 1:17 p.m.
Please remind them if you can. All of our jobs will be easier if there is not too much attention on us.

Kathy Hammond 1:22 p.m.

Assuming there's anyone around to do them. One of my guys didn't come back from lunch, and I've had to talk to three of the ones who are left to keep them around for the rest of the week. Tim wasn't the greatest gardener ever, but no one wants to work at a place where your coworkers can get killed by the bosses.

Jean Phan 1:22 p.m.

I understand. I don't think it will happen again.

Eddie Vasquez 1:25 p.m.

It'd be easier if we could get some kind of bonus for sticking around. I don't know about the other departments, but there's a lot of kitchen jobs open right now and it's hard to convince people to stay without a good reason.

Jean Phan 1:26 p.m.

I understand. But it's not a good time to ask about money.

Kathy Hammond 1:32 p.m.

Who would it come from anyway? Who even owns the house now?

Jean Phan 2:43 p.m.

I don't think that is a good thing for us to discuss on this channel.

39

Gertie sat at the table in the pool house, examining the disk, like she might be able to see the contents through its plastic shell. Then she held it under a lamp, in case there was more writing on the label that had faded away. But the exterior of the disk held no clues at all to its contents, making her more determined to find a way to read it.

There were places that could help with that, though none of them would be open on a Saturday night. In the meantime, she was going to need to keep the disk safe. That meant keeping it on her body when she eventually fell asleep. She was looking through the filing cabinets, hunting for something like a padded envelope, when she found them.

It was the stack of three very old laptops she had encountered when she was first exploring. Then they had been an amusing throwback. But now, with their built-in disk drives in their chunky plastic bodies, they presented a possible lifeline.

That is, if Gertie could find a way to plug them in. The

batteries were dead in all three machines, and there was nothing in the cabinet that could be used to charge them. She was wondering how hard it would be to get vintage power cords shipped to her overnight when she spotted a storage box under the desk. Through the cloudy plastic, she could see a tangle of cables, and from the old magazines stacked on top of it, she guessed it had been there for a while.

After twenty minutes of sorting, and more thought than she had ever given to power connections before, Gertie had two of the laptops plugged in.

The first laptop did nothing when she held down the Power button. Gertie tried a few times—she could hear something whirring, but aside from a flicker, the screen stayed dark.

"One down, one to go," Gertie said, then turned to the second laptop. It looked older, so she'd had lower expectations, but it booted up immediately, with a noise like a cat landing on a piano. And, after an excruciating wait staring at a start-up screen, the desktop appeared, looking out of date but recognizable.

It was what Gertie had been hoping for, but now, as she thought about what to do next, she suddenly felt very small and exposed. She had already locked the dead bolts on the pool house door, but even as she checked them again and closed the curtains, she was still aware of how vulnerable she was, in this place that had already seen two deaths.

It was late, and the house was mostly dark, though there were lights on in the upstairs wing where the four bedrooms were. Gertie didn't know who was where, so she couldn't say if anyone was gone or sleeping. She wondered if they were feeling the same urgency she did, knowing they had only one more day in the house. Or were they so confident that they would win in court, it didn't even cross their minds?

Not that she needed to be in the pool house for what she was about to do. Gertie brought the disk out of her bag and contemplated it. She could wait until morning, to find a computer expert with the right equipment to ensure she was handling it properly and whatever it was Arnold had been hiding for all this time wouldn't be lost. But that would take time, and Gertie didn't have that luxury.

So she took a breath, said a little prayer to any supernatural being that was listening, and slid the disk into the slot on the side of the laptop.

It went in with a click, and there was a minute of whirring while Gertie worried she had made a mistake. But finally it stopped, and an image of the disk appeared on the desktop, labeled "1995 Accounts."

There was one file folder on the disk, and the first thing Gertie did was to copy it to the hard drive. Then she double-clicked on it, unsure of what she might find. But the only thing that appeared was a new window, with a list of file folders, each dated with a different month.

It was from two years before she was born, around the time Arnold had left his first wife for her mother. She was suddenly uneasy and wondered if she really wanted to know what the folders held. What if this was some record he had kept of cheating his first wife out of the money she was owed in the divorce or payments related to Carla's own indiscretions? But Gertie had never had any illusions about her parents, and if all she was in danger of learning was that they had been lousy people in a way she hadn't been aware of, she could live with that risk.

But first she was going to have to figure out how to read what was in the folders. Each one contained a list of Excel files, which was fine; Gertie had learned to use that in college. But finding the program was challenging, because the whole computer seemed to be organized in a way designed to hide everything on it. Eventually, after a lot of clicking, she came across a familiar icon, and the program not only opened but loaded without demanding a password or a subscription.

Cautiously, because she didn't trust her luck to last, Gertie clicked through the tabs. She had chosen a file from the folder called "Jun95," because that was two years to the month before she was born. It would have been right around the time Arnold had met Carla at that pool party, six months before he started the process to end his marriage to Doreen.

So what had he been keeping in spreadsheets at that time? To Gertie's untrained eye, it wasn't immediately obvious. There were five tabs in the sheet, each with dates, names, and numbers that Gertie took to be dollar amounts. At first she thought each sheet was a duplicate of the others, but a closer examination revealed subtle differences—amounts that moved from one cell to another and names that were modified with extra numbers.

Gertie didn't know much about accounting, but she did know

that someone keeping different sets of records of the same transactions was a bad sign. It was going to take her some time to decode the data enough to be sure, and it would have been helpful if she had any way of getting the file off the computer, to send to a friend of hers who knew about these things. But the old laptop didn't seem to have any way to connect to Wi-Fi, and Gertie didn't want to spend the time hunting for another cable and somewhere to connect it. So, lacking any better options, she took pictures of the screen with her phone, trying her best to get the words and numbers clear in the images.

She was in the middle of composing a text to her friend, trying to explain what she wanted to know, when Gertie heard a noise behind her.

The computer was on the desk next to the file cabinets, which put her back to the front door. The floor behind her had been clear when she sat down, but now a folded piece of paper sat on the brown tiles, moving slightly in the breeze from the laboring air conditioner.

She picked it up and flipped back the curtain over the window next to the door, only to find herself looking at a louvered wooden panel. It took her a moment to understand what she was seeing.

"Someone closed the shutters?" Gertie wondered aloud. Whoever it was must have worked quietly—aside from the whir of the AC, the pool house was quiet, and she didn't think she could have been that caught up in her investigation of the disk.

Gertie unfolded the paper and read it.

You cause big problems. Something is about to happen. Lock yourself in and stay away from the windows. I come and find you soon. —Mrs. Jean Phan

Gertie stared at the note—nothing about it was right. Why would the writing of someone who spoke fluent English contain such an obvious grammatical error? Why not name the danger so she would know who or what she was supposed to avoid? How was closing the shutters and sliding a note under the door less obvious than knocking? And was she really supposed to believe someone as capable as Mrs. Phan couldn't get her phone number?

Her first instinct was to fling open the front door and find out exactly what it was she wasn't supposed to be seeing. But she didn't. Partly because there was a small chance the note wasn't fake and Mrs. Phan had communicated that way for reasons of her own. And partly because, if the household manager didn't write it, then the person who did would expect her to do one of two things. Either Gertie would do as she was told and stay put, or follow her first impulse and go out the door. They would have plans for both of those, and whatever they were, they would not be good for her. Two people had died violent deaths—she didn't think she was overreacting to not play into an unknown set of hands.

Gertie decided on option three.

40

The windows in the bedroom were large and close to the ground, but they led directly to the path that wrapped around the main house, and anyone looking out would see her. The bathroom window, on the other hand, was high in the wall and barely large enough for Gertie to fit through. But it opened to the back of the pool house, where the path was narrow and unlit, and it was overlooked by nothing but palm trees. It wasn't until she had climbed up on the toilet seat and squeezed herself headfirst through the opening that she remembered another thing about this window: it was located over her namesake grandmother's collection of rosebushes.

Gertie looked down at the dense foliage, glossy in the moonlight.

"Fuck it," she said, then pushed herself forward.

In the end, it wasn't that bad. Gertie managed to keep one hand on the window ledge and roll her body out the window, so she took the fall into the thorns butt-first. She ended up with some scratches on her arms and one on her face, and at least one of the rosebushes was going to need some reconstructive pruning. But she was out, and now she just had to decide what to do next.

Gertie's exit from the pool house had been anything but silent, and the patio she had been told to avoid was only on the other side of the building. If there had been anyone there, waiting to see what she would do, they probably had a pretty good idea now.

But the seconds passed, and silence reigned in the desert night. The possibility occurred to Gertie that she was being ridiculous, that the note had been just a prank, intended to make her panic and engage in exactly this sort of idiocy. But if that was what she had fallen for, then Gertie didn't care. Because the other things she could think of—like a "gas leak" in the pool house or an "accident" that might have struck her if she had come out into the courtyard—were worth risking embarrassment to avoid.

For the moment, though, it seemed her escape had gone undetected. After waiting for several excruciating minutes, Gertie moved out onto the path, stepping softly to keep her sneakers from crunching on the gravel.

Behind the pool house, the path was deep in shadow, and there wasn't much risk of being seen. But it wasn't long before Gertie reached the corner of the building, and she had to make a decision. The path branched there, with one going off into the darkness. She was pretty sure she could follow it and eventually work her way around to the employee lot. The keys to her rental car were in one pocket, the disk in another. She could start driving and never come back. She could take the disk to experts who could retrieve the data and advise her on what it meant. She could go back to the life she had been planning to have before that envelope had shown up in her mailbox.

Or she could go around the corner, into the lights of the house, hoping whoever had left the note wasn't looking through the reflections in the windows to see her coming closer, and try to find out what next thing had been planned in this place.

Once she was around the corner, Gertie tried to walk as normally as possible. There was no cover here, and any attempt to crouch or conceal herself would make her more obvious. But she did keep an eye on the windows, alert for any sign of light or movement. It took only a few strides for Gertie to make it to the side door to the kitchen, and despite her fears, nothing happened.

Stepping through the door was like waking up from a dream. Outside, Gertie had been in a world of unknown dangers, where any shadow could hold a threat. But the kitchen, bright and ordinary, mocked her nerves. Eddie, the chef, was bent over the sink, up to his elbows in soap suds, and around him was the ordinary detritus of a long day of cooking.

Eddie looked up at Gertie and smiled.

"Oh, hey, I was meaning to find you. My team is off tomorrow, so if you want—"

"Is Mrs. Phan still here?" Gertie interrupted.

She must have said it louder than she had intended, because Eddie recoiled slightly in surprise. The genial smile faded as he got a closer look at Gertie, his eyes dropping from the scratch on her face to ones on her arms and the damage to her clothes. Gertie was suddenly aware of how she must look—a total stranger who had shown up at this house with its carefully run systems, asked questions and made demands, and now was running around in the middle of the night looking like she had just lost a catfight with an actual cat.

But Eddie's expression was more alarmed than judgmental.

"Her office is downstairs. I think she should still be there. You want me to come with you?"

"Yes. Please." The chef was low on Gertie's list of suspects, and she had a feeling the less time she spent alone, the better.

She followed Eddie down a narrow set of stairs with white plasterboard walls and stark fluorescent lights. The treads of the stairs had been covered with cheap and shiny linoleum many years ago, with strips of black traction tape added later. Not the most stylish design, Gertie thought, but Arnold might have been better off if the stairs to his office had looked more like these.

In fact, this part of the house was so distinct from the rest of the building that she hardly would have believed it was the same place. At the base of the stairs, she found herself in a short hallway that opened into a larger room, lined with shelves and several large, industrial-looking washing machines and dryers. But Eddie stopped before they got there, knocking on the only door that led off the hall.

"Jean?" Eddie said. "I think we may have a situation."

The door opened so quickly that Gertie thought it must have

had some sort of automatic mechanism. But it was just Mrs. Phan, standing in the doorway of a tiny and pin-neat office. She took one look at Gertie and exchanged a knowing glance with Eddie.

"Come in," she said. "Tell me what happened."

PHONE MESSAGE LEFT BY ANDY BURNETT FOR GERTIE GLASS

Hey, kiddo, sorry to bother you so late, but I hope you get this message. I just heard from my neighbor back home that someone came around and was asking people questions. I thought at first it might have to do with a project I did in Florida, but he said they mostly wanted to know about you and your mom, if you'd been around lately, who your friends were, that sort of thing. He didn't tell the guy anything, but he did get a picture on his doorbell camera, so we can check that out later. Anyway, I thought I should let you know, so you can be on your guard. Nobody hires a guy like that so they can figure out what to get you for your birthday, you know?

I tried to warn your mom, but I don't know how much good that's going to do. You know how much she likes to talk. But I did tell her it might have something to do with this inheritance of yours—don't know if that's true or not, but I think it got her attention.

Anyway, I just got a line on this pop-up art show that's happening over by the Salton Sea, so I'm heading there to see if I can get some good photos, but I'll come find you when I get back, and maybe you can tell me who's got it in for you guys. Take care of yourself. Talk to you later.

41

"So, when this note arrived, I was suspicious," Gertie concluded. "It didn't seem like something you would write."

Unable to think of a better way to explain her decisions, Gertie had told Mrs. Phan and Eddie everything, from her accidental interruption of Brian and Haylee's encounter, through the overinflated tires, to her investigation of the disk from Arnold's office. They had both looked shocked when she described the car accident, and Mrs. Phan had smiled at her account of remembering the hiding place, but neither she nor the chef said anything until Gertie finished her story.

"You're right. I didn't write this," Mrs. Phan said, examining the note with clear distaste.

"Looks like nice paper. I wonder where it's from," said Eddie.

"Main floor office desk, top right drawer," the household manager answered promptly. "Black fine-point pen from the box under the lamp."

"So it was written by someone here," Gertie said, though she'd never doubted that. "But why?"

"Someone didn't want you going out of that house," said Eddie.

"And they closed the shutters," Mrs. Phan reminded him. "They didn't want her going out, and they didn't want her to see what would happen." She picked up a sweater from behind her desk and started for the door.

"I think we had better get up there and see what's going on," she said.

They had started up the stairs when a thought occurred to Gertie.

"Mrs. Phan, wait. I have something to give you."

The narrowness of the steps meant they had been walking in single file, with Eddie first, then Mrs. Phan, then Gertie. The older woman paused to let Gertie come up next to her and looked quizzical as Gertie handed over the disk.

"Can you find someone to copy what's on here and keep it somewhere safe? I think it might be important."

"Of course. I know just who can do that. And I'll take good care of it." Mrs. Phan looked briefly at the disk before tucking it into a pocket on the inside of her sweater. "Your father must have thought it was important, to hide it like he did."

They continued through the kitchen and out into the main room of the house. Despite the drama of the note, everything seemed peaceful. But as they approached the doors to the pool, Eddie held out an arm to stop them.

"That's where they didn't want you to go, right?" he asked Gertie.

"Right, but I don't— Oh no."

The other two saw it at the same time she did. The pool was lit up like it always was at night, but the clear rectangle of bright blue was interrupted by a dark figure surrounded by a spreading cloud in the water.

All three of them started running, but Gertie got there first. She dove in without hesitation, barely noticing the way the water stung her fresh scratches. The body was a man, and it was still warm when she got to it, but that was all she was able to register before she towed it over to the edge of the pool and the other two helped her haul him out.

"It's Mr. Brian," Eddie said, staggering back and staring at him in shock. "And his head is bleeding. Jesus, it's bleeding a lot. What happened?"

Mrs. Phan had no time for questions. She tilted Brian's head back and swept between his lips with her finger, then started breathing into his mouth with practiced confidence. After five breaths she switched to compressing his chest and looked up at the others.

"Call nine-one-one," she said to Eddie, then turned to Gertie. "And you get a towel and use it to stop the bleeding on his head. They're in the chest behind the table."

Gertie obeyed without hesitation and found the box, filled with towels that were perfectly folded and fluffed. As she placed Brian's head on one of them, she noticed the wound was squarely on the back of his skull. That wasn't a place a person would hit themselves if they were falling into a pool on their own, and she was about to say so when the lights came on in the house.

Maryann was the first out the patio door, followed by Neil.

"What's going on?" Maryann asked. "Oh my God, is that Brian?"

Mrs. Phan was busy with rescue breathing, and Eddie was speaking rapidly into his phone, so Gertie took up the answer.

"We found him in the pool, and we—I—pulled him out. He has a head injury, but I don't think he'd been in the water for very long. Eddie's already calling for help." A breeze picked up, and Gertie was suddenly aware that she was soaked to the skin.

"I think everything possible has been done so far," she finished.

"What the hell is going on?" Jennifer was the last to join the party, banging her shoulder on the frame of the sliding door as she stumbled out onto the patio. "Can't we have one peaceful night around here? God."

"Brian fell in the pool," Maryann said shortly. "We don't know much more than that yet. He might not even make it."

Jennifer seemed to be having some trouble processing that information. "Brian drowned himself in the pool? Here? Why would he do that? Is he dead?"

Mrs. Phan looked up from where she was still leaning over Brian's body. "Not dead," she said. "He's breathing, but he needs an ambulance. Eddie?"

Eddie moved the phone away from his mouth. "Ten minutes. I told them to send the police too."

"Why do we need the police?" asked Jennifer, turning angrily at the chef. "Who told you that you could do that? You should know what your job is around here."

Eddie finished his call and pointed to the towel behind Brian's head, which was already soaked through with blood. "That big dent in the back of his skull is what told me to do it, *ma'am*," he said. "You want to fire me for that, go ahead."

The force of his voice seemed to take all three siblings by surprise, and Jennifer even looked a little bit ashamed. She also looked like she was high, Gertie realized, with pupils like pinpricks, despite the low light.

But Gertie didn't have much time to consider that or what it might mean. The implications of Eddie's words were starting to sink in for the others too, and they were reacting in their own ways.

Maryann dropped her head and looked thoughtful, her fingers pressed against her mouth. She took a breath, like she was about to say something, but Neil beat her to it.

"Gertie," he said. "What did you do?"

42

Gertie stared at her half brother in disbelief.

"What did I do? I pulled him out of the water so Mrs. Phan could save his life. What are you talking about, what did I do?"

"We know you had a fight with Brian earlier today," Maryann said. "You can't blame us for being suspicious."

Gertie was beyond furious. "The hell I can't," she said. "Two men from this house are dead, which had nothing to do with me, and now a third one's only alive for now because we were there to find him. And all you can think is that I must have done it?"

She would have gone on, but Gertie was interrupted by the sound of sirens. The paramedics must have underestimated their arrival time, because it had only been only about five minutes between when Eddie hung up his phone and three men and two women in starched blue outfits were hurrying into the courtyard, attaching things to Brian and trying to get him to respond.

Brian's eyes were open, but he showed no signs of awareness

of what had happened. He responded to the EMTs' questions with blank stares and indistinct muttering, and when Jennifer tried to get closer to him, she got nothing but him silently moving his lips before the emergency workers pushed her back.

The police arrived as Brian was being loaded into the ambulance. After hearing the basics of the situation, they took over the courtyard, sending everyone to wait back in the house. The three siblings gathered in the conversation pit, where Maryann and Neil spoke in low tones and Jennifer leaned back on the sofa and stared into space. Eddie said something about his work and went back into the kitchen, and Mrs. Phan sat down at the dining table and began calmly scrolling on her phone. Gertie thought about joining her—she could have used a minute to collect herself for what was going to be a tough conversation with the cops. But then she had another idea, and with one last look at the police working around the pool, she followed Eddie into the kitchen.

"Can I ask you something?"

Eddie looked up at her from where he had returned to his dishwashing and tried to smile. His normal cheerfulness had obviously taken a hit, but Gertie appreciated the effort.

"Sure thing," he said. "What do you want to know?"

Gertie picked up a dish towel and started wiping a pot he had left on the drying rack. "The night before my father died, he had all four of his other children here for dinner. I have the impression he wanted to talk to them about something to do with the business. I'd like to know what they discussed and how it went."

"I see. And you think I might have been listening at the door, taking notes?" Eddie sounded annoyed, and Gertie didn't blame him. But she needed to know.

"I'm sorry," she said. "But you were here, right? And the servers would have been coming and going, and…"

"And you've noticed that some folks don't really see people like that? Yeah, you're not wrong. We hear all sorts of stuff we're not supposed to. The thing is, though, if you want to keep working in this business, you learn to act like you see them as little as they see you. We're allowed into these homes to do a job, and that only works for the clients if they know their personal business isn't going to be spread all over the country."

"I understand," Gertie said, but she felt deflated. She should have known better than to ask—Eddie didn't owe her anything. Certainly not enough to put his job in danger.

But the chef surprised her.

"That said," he went on. "To hell with it. People are dying left and right, getting pushed into pools. Like I'm going to care about what anybody thinks of me? So, what do you want to know?"

Gertie almost laughed, but she realized how out of place that would be. So she restricted herself to smiling gratefully and said, "The conversation at dinner the night before Arnold's birthday."

"Right, that. Actually, you're in luck. Harper was on that night, and she's putting herself through an MBA program, so she was interested in what they were talking about."

Gertie felt a surge of hope. "I should probably talk to her. In the meantime, can you remember anything?"

"Yeah, some. They weren't happy to be here. I saw that myself.

Mr. Glass liked me to come out at the beginning of the meal to bring the appetizers and talk about the courses, and when I did, it was obvious they'd already been arguing. I didn't catch much of it, except Neil saying no one respected his time, and Mr. Glass said it wasn't respect that Neil had come here looking for."

The voices from the living room were getting louder, and some were unfamiliar—probably the police coming in to ask questions. Gertie didn't want to let the others tell their stories first, but she also didn't want to miss this opportunity to learn more about the night before her father's murder.

"And the rest of the conversation?" she asked. "What were they talking about?"

Eddie set the pot he was washing back in the sink and gave Gertie his full attention. "I didn't get all the details. But the general gist was your father had a new idea of what to do with all the mall properties, something to do with research. He was sure it was the next big thing, but it was going to take a lot of money to do it, which meant borrowing, and the rest of them weren't going to get any more money from the business until it was all done. You can imagine how well that went over."

Gertie could.

"He was cutting them off?"

"I don't think it was cutting off all the money, exactly. Believe me, I was interested in that part. But no more big payouts or something? Anyway, they were all freaked out, and I've gotta admit, things got loud enough that I did do some listening. Everyone was talking at once, but one thing I did pick up on was your dad saying something like, 'I get to make the decisions. It's this or nothing.'"

Gertie thought about that, trying to fit it into the other things she knew. She wasn't surprised that the biotech lab conversion plan was what Arnold had wanted to discuss with his children—she had guessed that from what she had found on his computer. And she had hardly needed to be told they wouldn't be receptive to the idea. Had Arnold honestly not known that? Or had the meeting been more a matter of telling than asking, when it came to what he was going to do with the money that was supporting them all?

People had been killed for less. And Brian, even if he hadn't done the killing, might have thought it was in his interest to let Haylee take the fall for whoever had. So why had he been floating in the pool with a dent in the back of his head?

The pool that was just steps from the building where Gertie was supposed to have been at the time, with no one to alibi her. Gertie was suddenly sure she knew why the note had been left and the shutters closed; she was supposed to be blamed for the attack. And all she had to defend herself was a ridiculous-sounding story and the hope that someone could say Brian couldn't have been in the water for longer than the time she was downstairs with Eddie and Mrs. Phan. It wasn't impossible, but Gertie didn't like her chances.

The kitchen door opened, and Mrs. Phan looked in.

"The police want to talk to you," she said to Gertie.

43

Around two in the morning, the wind began to blow. Lying on the bed in her motel room, Gertie listened to it and wondered what it was doing to the garden. She was wondering a lot of things, actually, but for some reason, thoughts of the palm tree that Tim had damaged in his enthusiasm to be helpful kept intruding into her mind.

The interview with the police had gone about as well as she could have hoped. Gertie told them about her escape out the window, and why, and Mrs. Phan produced the note as proof. The detective didn't seem very impressed, but he took it and listened with more interest when she mentioned the closed shutters on the windows facing the pool. From the questions he was asking, it was clear someone had told him that Gertie had had an argument with Brian earlier that day, though not what it was about. Gertie didn't think it would be a good idea to tell him about the matter with Haylee, so she said Brian had been insisting she give up her inheritance. That didn't make her look good, but it was believable at least.

More helpful were the testimonies from Mrs. Phan and Eddie, who confirmed she had been in the house for ten or fifteen minutes before they had all found Brian together. The cop hadn't said that the fact Brian was alive was in her favor, but the search Gertie did on the internet after he let her go confirmed that survival was unlikely after that much time.

But statistics weren't proof, and Gertie was relieved when she had been allowed go back into the pool house to gather what was left of her things. If the officer who had been left to watch her wondered why she packed up a vintage laptop, he didn't mention it.

The detective had even said if she was willing to wait until the crime scene team was done, she could sleep there that night, but Gertie wasn't interested. After two murders, two near misses, and an attempt to frame her, she'd had enough of pushing her luck. So she threw the fresh clothes Mrs. Phan had found for her into her rental car and took off, skipping the first two motels she saw and choosing the third, just in case someone might try to find her. It was just off the freeway at the edge of the city, with a neon sign that promised cable TV and air-conditioning. In fact, the Desert Lion Inn had very little to recommend it, aside from the fact that if anyone was going to look for her, they wouldn't start there.

It wasn't until she had gotten herself settled into her temporary quarters, with the cheap desk pushed up against the door, that Gertie allowed herself to think about what had happened.

The note had come from someone in the house—Gertie would have been sure of that even without Mrs. Phan's evidence about the paper. The police had checked the gates, and there was no sign that anyone had broken in, and at the late hour, nearly all the staff had already left. Unless she was missing something, the only people with the opportunity to try to kill Brian were the six of them who had been in the house.

Gertie knew she was out of the running, and she didn't see how Mrs. Phan or Eddie could have done it either. The attack must have happened while all three of them were in the basement, possibly even when they were on their way back up the stairs, or else no amount of rescue breathing would have brought Brian back.

Maryann, Neil, and Jennifer had all been in the house, each alone in their separate rooms. None of them had an alibi, and they all presumably had the same motive. Brian was, after all, the person in the best position to undo the framing of Haylee, the point on which the person who had killed Arnold and Tim was staking their freedom.

Brian had been aggressively unreceptive to Gertie's suggestion he should give Haylee an alibi and restart the investigation, and she had taken that at face value. But what if she had underestimated him? What if Brian had known something about one of his siblings, and he made the connection when he realized Haylee couldn't be the killer? He might have reacted with anger in the moment and spent the rest of the day deciding what he was going to do with the information.

And if what he'd decided to do was to confront the person who had killed Arnold and Tim, that might have sealed his fate.

That was the idea that had sent Gertie to this motel room by the freeway, with its air-conditioning unit that sounded like it might either shut down or explode and a scratchy comforter she didn't examine closely. She wasn't expecting to be comfortable here, but she was reasonably sure that, unless someone had snuck an AirTag into her pocket or gotten access to her credit card, she should have at least until morning before anyone was able to track her down.

After all, there were currently three people who could disrupt the frame-up job on Haylee. One was in the hospital, one was in jail, and one was Gertie, barely having escaped being framed herself.

There were a few ways she could see of getting out of this. But the only one that didn't involve running far away was to find out who was behind all the violence.

At least Gertie thought she was starting to understand the motive. Even entering his tenth decade, Arnold had believed himself to be a savvy businessman, and he clearly wasn't willing to give up on the company he had built. Recognizing that malls weren't the way forward, he had settled on the idea of converting the properties into biotech research buildings. Gertie thought she could follow his reasoning—the articles he had saved touted that as the hottest thing in real estate, though she couldn't quite see it herself.

But Arnold must have, and that was what he had called his other children together to discuss. Having seen the budgeting for the project, Gertie could guess what he'd wanted to talk about. He was planning on borrowing against the company, and if Jules was right that it was already heavily leveraged, that could be a major risk. Even if it did work out, it would be a while before any of them could get their hands on a large amount of cash, which might have been a serious problem for someone.

And if it didn't work out, the whole thing could come tumbling down.

That counted for a motive, not just to kill Arnold, but to do it soon. He had a meeting with the banker that week—if he hadn't died before then, the money might already be tied up.

So who could have done it? Maryann had been away from the house when Arnold died, but she could have helped with the cover-up, and with framing Haylee. Even Brian might have been in on that part—maybe he had been told to make sure she was distracted from her missing phone, and he had chosen the only thing he knew? If Gertie hadn't gone looking for a fan just then, it would have been Haylee's word against his, and there was no question how that would look to a jury.

It wasn't a bad theory. Brian hadn't struck Gertie as an ethical person—would he really have posed a threat to one of his siblings, even if the question was their father's death? She could more easily see him being spooked by Gertie having caught him in his part of the scheme, and in his panic, he'd become a liability. At that point, his coconspirator might have decided to solve their problems in bulk, killing Brian and framing Gertie for the crime.

Her only comfort was that the attempt had been so sloppy. It was a consistent feature of the crimes, she realized. All of them relied on people behaving in exactly the way the killer wanted, plus some luck. They had failed spectacularly at their attempt to deprive Gertie of an alibi for the attack on Brian—ironically, if it hadn't been for the note, she probably would have still been sitting there in the pool house, completely unaware of what was going on.

On the other hand, if she had heard something or decided to leave through the pool house door, she might have caught them in the act. What would have happened then was a question she was happy not to have answered.

That line of thought wasn't doing her any good, so Gertie abandoned it and went back to thinking about what she did know.

Two weeks ago, Arnold Glass had invited four of his children to his house for his ninetieth birthday. They had had dinner together, along with his current girlfriend, and he had talked about his plans for the family business. The following morning he had fallen down the stairs from his office and been hit over the head with a sculpture that had been nearby. Then, the night before his funeral, a gardener from the house had been run down by the girlfriend's car, which was found with the sculpture hidden in the back. Gertie knew that neither Haylee nor Brian could have killed Tim, and one of the things she had done before leaving the house was to check the records from the gate that confirmed Maryann had been out of the house when Arnold died.

That left Neil and Jennifer as options for lone actors, but with conspiracy, the field was wide-open. Even Haylee was a possibility for Arnold's murderer, but Gertie didn't think much of that idea. To frame the person who could implicate you in a murder was dangerous no matter what. But there was no way anyone would have collaborated with Haylee on something so big, for the simple reason that the woman was dumb as a bag of hammers.

Gertie flopped back onto the bed and stared at the water stains on the popcorn ceiling. One of them looked a bit like Australia, which for some reason made her think about a book she had read when she was little, about a child who had a terrible day.

You have no idea, kid, she thought as a wave of exhaustion rolled over her. *This is what I get for opening the mail.*

WHATSAPP CONVERSATION BETWEEN EMILY ANDERSON, CPA, AND GERTIE GLASS

4:35 a.m. PDT

Hey, Gert! Wow, no offense, but you aren't the person I expected to be sending me spreadsheet screenshots in the middle of the night. Do you want to tell me what this is about?

Okay, you're probably still asleep on the West Coast. I'm in Antigua right now with Eric's family, and they all get up super early.

Anyway I took a look at those pictures. What else am I going to do, enjoy my time in paradise or something? 😄

[gif of fire juggler being hit on the head with a flaming torch]

I could tell you more if I had access to the complete files, but from what I'm seeing, it looks like someone was making different versions of some business accounts, with the money moving around into different categories. Also, I'm not sure from just what you have here, but it looks like the same payments are recorded more than once? There's a five-thousand-dollar invoice from something called "IntDev" that seems to be here at least three times. I'm not saying it's necessarily sketchy, but if this is a publicly traded company, let me know so I can short them.

Kidding!

What version of Excel is this? It looks super old to me. Are you doing some kind of historical research or something?

8:06 a.m. PDT

Hi Emily, sorry for not explaining before, I was kind of in a hurry. This all has to do with a thing with my father—it's a long story.

I took a bunch more screenshots and saved them in a shared drive, the link should be in your email. Can you take a look when you get a minute and let me know if there's anything that makes more sense to you?

I'm going to be offline for a while today. If you don't hear from me by tonight, can you try and get in touch with the police in Palm Springs and tell them about this? It might be important.

Sorry to put all this on you. I know it sounds totally crazy. It probably is.

11:43 a.m. PDT

Sorry I didn't see this, Eric's mom wanted us to all go on a plantation tour 😭

What do you mean, the police?

Shit, Gert, what the hell is going on?

Gertie?

44

When Gertie left the motel at eight thirty in the morning, she didn't exactly have a plan. But she did have some ideas, and after reading and rereading Emily's responses about the spreadsheets, she thought she knew what her first step was going to have to be. But she found a coffee shop first and loaded up on a double cappuccino and two pastries, because Gertie knew better than to try to talk to her mother on an empty stomach.

She found a parking spot in the shade of some trees, finished her coffee, and reflexively checked her face and shirt for crumbs before pulling up Carla's name on her phone.

Carla picked up on the third ring, and immediately there was an alert that she was requesting a video call. Gertie sighed, cursed herself for not disabling that setting on her mother's phone, and accepted.

"Sweetie! What are you doing? Did you get the money? How much is it?"

She was holding her phone up at an angle so it pointed down

at her face, the way the influencer consultant she had hired had instructed her to. Gertie wanted to tell her not to tire her arm out for no reason—no one was watching her now. But it wouldn't do any good, so she saved herself the trouble and got right to the point.

"Sorry I haven't been in touch," she said. "Listen, this is going to seem kind of out of the blue, but I've got a couple of questions about stuff that happened while you were married to Arnold."

As usual, Carla wasn't interested in anything Gertie had on her mind.

"That bastard," she said, tilting the phone some more so it would capture her cheekbones at the best angle. "He didn't write you out, did he? Because you're his daughter, I swear it. There was no other guy then. And anyway, they did all the tests."

"This isn't about the will," Gertie said, then inspiration struck. "But it does have to do with my inheritance."

She would have liked to leave that part out entirely, at least until she had a better idea of what exactly she was going to end up with and how to make sure Carla wasn't going to tell everyone her own version of it. But the best chance of getting the information she needed was to play to Carla's interests.

Gertie had guessed right. At the mention of money, her mother was suddenly all ears, even lowering her phone so she could look more directly at the screen.

"So you got something? How much? When does it pay out?"

"There isn't any cash," said Gertie, in what was technically not a lie. "But he left me part of the company. Not enough to have a controlling interest, but I'll have a say in some decisions."

"The company?" The way Carla's face fell, a person might have thought Gertie had just told her she had a terrible disease. "Why would you want to own a bunch of malls? No one goes to malls anymore."

"I know, but that's not important right now. What I need to know is, was there anything funny going on with the company while you and Arnold were together? Anything he mentioned to you?"

It was a long shot—no one who had known Carla for long would try to tell her anything important. But at her best, Carla could be an attentive listener, in the way that made the speaker feel like he was the most interesting man in the world. (It was only ever a man, with Carla.) Those were the times when she learned things they might not have intended to share and which she would happily repeat whenever it occurred to her.

Unless, of course, she forgot them entirely. Which was what Gertie was starting to suspect had happened here, as the minutes dragged on and none of her prompts drew any memories besides the old grievances she had heard a thousand times before.

"And when I wanted to change the floors so I could have my yoga studio in the living room, the housekeeper told me I couldn't do that. Like, she's the housekeeper! She doesn't get to tell me what to do. But Arnold let her control everything, and he wouldn't listen to me. I don't think they were having an affair, though. She was an old Chinese lady and kind of fat. She liked you, though. Is that a crumb on your face? You need to watch that video I sent you about carbs, honey—they kill your brain."

"And there was nothing about trouble at the company?" Gertie asked through gritted teeth. She wanted to yell at Carla, that Mrs. Phan was neither Chinese nor fat, that Carla wasn't very good at yoga, and the Earth would crash into the sun before Gertie watched any of those videos. But it was getting late, and she wasn't sure how much time she had to get the information she needed before the next disaster occurred, so she gave it one last try.

"The business was always having troubles. It was about to go under," Carla said blithely. "I should have known that when I met Arnold, but of course, I thought it was great then. I used to love the mall."

She got a faraway look that Gertie recognized, so before Carla could start with her hairspray-tinted eighties memories, she cut her off.

"What do you mean 'about to go under'? How did the company survive?"

This time Carla did look like she was making an attempt to remember—if it hadn't been for the Botox, she might have been frowning.

"That was weird," she said at last. "Because the money turned up, but he was mad about it. And I was like, why are you mad about money? Who cares where it came from?"

Gertie could just hear Carla saying that—it was as close to a personal philosophy as she was likely to have.

"Where did the money come from?" Gertie asked.

But, in this matter at least, Carla was consistent.

"I don't know," she said, as indifferent as ever. "Some sort of billing thing? All I remember is that Arnold was so mad, and he kept saying things like, 'She's not as smart as she thinks she is.' And I just thought, Who is? Except you, honey."

TEXT FROM JENNIFER GLASS TO GERTIE GLASS, 9:15 A.M. PDT

Hi Gertrude, this is Jennifer. Could you stop by the house sometime this morning? I think there are still some of your things here that you left. Thanks

SATURDAY, AUGUST 24

FIFTEEN MINUTES BEFORE THE DEATH OF ARNOLD GLASS

Arnold took another sip of his coffee and stared at the numbers on the computer screen. It was going to cost a lot, no question. He had known that, of course, but until he started to put the estimates together, he hadn't fully grasped how much it really was.

Not that he couldn't manage it. Of course he could, just like he'd managed everything else in his career. There had been plenty of times people had told him his ideas would never work, and hadn't he always proven them wrong? Well, almost always.

He added up the columns again, as though the result might change. Of course it was a risk—everything worth doing was. That was no reason for his children to react like he had gone crazy for wanting to save the company he had built.

Worse than crazy, they had thought he had gone soft in the head. Neil had nearly said as much, like he had anything to say about a person being soft. And he had the nerve to suggest that Arnold shouldn't be taking on any new projects "at his age." As if Arnold wasn't as sharp at ninety as any of them would ever be.

But Arnold wasn't fooled. He knew perfectly well what his children were worried about, and it wasn't his mental health. It was their money, or rather his money, that they had gotten a little too comfortable spending. Well, they could have a try at living leaner for a while, maybe that would teach them something about life.

He leaned back and looked out the window, across the desert to the city in the distance. The people who'd built that hadn't given up, had they? If anything seemed impossible, it was making a livable place out of this barren, baking wasteland. But they had done it, and they had made a lot of money in the process. Arnold didn't know who "they" were, but it stood to reason.

And they'd probably had people standing in their way too. That was always the worst part—not the logistics or the costs of a thing, but the human element. That was why Arnold had taken to collecting things, documents, pieces of information, even if he didn't know what he was going to do with them at the time. Those were his insurance policies, as he liked to think of them. Something he had learned early in his career was that when you had an advantage over someone, you didn't always want to use it right away. It could be months or years, but it was amazing what you could do with a little leverage.

He gave his hiding place an involuntary look. That was one he didn't want to have to use, but extreme provocation called for an extreme response. No one was going to take control of his company from him, not while he was alive.

And not afterward either. Hadn't Jules been surprised when he had given Carla's daughter the shares! But he had leverage there too. The girl might turn out to be useful after all. Changing the will had absolutely been the right choice; Arnold's only regret was that he wouldn't be around to see their faces when they found out.

He was less sure about young Gertrude as the one to carry on his legacy, but who else was there? It was a shame she hadn't gotten any of her mother's looks, but at least she had his brains. Even for a girl, that was something. Not that she could be expected to understand everything. That was why he had given Jules the second letter, to mail to her in the event of his passing. It had been an afterthought, but now he was glad to have included it. No point taking chances with something so important.

Arnold's musings were interrupted by a sharp rap on the tower door. He looked up, surprised and annoyed. The only person who was allowed to bother him here was Mrs. Phan, and he already had his coffee. But she had said she was about to leave to run the party setup when she brought it, and everyone in the house was going with her.

But someone must have stayed behind, because they were knocking again, more insistently this time. He thought about shouting through the door that he was busy and hoping the visitor would give up and go away, but something about the sound of that knock suggested someone who wasn't going to be put off so easily.

"All right, hold your horses. You're not on fire."

Arnold closed the windows on his computer, just in case, and got up, grumbling. This was positively the last interruption he was going to tolerate.

45

For the trip back to the house, Gertie drove carefully and stayed alert. She thought she had almost everything she needed, and after one more stop, she would know if she was right. But her evidence was thin and circumstantial, and her suspect had plenty of resources. At this point, Gertie thought her best chance was to get some key allies and hope she could make her case before the person she was up against made their next move. By now she knew they were desperate, determined, and unafraid to take almost any risk to get what they wanted. Gertie's only hope for her own safety was to make sure as many other people as possible knew what she knew, but her best chance to put the matter to rest for good was going to require a more direct approach.

If you can't join them, Gertie thought, *then beat them.*

The stop Gertie had to make was on the way. She pulled into the parking lot of the park's visitor center just after nine, relieved there were no other cars there besides a green truck with the park logo.

She found Ranger Boyd behind the desk, trimming his fingernails over a piece of paper. He looked up as Gertie came in and covered the evidence.

"Welcome to Las Palmas Desert Park," he said. "Can I help you?"

"I hope so," said Gertie. "I came by here a couple of days ago—from the house up the road?"

Gertie felt a small surge of pleasure as his eyes lit up with recognition. "Oh sure, Gertrude, right? What can I do for you?"

There wasn't a graceful way to approach her question, so Gertie dove right in. "When I was here the other day, you started to ask me about the uniforms the staff at the house wear. Was there any reason for that?"

The ranger looked surprised. Whatever question he had been anticipating, that wasn't it. "Oh yeah, that's nothing really. Never mind about it."

"I'm sorry, but I think it really might not be nothing. Humor me?"

Boyd folded up the piece of paper with the nail cuttings and carefully transferred it to the trash without meeting Gertie's eyes. There was clearly something on his mind, and she left him alone with it.

"I'd rather not get anyone in trouble," he said.

"You aren't," Gertie lied, sort of. "Would it help if I guessed?"

The ranger didn't say anything, so she went on.

"I think maybe you found some clothes around here somewhere, about two weeks ago? They'd been discarded, probably in the bathroom. And it seemed weird, but it's none of your business what people do with their clothes. But still, you'd been wondering, so that's why you asked me about the uniforms. Am I close?"

The ranger looked relieved.

"Well, since you know all about it already," he said. "Yeah, that was pretty much it. We've got a cleaning crew that comes in every day, mostly to deal with the public areas around the visitor center. Things can get weird out here, so anything out of the ordinary, they know they can bring it to the ranger on duty and we'll deal with it. Anyway, one of them comes to me, says they found these clothes, and what do I want them to do with them. So I take a look, thinking it's going to be, like, a shirt that someone got hung up on a cactus and didn't think was worth taking home. But it's a whole outfit, completely pristine—a black polo shirt and nice pants, with a logo on the shirt."

"And you looked it up and figured out it was the uniform that the people who work at the house wear," Gertie finished for him. She didn't mind chatting with Ranger Boyd, but he did talk slowly, and she was in a hurry.

"That's pretty much it," Boyd agreed. "My feeling was, I didn't know what it was about, but no one seemed to be hurt or missing, so it was none of my business. But I did wonder about it, which is why I brought it up with you."

"I'm glad you did," Gertie said. "It might be important to a much bigger problem. Do you remember what day you found the clothes?"

Now that he was confident that Gertie wasn't using him to narc on some hapless employee, Boyd was eager to be helpful.

"Let me see," he said. "We're a little shorthanded lately, so I've been working some extra weekend shifts. I remember I was running late that day, because it was the only time I could get into the laundry at my building, and I had to wait for the dryer to free up. So I was already worried about what I might have missed, when Rosa came to me with the clothes. That was a Sunday, definitely. The twenty-fifth."

The day after Arnold died. Gertie nodded; she had already been sure of it. She was also fairly certain about what she was going to hear next, but she still had to ask.

"What time does the cleaning crew come through on the weekends? If something was left in the trash on Saturday, would it still be there on Sunday morning?"

"Oh, definitely. They come in the morning—they're usually done by eight. We have extra crews in the high season and on holidays, but during the summer, it's not worth it. And anyway, we don't want to have them working in the heat of the day if they don't have to."

"Of course," Gertie said. From the way Boyd was looking at her, she knew he was dying to ask what this was all about, and part of her wanted to tell him. But she still needed one thing from him, and she thought she had a better chance of getting it if he was still curious but not convinced she was insane.

"The last time I was here, you mentioned you had seen a mountain lion on the trail camera that was set up between here and the house. I was just wondering, how long do you keep the images from that camera?"

"It depends. I mostly go through and clear out anything that's not relevant if the hard drive is starting to get full. But we keep the wildlife pictures indefinitely—we've got a backup drive for those."

"Right, well, it's one of those irrelevant photos I'm interested in. From that Saturday, the day before the clothes were found in the trash, between eight and ten in the morning. There might be something on that camera that could answer a pretty big question for me." Gertie knew she needed to explain herself better, but she hesitated. If the park's camera had caught what she hoped it had, it would be as close as she was going to get to definitive evidence against the killer. But there was no way to explain it to Boyd without telling him everything, and Gertie wasn't sure how he was going to take that.

But she was about to find out.

"Okay," he said, as he got up from behind the desk. "I don't know if you're crazy or I am, but there's no way I can't go look now. One thing, though—it's not nudists again, is it?"

"No nudists," Gertie assured him. "In fact, you could say the whole thing is a cover-up."

46

Boyd must not have meant the part about thinking Gertie was crazy, because he let her follow him into the office and watch over his shoulder as he connected to the server for the trail camera. It took a few minutes to find what they were looking for, and as Boyd clicked through the folders, Gertie was aware that the cooling system in the small office was struggling, and the sweat was running down her body.

Boyd on the other hand, seemed unbothered.

"Saturday the twenty-fourth, right?" he said, scrolling down the list of dates. "Not too many captures on that day. We get less in the warm season—most of the animals that are big enough to set off the cameras move into the hills where it's cooler. But here's one at eight forty-six a.m., so let's see if that's it."

Gertie tensed up, suddenly aware that she was holding her breath. But the ranger hovered his cursor over the label for the file without clicking on it.

"One thing," he said, turning back to look at Gertie. "If this is what you want it to be, you have to tell me about it. I think that's fair, don't you?"

"More than fair," Gertie agreed. "But it's a long story. Can I give you the short version now and follow up with the full details later? I'll buy you dinner."

Boyd smiled and nodded. "Deal. I probably shouldn't be away from the desk for that long anyway. Okay, let's see what we've got."

Gertie shouldn't have been surprised. She had put the pieces together, made most of the connections even before Carla had come through with her memories. But she still heard herself gasp when the picture resolved on the screen.

Maryann was clearly not a very experienced cyclist. Her seat was set too high, and the way she was leaning forward wouldn't do her much good if she hit a rock on the trail. But the woman who was supposed to have driven away from her father's house an hour earlier was clearly riding a bicycle less than three miles from the building, dressed in the uniform of the household employees.

"I'm guessing you found what you were looking for," Ranger Boyd said, when Gertie had gone about thirty seconds in silence.

She nodded, not trusting herself to speak. But this time, it was Boyd's turn to fill in the details.

"This is about the deaths, isn't it?" he said. "The old man a while ago, and the gardener the other day. I'm not dumb; I pay attention to the things that are going on around here. Particularly when they have to do with privately owned property on what should be park land, where people are suddenly dying under questionable circumstances. I know they arrested someone for the murders, but I'm guessing you think there was more going on."

Gertie nodded again, then finally found her voice.

"Yes, you've pretty much got it. The person in this picture," she said, gesturing at Maryann. "She was supposed to be away from the house at the time of the first death. I think she used Tim—he was the gardener—to help her set up her alibi. And then she killed him and framed someone else."

"Why?" said Boyd. "Those people are rich, right? What did she need so badly that she did all that?"

"I'm not sure. I think she started out thinking she was doing what was necessary," Gertie said slowly. "And then, when she didn't get what she wanted, she tried to make it work out the way she thought it should."

"By killing people," Boyd finished for her.

"By killing people," Gertie agreed. "And things still aren't working out very well for her."

She stepped away from the desk and looked out the window. The light in the room had suddenly dimmed, as a blanket of clouds rolled across the sky.

"Can you do me a favor?" she asked. "The police should see this, plus the clothes. I don't know how seriously they're going to take it, but I think it would be better if you gave it to them directly."

"Sure, of course." The ranger smiled at her. "Believe me, it wouldn't be the first time I had the cops thinking I was crazy. Probably won't be the last. But why don't you come with me? You can explain the whole story then."

Gertie shook her head. "Even with all this, I don't think it's going to be enough. Not when it comes to the sort of person we're dealing with here. I need some more help, and the only place I can get it is back at that house."

She started toward the office door, and Boyd got up to follow her.

"I hope you don't mind me saying, but that seems like a really bad idea."

"I don't and it is. But it's the best one I've got right now." Gertie turned back and smiled at him. "And don't worry. I can take care of myself. I always have."

47

Gertie parked in the driveway. This time, no one came to greet her or take her bags, and there was no activity around the house. Gertie wondered at the change, until she remembered passing remarks from Kathy and Eddie, that they were going to be off today. In both cases she hadn't questioned it, because she'd had other things on her mind, but now the timing struck her as suspicious.

She left her car and crossed the front yard in silence, with even the cicadas quiet under the cloudy skies, and for the first time, Gertie began to seriously doubt the wisdom of her plan. But she was here now, and having come this far, there was nothing else to do but go on.

It had been only three days since the first time she had approached the front door, but it seemed like a lifetime had passed. She had a moment of déjà vu as she came up the path, but of course things were different. Not just that she knew what the house was like inside—she could even see in. Where the bright sunlight had turned the windows into mirrors for her first arrival, now the clouds reversed the effect. She could still see the reflections of the cacti and palms that dotted the front garden in the glass, but through them three figures were visible, scattered around the main room like dolls in a diorama.

Neil was in the conversation pit, on the sofa, and Jennifer was sitting at the dining table, with a plate of something in front of her. Only Maryann moved when Gertie approached, coming forward from where she had been standing by the office stairs like she was going to meet her at the door.

But Gertie still had the keys, and she let herself in.

The surprise on all three of their faces as she came through the door on her own was undeniable. Neil just looked startled, but Jennifer nearly snarled at her, and even Maryann drew back, like Gertie had brought a bad smell in with her.

Looking at Maryann with new eyes, Gertie wondered at her level of calm. Could a person really kill her father and an innocent bystander, and try to kill her brother, and stay calm enough to hold a glass of iced tea without her hand even shaking?

"Thank you for coming," Maryann said. "I'm sure you've got things in your life you want to get back to. I just thought we should have one more get-together to iron out some of the outstanding issues."

"You did?" Gertie asked. She was only a few steps in from the door, but she was very aware of it closing heavily behind her. "The text I got was from Jennifer. She mentioned that I left some things here."

Maryann dismissed that inconsistency with a wave of her hand.

"What matters is you're here now. Have a seat?" She gestured at the conversation pit and started to lead the way over.

Gertie was not a stupid person, but she was starting to think she might have acted like it. She had come into this situation thinking she held all the cards, but there was no question that Maryann was the one who thought she was laying a trap.

One of us is about to have a rude awakening, Gertie thought. *I hope it's not me.*

Aloud, she said, "I'll just stay where I am, thanks. I won't be here long. There's just a couple of things I wanted to ask, before I go."

Despite her words, Gertie did come a few steps farther into the room, so she was past the shelf with its array of decorative objects. The space that had held the unmatched bronze statue had been filled, and three modernist candlesticks now sat next to the oversize geode.

"All right," Maryann said. She was maintaining her cool amusement, but Gertie thought there might be an undercurrent of worry there. Did Maryann think Gertie had come here on a bluff? She must have, to have both Neil and Jennifer sitting by, ready to be witnesses to whatever she was planning. That was fine with Gertie—it was what she wanted too.

In spite of her earlier theory about the siblings working together, Gertie was sure now that Maryann had acted alone. There would have been no reason for her elaborate charade otherwise—to trick Tim into driving her car away from the house while she stayed behind, dressed in a staff uniform so if anyone did catch a glimpse of her, she would have gone unnoticed. At the very least, whoever was helping would have managed an alibi of their own, and Neil and Jennifer had none.

But more than that, Gertie had the idea that the crime had been about Maryann and Maryann alone. She had cooked the books to save the company, and it was to have power over her that Arnold had kept those records for all these years.

Just like he had kept Gertie's IOU.

Gertie cleared her throat and looked Maryann straight in the eyes. "Did you know the park district has a trail camera set up on the path that leads to the visitor center from here? They mostly use it to track things like mountain lions and bobcats, but it can pick up other predators too. For example, someone riding a bicycle from here, to change her clothes and have a gardener meet her with her car, so she can look like she was far away when she was actually in the house, killing her father."

For nearly a minute, silence reigned. Maryann stayed frozen where she was, holding her iced tea halfway toward her mouth, half smiling and looking like she was doing some very fast mental calculations. Jennifer was still seated at the table, slack-jawed and staring through the hair that had fallen across her face.

It was Neil, in fact, who was the first to respond.

"Are you high?" he said. "What the hell are you talking about?"

"Sorry," said Gertie. "Let me take that from the top. Maryann claimed to have been away from the house on the morning when

Arnold was killed, but she was here, killing him. She convinced Tim to leave in her car on some pretense—probably something to do with wanting to get into cycling without letting anyone else know. He was supposed to pick her up at the visitor center in the park, and then he got permission to go riding himself." She risked a glance over at Jennifer. "From the little I knew of him, I'd say he was a credulous sort of guy who did what he was told. Maryann even changed into one of the employee uniforms so that if anyone saw her, they wouldn't think she was a member of the family."

"Okay, back up a second." Neil was coming closer now, looking concerned, as both his sisters held their distance. "The part about Maryann killing Dad—where are you getting that? Because even if she did go out for a bike ride, I don't think that's exactly the smoking gun you think it is."

That was true, and this was where Gertie's argument got onto shaky ground. And it was where she was going to need to convince Neil and Jennifer, or at least raise enough doubts in their minds that the family wouldn't present a united front when she took her evidence to the police.

"I'm sorry," she said. "I know this is a lot. But you have to understand, it goes way back, to before I was even born."

To her surprise, Jennifer barked a laugh. "That's not long," she said. "Seriously, Maryann, do you really want to let her talk like that? We don't need to sit here and listen to this."

Maryann hadn't moved, but now she came to take a seat at the table with Jennifer. "I think she's going to make sure we hear it no matter what we want," she said in a level voice. "We might as well let her get it over with."

Maryann turned her gaze to Gertie, bored and slightly contemptuous, which scared Gertie more than anything. A person shouldn't be that calm when they were being accused of killing their father, even if they knew it was coming, and there was no way the dissolution of her alibi wasn't news to Maryann. But she was acting like Gertie was just an excitable child, telling them her latest ideas about the moon.

Neil, at least, was interested. He looked more concerned than anything, as he drew closer to Gertie, holding out a hand as if to slow her down.

"This stuff you say happened in the past—how do you know about it? What is it?"

"Arnold left a disk. It was hidden in his office, with evidence that someone had been committing fraud on behalf of the company. It happened back in the nineties—I'm not sure what set it off, but money was running out, and the company was in trouble. Arnold found out about the fraud and kept the evidence, but he didn't say anything, except to complain to my mother about it."

"Your mother! Yeah, there's a reliable witness." Jennifer sounded contemptuous, but she kept glancing at Maryann like she couldn't believe what she was hearing.

Gertie took some encouragement from that. Her youngest half siblings might not like her, but they had to realize she wouldn't be saying these things without something to back it up. That was what Gertie had to count on, that they would be able to overcome their dislike of her to understand the seriousness of what she was trying to tell them. Speaking directly to Jennifer, she went on with her story.

"He didn't tell anyone else, but he held on to the evidence," she repeated. "And I think when Maryann confronted him about his plans for the company, he played it as his trump card. He knew what she had done, and if she didn't fall in line, he was going to use it against her. Even for the damage it might do to the company—it was all or nothing. If he couldn't get his way, then no one could."

"And for that reason, plus my going for a bike ride, you think I killed him," Maryann finished. "Well, it's certainly creative, I'll give you credit for that. But I don't think you're going to get very far with it. After all, the police already have a suspect in custody, with much more convincing evidence against her."

"What about Brian?" Gertie said, still addressing her words to Jennifer. "You know someone in this house attacked him last night. That was because he accidentally provided an alibi for Haylee. They were having sex in the office here when her car was being used to run down Tim. I had the misfortune to walk in on them when I came in to look for a fan."

That got an unguarded response out of Jennifer, who laughed. She was about to say something, but she caught Maryann looking at her and shut her mouth with a snap.

It was time for Gertie to make her final appeal.

"Look," she said, turning to Neil. He hadn't said anything for a while, and as Gertie spoke, his look of concern had been deepening. "Haylee didn't attack Brian—she couldn't have. He told me he wasn't going to support her alibi when I talked to him, but I think he must have done some more thinking and gone to confront the person he suspected himself. And it's only luck that he's still alive in the hospital now. So, of the people who are left, you've got yourself and two others, one of whom went through elaborate steps to make it look like she couldn't have been the one to kill your father. Our father. And as long as you know that, none of you are safe."

It was a long shot—Gertie had known that before she started. But she thought she could feel the mood in the room subtly shifting as she made her case—Jennifer had stopped sneering at her and was staring out the patio doors, and Neil honestly seemed to be listening.

"You have to believe me," she said, coming toward him. "This is serious."

Neil smiled gently and met her eyes.

"I do believe you. The thing is, Maryann already told us," he said, then swung his fist into Gertie's stomach.

48

Gertie staggered, gasping for breath that wouldn't come, and crumpled to the floor. A distant voice in her mind told her she had to fight, to defend herself, to get away, but no part of her body would respond. She felt her head bounce on the marble tiles and came to rest staring under the credenza.

Someone left their phone down here, she thought senselessly. Then hands grabbed her from above, hauling her roughly to her feet and twisting her arms to pin them behind her back.

"Damn, she's solid," Neil was saying. "How can someone so thin be so heavy?"

"Because unlike some of us, she's been staying fit by exercising, not taking shots." The clouds in Gertie's eyes had begun to clear, and she could see that Maryann had gotten up, leaving her tea on the table to come over and examine her.

"Make sure you've got a good grip," she was saying to Neil. "Our little sister here has already proved to be quite the escape artist."

Gertie knew she was supposed to be thinking and feeling things about what was happening to her, but her entire conscious mind was still focused on trying to get air into her lungs. Finally, the tension in her chest released, and she was able to take a breath.

"Why?" she croaked, trying to look back at Neil, who had her arms pinned behind her back. "She killed—"

"Our father, yes, you've mentioned it," Neil said sourly. "It wouldn't exactly have been my choice of solutions to the problem, but you have to admit it was effective. And what he was planning to do—it would take all the cash that was left and then some."

Her head began to clear, and Gertie took in the magnitude of her mistake. She had thought that being forced to confront their sister's crimes would turn Neil and Jennifer against Maryann, clear the way for the police investigation. But of course, Maryann knew them better than Gertie did. What's a little matter of people's lives, when money is everything?

"Look, he was old." Jennifer was still over at the dining table, and now she was fishing through her oversize handbag, pulling out a small case and a vial. "How much longer was he going to live anyway? If he didn't want to die, he should have thought about how what he was doing was going to affect us. Anyway, like Maryann said, it's done now. Nothing we do is going to bring him back to life, so we need to look out for our own interests."

She said it mechanically, like she'd had the words repeated to her several times in the process of coming to believe them. That made Gertie optimistic, that maybe Jennifer wasn't as bought into the idea of killing as the other two, but any hopeful feelings were immediately drowned by the sight of the syringe Jennifer took from the case, carefully removing the cover from the needle.

"Are you all completely insane?" said Gertie, as she strained against Neil's grip. "Did you miss the part about where she tried to kill Brian for being a risk to her? Or how she used the company to commit her fraud?"

"I *saved* the company. For all of us, and particularly for Mother. You have no idea how hard she worked, keeping everything together for all those years, just so he could toss her aside as soon as he was rich enough for some whore to wiggle her ass at him. He didn't kill her, but he might as well have."

Gertie hadn't been focusing on Maryann, to save her energy for where she might have more of a chance. But she looked directly at her now, and if anything could surprise her at that point, Maryann's expression would have done it. Despite everything, she was still calm, but it was the calm of pure fury, and the way she looked at Gertie held more hate than she ever could have imagined.

"It happened before you were born, you said," Maryann went on. "That's true enough. While I was risking my life and career to try and save the family, your father was happily off screwing the bitch who whelped you. And was he even grateful? Of course not. He just held on to it, hoarded it like he hoarded everything, so he had it to use against me the next time I tried to save him from himself."

"You're a real humanitarian," Gertie said, as she watched Jennifer fill the syringe from the tiny glass bottle. "How many people are you planning on killing to cover for your mistakes?"

"It's a shame Dad never got to know you," replied Maryann. "He would have appreciated your arrogance."

She turned to Jennifer, who had finished preparing the syringe and was standing by, holding it carefully in front of her.

"Is that enough?" Maryann asked.

"Yes, it's totally enough," said Jennifer.

"Are you sure?"

"Look, I know what a fatal dose of fentanyl looks like, okay? Can't you just trust my abilities this one time?"

"Fentanyl?" Gertie asked. "I thought blunt force trauma was more your thing. Why not just run me down with someone else's car, like you did to poor Tim?"

"Careful how you hold her. This will go easier if we minimize the bruising." Maryann ignored Gertie, directing her comments to Neil.

At this point, bruises were the least of Gertie's concerns, so she gave her right arm a good yank and tried to elbow Neil in the stomach.

"Would you hurry up?" Neil said to Jennifer, who was hesitating a few feet away. "This is like trying to hold on to a cat."

"Well, you've got to keep her still. It's not going to look like she took it herself if I just stick her anywhere."

"I'm supposed to have done this to myself?" Fighting wasn't getting Gertie anywhere so far, so she switched tactics. Maybe if she could keep them talking for long enough, at least one of them would realize what a bad idea this was. She didn't have a lot of hope for that, but it was the best she had at the moment. "How gullible do you think the police are, anyway? At this point they're just going to count down and arrest the last person left alive here."

Ignoring her words, Maryann picked up Gertie's bag from where it had landed on the floor.

"You were a drug addict who came up with increasingly contorted lies to cover for your desire to claim the house. In doing so, you recruited people like Haylee and the gardener to help you. When you finally thought you had gotten what you wanted, you got hold of a large supply of your drugs and tragically overdosed."

"And the clothes? The trail-camera photo of you riding through the park when you were supposed to be miles away from here?"

Maryann smiled, her lips curling up over her teeth. "I think you'll find that this ranger friend of yours has some unsavory episodes in his background that make his testimony less than reliable. And if he doesn't, he will soon."

Gertie went cold all over. More than even the sight of the needle that Jennifer was still bringing closer, Maryann's words drove home how utterly they were planning to destroy everything Gertie had tried to do. Not only her, but anyone who had been stupid enough to help her.

The grand prize for stupidity was definitely going to Gertie at this point, but she thought there were a couple of runner-ups in the room with her. Jennifer might have thought the same thing, because she hesitated again. Gertie took that as an opportunity and tried again.

"Jennifer, can't you see she's setting you up to be framed if this goes wrong? The text telling me to come here came from your phone, and you're the one who got the drugs that are going to kill me. What do you think is going to happen to you if the police don't buy her story?"

It didn't work. Jennifer paused for a second longer, but a wordless look from her sister urged her forward, and she started moving, holding up the needle with practiced ease. And in a last, desperate burst of inspiration, Gertie found the nuclear option.

"If you kill me, my mother gets the house."

That got to them. Jennifer gasped and took a half step back, and even Maryann's sneer faded. And, most importantly Neil's grip relaxed, just for a moment, but enough that with a surge of strength, Gertie was able to pull herself free. Maryann moved to block the route to the door, but that wasn't Gertie's goal. Grabbing the geode off the table, she heaved it through the nearest plate glass window.

49

The glass seemed to break in slow motion, the cracks spreading out from the cannonball-sized hole until they reached the sides and top, then collapsing in an avalanche of razor-sharp fragments and sheets.

Gertie ran through it, covering her head with her arms and ignoring the sting of the shards hitting her skin. Neil was close behind her, but a piece of glass a foot wide fell between them, barely missing Gertie, and he jumped back with a yelp.

As soon as she was out in the open, Gertie picked up speed. She was sure she was a faster runner than any of them, but they would get to their cars soon enough. Her best bet was to strike out across the park, to try to make it to the visitor center before she collapsed in the heat. She had no other options—her own car keys were back in her bag, along with her phone, and there wasn't enough traffic on the road to the house to count on finding help there.

At least, not usually. Coming out of the front yard, Gertie

crested a low rise and was looking for a clear path through into the park when she noticed movement in the distance. Not one car but three, and at least one of them had lights on top. Her pursuers must have seen them too, because behind her she heard the skidding noise of feet stopping quickly on gravel, plus the clear sound of Neil saying, "Shit!"

"New plan," Gertie gasped under her breath, then started running at full speed down the road.

———

Gertie had only gone about eighty yards when she heard the engine behind her. She hadn't forgotten about the cars, and she was ready for it, quickly leaving the shoulder for the rougher ground off the road, where only a very determined or foolish driver would follow.

But Jennifer didn't even look at her as she passed, pushing the acceleration of her luxury SUV to its limit. Her eyes were focused ahead, and she was driving like she was counting on the police not caring about her when they had other things to do.

"Good luck with that," Gertie muttered as she returned to the pavement.

In the end, she didn't do much running. Which was for the best, because even under the overcast skies, the temperature in the desert was approaching a hundred. No other vehicles came from the house, and it was only a few minutes before the police cars met her. There were two of them now, one unmarked and one black-and-white. Gertie waved them down, noticing a sharp pain in her shoulder as she did. Her vision was starting to get fuzzy again, but she saw several figures get out of the cars and come toward her.

"Ma'am, are you all right? Ma'am?"

"Of course she's not all right. She's got pieces of glass in her all over!"

That sounded like Mrs. Phan's voice, which didn't make sense, but Gertie was tired of trying to get things to make sense. So when she found herself sitting on the ground, leaning up against a warm tire with the household manager's concerned face bent over her, she just went with it.

"There's been some damage to the living room window," she said through gasps of breath. "I think we should look into getting safety glass put in there."

50

"So it was your phone I saw on the floor."

Gertie had expected the police to take her back to the house with them, but that wasn't how it worked out. Mrs. Phan stayed with her until the paramedics arrived, but she refused to answer any questions, saying Gertie should rest and everything would be explained later. Then she was called away, and several firefighters lectured Gertie on the dangers of walking into glass doors. Gertie considered explaining to them that it would have been more dangerous for her not to, but that seemed like a lot of work, and she was suddenly very tired. So she just nodded while they cleaned and bandaged her wounds, then sent her off to the hospital, where she got another lecture and some stitches.

Eventually, the medical professionals got tired of poking her and telling her things, and Gertie was left to sit in the lobby and wonder who she could call to come pick her up and if her insurance was going to cover this.

The first question, at least, was dealt with when Mrs. Phan

came through the door, walking into the hospital like she owned the place. Somehow she made the paperwork vanish, and soon they were settled into Mrs. Phan's personal car, a newish hybrid with a tree-shaped air freshener hanging from the rearview mirror. They were going to the police station, Mrs. Phan explained, because there were still some questions, even though the police had heard everything that had gone on in the house that morning.

"It was my phone," Mrs. Phan agreed. "Not a very good hiding place, but it needed to be somewhere that it could get the sound and the signal. And I know about them—they never look under anything. I could have been hiding under that furniture, if I fit."

Gertie laughed. "So, do you always bug the house, or only when your employers are planning on murdering someone?"

"Only then." Mrs. Phan laughed too, then fell suddenly serious. "I'm sorry. I should have warned you. When they dismissed all of us for today, I knew something must be happening, but I didn't know what. So I got the idea to leave my phone and listen so I could find out. But I never guessed they would actually try to kill you."

"That makes two of us," Gertie said. "I was suspicious too, but my great plan was that I was going to reveal what Maryann had done, and the other two would fall in line. Not my brightest moment."

"No, but you couldn't have known." Mrs. Phan put on her turn signal and waited for a pedestrian to clear the crosswalk before continuing. "Brian isn't the nicest of them, but he is the only one who is willing to think for himself. He's doing better, by the way—awake and talking. He doesn't remember who hit him, but when the police asked about Haylee, he told them everything."

"I guess people can still surprise you," said Gertie. "In a good way, I mean."

"Sometimes," Mrs. Phan said. "But not always."

"No, not always." Gertie shifted to relieve the pressure on the stitches in her shoulder. "What happened to the rest of them? I saw Jennifer driving away."

Mrs. Phan made a derisive noise. "Yes, and she didn't get far. The highway patrol stopped her trying to go the wrong way up an exit ramp to the freeway, and they found the drugs when they searched her car. And I was with the police when they went to see Maryann and Neil. They tried to say it was you and Jennifer who did everything, but of course they didn't know my phone was there."

"Are you going to get into trouble for that?" Gertie asked, while she tried to work through the potential legal implications. Mrs. Phan just shrugged.

"I don't know; we'll see. I'm sure it will be fine. Anyway, once they knew it wasn't working, Neil turned on Maryann, and she tried to make it seem like it was all his idea, and they all got arrested. The police said they would be done with the room by this afternoon, so I called a contractor to bring in some wood to cover the window. It won't be pretty, but it'll do for now."

"That's a good idea, thank you," Gertie said. It was a trivial response, but she didn't know what else to say.

She sat in silence as they stopped at a light and then started again, the hybrid's electric motor whirring up to speed.

"Mrs. Phan," Gertie said, staring out the window at the pale stucco buildings as they passed them, "what am I going to do now?"

Now it was the older woman's turn to fall silent.

"You'll do what needs to be done," she said at last. "The same as I would."

51

Mostly what Gertie did for the next two weeks was answer questions. Questions from the police, from the insurance companies, from more lawyers than she cared to count, and from her friend Emily, who had managed to get everyone Gertie knew from college worried about her by the time she got her phone back.

Most of that had been done from her motel room, so by the time Jules called and told her she was cleared to take possession of the house, Gertie was more than ready to leave behind the rattling AC unit and mysterious stains and go back there. It may have been the place where her half siblings had tried to kill her, but at least it was clean.

The house looked the same as she had left it, except for the sheets of plywood covering the missing window and the cardboard boxes next to the front door. That had been Mrs. Phan's suggestion, to have the staff pack up any personal items from the bedrooms so they could be returned to their owners with minimal trouble. One of Brian's children had already been by for his things, seemingly more concerned about his watches than the fact her father was still in the hospital, though she did say he was "doing okay" when Gertie asked. That was more than she got from the courier who came by on behalf of Neil's husband, who would only hand her the paper authorizing him to pick up the listed items and refused to speak to her at all.

Gertie had thought she was done with distributing boxes for a while and was heading to the downstairs office to return a call from the window contractor when an Uber dropped Haylee off at the front gate. She didn't knock but tried her own key, then rattled the door when it didn't work.

She was even more surprised when Gertie opened it to let her in.

"What are you doing here?" she asked. "I thought you left."

"I came back. This is my house, after all." Gertie didn't bother asking why Haylee was there; she thought she had a fairly good idea about that. Instead, she said, "I see the police released you. How was jail?"

"What? Oh, it was okay, I guess. Really boring, and they wouldn't let me have my phone."

It was true: Haylee's time behind bars didn't seem to have affected her. Her hair had lost some of its luster, and she was dressed in a relatively modest outfit of jeans and a micro tank top, but otherwise she wasn't very different from how Gertie had first seen her, mincing down the stairs.

Her priorities hadn't changed either.

"Anyway, I'm back now. I'm going up to my room. Tell the staff to send me up a smoothie. And they'd better not put kale in it. Watercress only."

"No," said Gertie.

"Okay, wheatgrass then. But don't let them tell you they don't have it. Those people always lie."

She started toward the stairs, but Gertie blocked her path.

"I don't think you understand. No one is going to be making you anything. You don't have a room, because you don't live here." Gertie pointed to the largest pile of boxes near the door. "Your things are in here; if there's anything missing, have your lawyer give us a call."

It couldn't have been the first time Haylee had been kicked out of a place, but she made a good show of being shocked.

"But I live here! You can't just throw me out." Even she must have realized that wasn't true, so she tried another argument. "Your father wanted me here. You wouldn't go against what he wanted."

"If he wanted you to have the house, he would have left it to you." Gertie almost felt bad for the woman; she knew what it was like to be suddenly cut off from the place you had been calling home. But she also knew what it was like to have someone living off you parasite-style, and in that situation, brutality was the only option.

As if she could read Gertie's mind, Haylee pouted and said her thoughts out loud. "I thought I reminded you of your mother."

"You do. That's why I want you off my property in the next five minutes."

52

Gertie tried working from the downstairs office, but everything about the room reminded her of some part of what she had been through, and it was impossible to focus on tax documents when every few seconds, she was thinking about Maryann trying to bully her out of her company shares, or if that spot on the carpet was just a shadow or had been left there by Haylee and Brian's activities. So she finally gave up and took her laptop to a shady spot by the pool.

She had finally heard back from Harper, the server who had been working the night before Arnold's death, and she had filled in some of the missing details. Most were things Gertie already knew or guessed, like that the reactions to Arnold's plans had been strongly negative and that Arnold hadn't taken that very well at all.

But one thing that had closed a loop for her was an exchange Harper had caught as she was clearing the dessert plates. The rest of the party had gone out to the courtyard for drinks, but Arnold was going up the stairs to his office, talking to Maryann as she left the table. Arnold had said something like, "You don't think much of my ideas right now, but you'll see! And it's better than the alternative."

Harper hadn't remembered the exact words, but she had been very clear on the way he had laughed.

That was what Gertie was thinking about, as she looked back through the patio windows into the empty house. She had been convinced that the money was at the heart of the crimes, but really, the money was only part of it. Money was the only means of communication anyone in the family cared about, and it was the way Maryann had found out how much her father had valued her. And when she knew it was not at all, there was nothing left for her to do but take the money itself.

Gertie looked up at the tower office and the blue sky beyond it. Was that what life had been like in this place? A balance sheet for every relationship, with no mercy if the numbers didn't add up? When she'd arrived, it had bothered her that she didn't feel like she belonged here; now she was more than grateful.

There was a rustle of feathers, and a raven flapped down to the edge of the pool. It started drinking, keeping a wary eye on Gertie, as she did the same, wondering what it thought of her. The large black bird looked as out of place in the pristine surroundings of the courtyard as she felt. Everything about it was adapted to the hard life of the desert, and here it was, sipping the water like it thought the pool had been put there just for this.

And why shouldn't it? That's what successful creatures did, didn't they? They adapted.

Having drunk its fill, the bird flew away, and Gertie was still staring at the spot where it had been when Mrs. Phan found her.

"What are you doing, working so hard out here?" she admonished. "You should be resting, after all that you've been through."

Gertie hit Send on the email she had been composing and closed her computer, smiling. "I didn't go through much that wasn't my own fault. And there's a lot of work to be done. I'm afraid there are going to be some changes around here."

"So I've heard." Mrs. Phan took a seat at the other side of the patio table and folded her hands in front of her. "It sounds like you have big plans for this place."

Gertie nodded. "It doesn't make sense, me living alone in this big house, with all the staff to take care of just me. And honestly, I don't want to. But the terms of the will make selling difficult, and anyway, I've been looking for something to do for a career. And," Gertie added with a smile, "with all those extra rooms, it would be hard for me to keep Carla from moving in."

Mrs. Phan laughed. "That much I can understand. So, what are you going to do instead?"

"I'm still working on finalizing the plans, but I think the main house is going to be some sort of event or meeting space, with artist studios in the current bedrooms. I'm keeping the tower office for myself, and I'll live in the pool house, with a few upgrades. Kathy has agreed to stay and work on making the garden a showcase for low-water and desert planting. If we can open it to the public, that should help with the nonprofit status. And Eddie is looking into the possibility of running some catering out of the kitchen.

It might need some work to bring it up to commercial standards, but I think it'll be worth it."

Gertie stopped and took a breath, aware that she had been speaking faster and louder as she got more into her ideas. "There are a lot of details that still need to be handled," she added. "But it should be doable."

Mrs. Phan patted her hand. "And if it is, you're the one who's going to do it. Your father was just the same way when he had an idea. Once the vision was there, nothing could stop him."

"Until something did," Gertie said automatically, then regretted it. "I'm sorry, I shouldn't have said that."

"But you're right." Mrs. Phan shook her head. "That was your father's big problem. He never thought about how his plans would affect other people. And that's where you're going to do better than him."

"Speaking of that," Gertie said, feeling suddenly awkward. "I guess you want to know what your options are for your job? I'm sorry for not talking to you sooner, but we were still ironing things out."

"Is there a place for me to work at the new business?" Mrs. Phan said, but she didn't look enthusiastic about the idea.

"Of course. We're still going to have an on-site staff, though a smaller one, and they'll need to be managed," Gertie said. "Or you could retire and take your pension. Which you have, by the way. Fully funded and vested, as of today."

"I don't understand. Your father...?"

"Left me a sum of money to fund the running of the house. A

very large sum, as it turns out, thanks to some assets that were held in the trust doing better than anyone expected. I've been over the will with Jules, and he agrees that employee benefits fall within the terms of the bequest. He can go through the options with you, but based on your years of service, you're eligible for monthly payments equal to your current salary or a prorated lump-sum payment. I'm sure he can explain it better than me."

"Well." Mrs. Phan sat in silence for a moment, apparently digesting the idea.

"It's no more than you're owed. You deserve it, for all your work."

Mrs. Phan thought about that, then smiled. "I do, don't I?"

She turned and looked back at the house. The late-afternoon sun was reflecting off the windows of the tower office, making it look like a lighthouse beaming across the valley.

"I wonder what your father would have thought of all this. He was very proud of the house, but he never wanted to let too many people come and see it. I'm not sure he'd like having strangers in there, doing their own things."

"Possibly not," Gertie agreed. "But he spent his whole life getting what he wanted. I think the best way to honor his memory is for me to have what I want."

LETTER FROM ALBERT GLASS TO GERTRUDE GLASS (DELIVERED TO THE WRONG ADDRESS AND THROWN AWAY UNREAD)

Dear Gertrude,

You should be receiving this letter after my death, and once the will has been read, for which I expect you will have been in attendance, you may be surprised to find that I have willed you my house, the thing I consider the greatest achievement of my life, considering that our relationship has been anything but close. The truth is, I have been following your educational career for many years, and I have been pleasantly surprised by your success. I can only conclude that you take after me more than your mother, who is frankly subhuman when it comes to intelligence.

In fact, it is this resemblance that motivated my decision to leave my house to your care. None of the children of my first wife have the character to understand what it means to take on this kind of responsibility. They are, sadly, too concerned with the comforts my money has bought them. The person who will carry on my legacy must be able to recognize the value of hard work and why the visionary men of this world deserve to be celebrated.

As the new custodian of the Glass House, I expect you to respect it for the achievement it is, and preserve it accordingly. No element should be changed; even the slightest alteration would be fatal to the purity of my design. In my lifetime, the so-called architectural establishment has not been receptive to this kind of innovation, but I expect they will in the future, and you will be there to ensure that credit is properly assigned. This building is my entry into the hall of the immortals, and I am placing the responsibility on you to keep my memory alive in its perfect preservation.

Sincerely,
Arnold Glass

READ ON FOR A LOOK AT
***SHE LEFT* BY STACIE GREY**

Available now from Poisoned Pen Press

THE GIRL

Amy slammed the door behind her and stalked out into the night. She should have known. Obviously, she should have known. They would say they were her friends, but they weren't really. Not as long as Jenna was in charge.

She stopped in the shadow of the trees and looked back at the cabin. The problem was, they had all come up here in Chris's car, and right now Chris was leaning against Jenna's knee and laughing at how stupid Amy was. Plus, he'd had at least three beers, so even if there was a universe where Amy could go back in and ask him to drive her home, there would be too much risk of being caught in one of the holiday checkpoints that were all around town to catch drunk teenagers just like them. Amy should know—her dad was manning one of them right now.

So she couldn't drive. And she couldn't go back. And the cheap brick phone that was the only kind her parents would buy her didn't get any signal out here, so even if they weren't both working and she did have someone to call, she couldn't. Which meant that Amy only had one choice. She turned around and started walking.

It probably would have made sense to take the road. There were no streetlights this far from town, but the moon was almost full, and out in the open, there was plenty of light to see by. Plus, if anyone wanted to find her, that was where they would look.

But the road went all the way around the park, probably four miles. And anyway, Amy didn't want them to come find her. That would be pathetic, making herself walk all that extra distance, just because she was hoping they would be sorry. They weren't sorry; they were having a better time without her. She would go through the park, just to show them how much she didn't care.

It was darker than she had expected under the trees. Amy went slow at first, keeping her eyes on the path and listening carefully for the sound of anyone coming after her. A couple of times she thought she heard something—a footstep, or some branches breaking—but no one called her name.

Eventually, Amy's eyes adjusted to the darkness, and she was able to pull some of her attention back from the ground in front of her to the bigger picture of what she had done. There were only two weeks left in the school year, but that was enough. She could just hear them all laughing about how Amy Brewer got so mad about a dumb joke that she walked for miles on Memorial Day night, literally running home to her mommy. She could try to tell her side of the story, but who would care? She had been one of them; she got what she deserved. Amy thought about the I-told-you-so looks she would get from her former friends and almost cried. She couldn't imagine anything worse happening to anybody.

Any other time, when things were bad, Amy at least had sports to fall back on. People forgave a lot when you were scoring goals and winning races. But the soccer season wouldn't start until November, and she'd had her final track meet last week. As she walked, she wondered if it would still be possible to sign up for a summer team, maybe swimming? It was worth a try.

Her route took her through an open-space park, one of a dozen or so that ringed the suburbs east of San Francisco where Amy had lived her whole life. She had thought of it as a familiar place, ordinary and kind of boring, but it didn't feel that way now. It wasn't even the first time she had been out here at night, but this was no nature hike with the hippie lady from the ranger station. This part of the path hadn't been maintained, and trees leaned low over it, while bushes reached out to scrape her legs below her shorts. (Probably poison oak, Amy thought. Why wouldn't it be?)

That was bad enough, but the worst part was that every time she moved, she thought she heard another footstep from somewhere behind her or to her right. She would stop, and the noise stopped, too, and no matter how quickly she turned to look back, she couldn't see where it was coming from.

It's just the echo of my own steps, she told herself, but she wasn't convinced. Since when did bushes echo?

Then there was another sound, a very definite crunch, and Amy jumped. Did mountain lions hunt at night? She thought they might. Right now, night seemed like a time for hunting. She wanted to run, but she fought the impulse. Amy was pretty sure animals would chase you if you ran. They had to; it was just instinct. So she kept her pace steady and made herself look as tall as possible, stomping with every step to sound big and heavy.

Eventually, she came out from among the oak and bay trees into a eucalyptus grove. Here, the undergrowth vanished—she remembered the ranger telling them it was because the trees poisoned the ground below them. The ranger had also said the creaking noises were from the wind rubbing the branches together, but Amy had liked to make up stories about how they were doors opening in the woods. Now she wished she hadn't. She wasn't a kid anymore, and she didn't like to think about anything coming through a door right now, even an imaginary one.

The more she walked, the colder Amy got. She hadn't brought a jacket, and even though it was almost summer, the dry air didn't hold enough of the daytime heat for her shorts and belly shirt to be comfortable. There was an emergency blanket in her backpack, left over from her mom's Y2K supplies, but she didn't have to think very long to decide that even the small chance of someone seeing her hiking through the park wrapped in crinkly Mylar wasn't worth the risk.

Aside from the creaking trees, the park was quiet, but further away Amy could hear the pops and bangs of illegal fireworks going off all over town. That was why the mayor's office had decided to put on the official fireworks show, according to Amy's mom, who had to set it up. It was supposed to give people something better to see so they wouldn't go around scaring their neighbors' dogs and risking starting fires in the dry grass. From the way things were sounding, Amy didn't think it had worked.

Another blast went off, close enough that the ground shook. Amy stopped and looked around to see if she could spot where it had come from, but there was nothing in the sky, just the shrieking sound of whistlers in the distance.

In a weird way, hearing the fireworks made her feel better. It was a reminder that even though it seemed like she was in the wilderness, she wasn't really that far from people, and home, and all the parts of her regular life. She walked on through the cough drop–scented air of the eucalyptus grove and tried to imagine what that life was going to look like now.

"I get everything." Jenna had said it while she was looking straight at Chris, who was peeling the label off a beer bottle with his long fingers. He had just glanced over at Amy when Jenna made her declaration, and Amy almost hadn't heard her over his smile. But, of course, Jenna had gotten herself right back into the center of everyone's attention. She didn't explain what she meant by the comment; she didn't need to. Jenna was pretty and thin, and her dad was rich enough to buy her anything she asked for, and most things she didn't. She got everything, and she always would. Amy couldn't even remember what had brought it up; it was just the sort of thing Jenna said. And now, Amy thought, one of the things Jenna was going to get was the ability to ruin her senior year. It wasn't fair, but then nothing was.

Or maybe not. Amy slipped her hand in her pocket and wrapped her fingers around the small plastic bottle there, feeling its contents rattle as she walked through the trees. Maybe, just this once, Jenna was going to find out that she wasn't as untouchable as she thought she was.

Down out of the hills, the ground started to level off. The trail was more developed here, with signs reminding hikers to leash their dogs and cyclists to yield to horses, and the brush on either side was cut further back, so she didn't have to move branches out of the way or watch for leaves that would brush her ankles.

Still, Amy felt an uneasiness she couldn't quite shake. She had just about managed to convince herself that the rustling noises that seemed to follow her were nothing but the wind, and if anything had been stalking her, there was no reason for it to have waited this long, but there was still a prickling on the back of her neck that wouldn't go away.

As she made her way to the road, she was tempted to see if her phone had any signal yet. This probably wasn't the kind of emergency her parents had in mind when they bought it for her, even after seeing what it cost, but one of them would find a way to get out of work to get her, and then this whole stupid night would finally be over. But she didn't, partly because she wasn't ready to explain what happened yet, and partly because, in the only piece of good luck she had had all day, she had just gotten to the place where the park drive joined the main road when a late-night bus turned the corner and stopped. Gratefully, Amy climbed on, paid her fare, and sank into the hard plastic seat as two police cars flew by, blaring their sirens.

She was thinking about what she was going to say the first time someone asked her at school about what happened when her phone started chiming from the bottom of her backpack. Amy's first instinct was to lunge for it, and her fingers had wrapped around the plastic brick before she paused to think. The only people who were going to call her right now were the five she left back at that cabin. Maybe they wanted to play with her some more, or maybe they were worried she was going to tell someone and get them in trouble. Either way, Amy wasn't going to give them the satisfaction of answering.

She pulled her hand out of the backpack and folded it over in her lap to muffle the sound.

It wasn't far from the bus stop to Amy's house, which was one of the many ways it was different from where Jenna lived. The ranch-style stucco houses of the mid-century subdivision were all anyone needed to see to know this wasn't a rich neighborhood, but for once that didn't bother Amy. All she wanted was to get inside and forget this night had ever happened.

She was standing in the kitchen, holding a box of graham crackers, when someone started banging on the door. Still carrying the box, Amy walked slowly down the hall, unsure if she should even answer it. There was no peephole in the door, but there was a window in the hall bathroom next to it. Amy looked out, but all she could see was a hooded figure, banging on the door with one hand and holding something to their mouth with the other.

Then they stopped and started looking around on the front step. It didn't take long for the figure to find the key in the hollow rock (Amy's dad hated that thing), and before Amy even had time to run or lock herself into the bathroom, the door opened, and the figure swooped through and grabbed her.

"Oh, thank Heaven, thank Heaven!"

It was her neighbor, old Mrs. Andrews, dressed in one of her husband's oversize sweatshirts and clutching her cordless phone as she hugged Amy tightly to her generous bosom.

"It's okay, she's here. She's right here in the house," she shouted into the receiver. "Oh, honey, you had us all so worried!"

Confused, Amy pried herself out of the hug.

"Worried? Why were you worried? Did they tell you I did something?" That was a possibility she hadn't even considered, that the others would take it even further by trying to get her in trouble. This was worse than she had thought.

"Oh no, no, no. You don't know? Oh, honey, they're all dead."

READING GROUP GUIDE

1. What is it like to return to a location you haven't visited in years? Do you have memories of that location? What kind of memories are they?

2. What is it like to meet family members again after an extended period? How would you go about interacting with them?

3. Gertie and her half siblings don't have the best relationship. How do you think rifts among siblings are best handled? How would you try to mend this kind of rift?

4. Gertie's mother is not portrayed as the most responsible person, with Gertie having to grow up very quickly and often act as the "mother" in situations. How do you think growing up this way affected her decision-making during the events of the novel?

5. There are a few sections from Arnold's perspective scattered throughout the book. How do these sections add to the story?

6. How would you react to receiving a fortune in a will (that you didn't know about prior to the reading)?

7. Gertie is offered a financial compromise to leave the siblings and the house alone, but she refuses it. Why does she do this? Would you refuse?

8. Gertie remarks on the household staff taking care of the details for her, like ordering food or having breakfast prepared. What would it be like to have someone organize those "details" for you? Would you be comfortable with it?

9. There's a clear divide in Arnold's household between the staff and Arnold's family. How do the people on different sides act toward and treat each other? What is the right way to treat someone who is your employer or employee?

10. Did you deduce who killed Arnold before it was revealed?

11. What would it be like to measure a person's worth only by how much money they make or are able to make? What kind of pressure does it put on Arnold's children to have their value measured by wealth?

12. Many characters comment on Gertie's similarities to her father throughout the book. How is she similar to Arnold, and how is she different?

A CONVERSATION WITH THE AUTHOR

Where did the inspiration for this book come from?

Like most books, *She Didn't Stand a Chance* can trace its heritage to a number of sources from the perennial tabloid fodder of old men with young wives fathering babies they can't possibly expect to see grow up to the British television series *Grand Designs*, which features some of the most outrageous domestic architecture around. Ultimately, I wanted to write a modern version of the classic country-house murder mystery, where a group of people are gathered for an event and one of them ends up being killed, and give it a darker California twist.

How did writing from Gertie's perspective differ from writing from Arnold's?

It was an interesting experience because I wrote Arnold's sections after I had written the rest of the book. So while Gertie's personality developed over the course of the drafts, by the time I got to Arnold, I had a pretty good idea of who he was and how his personality would play into his death.

Agatha Christie famously had Poirot say that the key to any murder lay in the nature of the person killed. While that's not true in reality, it's an interesting way to approach the question in fiction because of the agency it gives to the victim.

Do you have a favorite character?

I always end up falling in love with my secondary characters, and this book was no exception. I enjoyed writing all of the Glass House employees from Kathy's no-nonsense attitude and love of plants to Eddie's joie de vivre. But my favorite was definitely Mrs. Phan. She's seen everything, can do just about anything, and always knows exactly the right thing to say. I wish I could be her. But failing that, I'd love to have her around.

What do you want readers to take away from Gertie's story?

I would like them to come away cheering for her and feeling glad that she was able to take control of her own story. From that, I would hope the reader might think about the ways they might be able to define themselves *by themselves* and not by their family of origin. And, of course, I want them to feel satisfied by the mystery and distracted from their own lives, if only for a while.

What are you currently reading?

Some favorite recent reads are *Silver Nitrate* by Silvia

Moreno-Garcia, *The Examiner* by Janice Hallett, *Emily Wilde's Map of the Otherlands* by Heather Fawcett, and *The Full Moon Coffee Shop* by Mai Mochizuki.

ACKNOWLEDGMENTS

Books are funny things—as much the product of teamwork as they are individual creations. There were many people behind this one, and I would say that no more than half of them corrected my use of commas.

Thanks to my agent, Abby Saul, who has been a fantastic supporter while she pushes me to be the writer I can be and is eternally patient with my endless questions and neuroses. And Anna Michels brings her excitement to each book as well as her strong editorial eye that invariably makes them stronger.

And to the copy editors, cover designers, book designers, publicists, and everyone else at Poisoned Pen/Sourcebooks, I would like to say thank you, and also I'm sorry for coming up with so many weirdly formatted bits in *She Didn't Stand a Chance*. I can't promise I won't do it again.

It takes a lot of people to produce a book but even more to produce a writer, or at least to prevent her from losing her mind. For this, I have to thank my writing tribe—Laurie, Michelle, Tammy, and Mysti—for the accountability and support they provide on Saturday morning write-ins and for not commenting on my hair. To Karen and Karen, who have known me and my writing for longer than any of us would like to admit: I still think the squid were a good idea. And to all of the Larkies, I just want to say: You're a bunch of fabulous weirdos. Never change.

I would like to thank Sue Trowbridge for giving my web presence a professionalism my personality absolutely does not support. Thanks also to the members of the Mystery Writers of America and Sisters in Crime Northern California chapters for being a great and supportive community throughout my writing journey.

Thanks to Mom and Dad for being absolutely nothing like the parents in this book.

Sometimes, when you're stuck on a scene, the best thing a writer can do is to go for a walk, and Zaphod is always ready to help with that. It's impossible to have an existential crisis when you've got a labradoodle pogoing down the street.

And thanks especially to Cameron for supporting me, cheering me on, and reminding me that I always say the book is a disaster around the halfway point.

Finally, a book isn't truly finished until it is read. So thank you to all readers, past and future, for letting my characters come to life.

ABOUT THE AUTHOR

© Andrea Sher

Stacie Grey is an author and fan of mysteries who lives in Alameda, California, with her husband and dog. In what passes for normal life, she works in biotech research. She mostly posts to Instagram and Mastodon and occasionally writes a newsletter.